Thrown Under the Bus

THROWN
UNDER THE BUS

THE RISE AND FALL OF
AN AMERICAN WORKER

TERESA ZERILLI-EDELGLASS

ACKNOWLEDGMENTS

Thank you, wonderful, supportive family and especially you, Mom, who has tirelessly listened to me endlessly yammering about my book and life in general!

Thank you, beautiful baby dog and love of my life, Toto. I miss you like crazy every day!

Thank you, all of my four-legged furry babies, past and present, whose unconditional love and companionship helped keep me sane.

Thank you, wonderful "life" friends, for always being there. You know who you are.

And most of all, thank you Stoney, Joe, Wayne, Jackie, and Obie, my dearest work buddies without whom I seriously don't know what the heck I would have done. Do you have any idea how great you all are? You got me through the roughest of rough times without fear of retribution, while others frantically ran for cover. You are brave, selfless souls, to whom I owe undying gratitude. I love you guys!

INTRODUCTION

WHAT DOESN'T KILL YOU makes you stronger. I've heard this expression so many times throughout the course of my life that it's darn near lost its meaning—it's practically cliché. Be that as it may, I'm here to proclaim that there couldn't more truth to this axiom for me—and I suspect for a lot of you too.

When confronted with adversity, most of us get so caught up in the moment (or in my case, years) that we fail to realize that every minute of survival translates into experience that can, without warning, quickly add up to an arsenal of strength. The positive, cumulative effect of being beaten down is unfathomable and, as in my experience, not evident until long after the fact. It's hard to imagine anything so negative resulting in such an invaluable positive. At best, you swear you're going to drop dead from the stress. But while you're busy fighting for whatever it is that moves you to do so—pushing through each moment, each day, each year—your mere endurance is a testament of your ability to survive *and* thrive. Tragedy might pull the proverbial rug out from under your life, but it also builds immense character and fortitude … if it doesn't kill you.

We live in a time where tragic stories of crazed gunmen, teen suicide, and other such atrocities seem to have become commonplace. The media quickly pounces on every opportunity to exploit these tragedies. In time, this can equate to the perception that society has gone completely mad and that everyone is on the verge of lunacy. But in reality, these events are, fortunately, still by far the exception, not the rule. Of course, there always will be those among us who sadly slip through the cracks of society, who become unable to cope and simply go off the deep end. Most of us, however, manage to pull ourselves along somehow, knowing that though we've been wounded, we will move on. Time will serve to heal, and in some cases, we rise to give back, to turn a horrific negative into a gleaming positive.

For me, life took the most unexpected turn just at a time when I thought I knew exactly where I was headed. What I thought would be the best, most fulfilling part of my personal journey—a point I invested so much of myself to get to—ended up the worst, most nightmarish time I could never have imagined in my wildest dreams. But make no mistake. While my story is one steeped in workplace harassment, it is by far more a cautionary tale about how easy it is for anyone similarly situated to end up just as I did. It *can* happen to you!

My saga is one I deem for the record books—and one I've yet to fully digest. For instance, can you imagine being made to walk around your workplace—one full to the brim with men, no less, in a skirt stained with menstrual blood? Or receiving a lousy performance evaluation for leaving dirty dishes in a sink? How about your boss telling you he could "use you" for whatever he wanted? I'm *still* in disbelief.

Spending the better part of nineteen years holding my breath, trying desperately to get back on track after those (and countless other) incredible encounters took an immense toll. It was like climbing a ladder but never quite reaching the next rung as depraved, vicious beasts desperately tried at all costs to pull me down to my demise once and for all. Although I fought back with the tenacity of a crocodile, the odds against a public-sector giant backed by a justice system very much gone awry were staggeringly low no matter how I sliced it.

When I think about it still, I'm amazed at how I managed to survive without going totally off the deep end. Perhaps I underestimated myself. Perhaps I started out stronger than I realized. And perhaps the strength I amassed along the way was greater than I was able to recognize until long after the dust settled. All I know is that in the end, I truly proved to myself that no matter what is thrown at me, no matter how utterly horrific the circumstances, I can come out the other side better for it—a bit beat-up perhaps but better—and I have no doubt you can too.

"Your enemies grow strong on what you leave behind" is a line from an Elton John/Bernie Taupin song (two guys for whom I have the greatest respect and without whose music my life simply would not be the same) that brilliantly sums up the means by which I was able to survive this whole ugly ordeal in a way I never could. Borrowed from Michael Corleone in *The Godfather, Part III* (1990), it is a sentiment so incredibly profound it's almost silly. Just stop and take it in for a moment. It is, in essence, saying that there may be times in your life when someone with whom you've had difficulties unwittingly taught you techniques you could then parlay into an array of means with which to fight back. (And when there is a long, acrimonious history between you, this can go a long way toward survival.) Truth is you *can* and *do* learn and grow from the tidbits your enemies leave behind, whether or not you know it.

My "enemy" fueled me with knowledge, fueled me with determination, and fueled me with purpose. They forced me to develop survival techniques—a virtual arsenal of legal knowledge and mental fortitude that I don't think I ever would have had the wherewithal to conjure up otherwise. Their evil plotting left a distinct trail that, with immense determination, I was able to turn, very gradually, into a force for good. As the song goes, I grew strong on what they left behind. It's a very simple yet mind-blowing concept!

While I might not have emerged the victor from each of the battles in this war, I certainly learned to hold my head high after being reduced to the pile of emotional mush I was ashamed to have become for so long. In the end, I came to know where I stood—and stand I still do—without the angst and despair that once all but consumed my existence.

I've heard many stories over the course of my life about women hitting the glass ceiling, about minorities being passed over for promotions, and about all degrees of sexual harassment in the workplace. No doubt many careers, and perhaps lives too, were destroyed. But I can honestly say that injuries aside (as I would never be so callous as to try to measure another's pain), I know no story quite as bizarre as my own—and I'm willing to bet you don't either. Had I not lived it, I'm not sure I'd even believe it. Even now, there are times I step back in amazement as I try to process the whole thing. To lose so many of what should have been meaningful, productive years to a seemingly never-ending series of counter-productive, mean-spirited exchanges that ultimately obliterated my career and changed the course of my life forever, for no other reason than being female, was and still is inconceivable.

Writing this book was the most cathartic thing I've ever done despite that it forced me to repeatedly relive incidents I'd much rather forget. At times, the incredibly painful memories the process dredged up made me break down and cry like the whole thing just happened all over again. But I suppose that's precisely the kind of stuff a cathartic process is predicated on! Whenever I felt that old, familiar darkness creeping in, I pulled back and reminded myself of how many hours, days, weeks, months, and years I wasted in fighting with an entity with which I should have parted ways long ago. I told myself that I am done with allowing anyone or any thing to have such control over my happiness. This would be my declaration of independence; nothing would stand in my way going forward, especially not the remnants of years of emotional despair.

I wish my first book could have been about something far less personal—and far more uplifting too. But it is what it is—and I feel strongly that sharing it will prove beneficial to many. Whether you are a fellow-disgruntled employee, someone facing a challenging time of any kind, or just someone who simply enjoys a story of triumph over tragedy, I hope you will take something useful away from it. I know in my heart that God sent me on this crazy journey for a reason, and I'd like to believe that reason extends far beyond the trials and tribulations of my own life.

CHAPTER 1

BORN TO BOOGIE

I WAS BORN IN THE 1960S on Staten Island, the "forgotten borough" of the five boroughs of New York City, where I spent the first thirty-four years of my life. I am the oldest of four children—two brothers, as well as a sister from my father's second marriage. My two brothers and I were born within the short span of two and a half years; my sister came along some twenty-five years later.

My childhood was spent living in my maternal grandparents' two-family house, once the single-family house in which my mother grew up. My grandparents and aunt lived downstairs—the five of us upstairs in a small four-room apartment. My mother's brother and his family lived across the street. I guess you could say this was the quintessential Italian-American arrangement, one commonly found in that geographic region. I doubt, however, we would have resided within the confines of my grandparent's house if not for my father's general disinterest in our home life, however. He wasn't exactly "Father of the Year" (or Husband of the Year for that matter), to which I know he would attest.

My father spent most of his time running a business that required his attention at all times of the day and night and the remainder *fadoodling around*—my way of saying he had better things to do away from home. When I was five years old, and my brothers four and three, our father met a teenage girl who would, some dozen or so years later, become his wife. We barely saw him except for Sundays when he would spend a few hours milling around the house before taking off for the day. My brothers and I had no relationship with him to speak of; we barely had any interaction with him aside from answering him when spoken to. Obviously, my dad made some bad choices—and we all suffered as a result.

My father died in December 2001, shortly after the horrific 9/11 attacks that shook our great nation to the core. Prior to his death, he admitted he had not been the father he should have been. His pain was obvious, and I saw him cry for the first time—I didn't know he could. He told me how proud he was of me and that of all the women he'd ever known, he held me in the highest esteem; he said I had my head "screwed on straight." He went on to say some other very poignant things that he previously never dared utter. I cannot express what an impact this had on me. I think in some ways it made up for all the years when he said nothing. It was an immensely bittersweet experience, for, while he was slowly dying, my father provided some greatly needed closure (to our fractured relationship) at a time when I needed it more than ever.

In addition to my father's philandering, he failed to provide us ample financial support. Early on, he worked on the tugboats off the coast of Staten Island, a job that took him away for long periods at a time. Years later, he started a commercial heating, ventilation, and air conditioning (HVAC) business he named after my brothers and me. That was an exciting time—I remember it like it was yesterday— his freshly painted work truck pulling up to the house with "TRC

Air Conditioning and Refrigeration" splashed across the front and side. It was one of the rare times I actually felt important to him. I was so proud, strutting about the place like I'd just won a prize. Nevertheless, despite his modest success as a small business owner, we—as a family—weren't any better off from a financial perspective than we had been prior.

My mother did the best she could, trying to make up the difference in other ways for our living in poverty. But as a stay-at-home mom, she had no choice but to rely on my father for financial support. Much to her credit, she never carried on about what we (or she) didn't have but rather persisted until she secured what her children needed to get by. Parenting three rambunctious kids, pretty much alone, she had the difficult task of balancing protecting her kids from "grown-up" stuff with scraping together enough financial resources to keep food on the table and clothes on our backs. Fortunately, when all else failed, my generous and caring aunt and grandparents picked up the slack that got us by.

None of this seemed to affect me much, except for the occasional jealousy when one of my friends got something we couldn't afford. I recall wanting a parakeet and hanging banners all around my bedroom, petitioning for it. When my best friend got a parakeet but I didn't, I was pretty deflated. Or there was the time I wanted my ears pierced and she got hers pierced instead. Frustrating, yes. But overall, despite a handful of bouts of envy over non-essential, material things, there was a lot to be thankful for, and the absence of a parakeet or a couple of holes in my earlobes didn't detract much from the big picture.

A well-rounded kid, I kept myself busy with a variety of activities such as learning to play a musical instrument or two, attending dance school, skating, writing poetry, art, crafting, crocheting, sewing, acting in school plays, and a host of other good stuff. In fact, I was an accomplished seamstress of sorts by the time I was in sixth grade (thanks to my aunt Marie), such that I was already wearing my own creations to school while the other kids in our sewing ("shop") class poked holes through loose-leaf paper with an empty sewing needle. Then, as if my plate wasn't full enough, I did my duty as a Brownie, Girl Scout, *and* Cadet—all this and a straight-A student and formidable athlete too. I recall how incredibly proud I was each year when I won the Presidential Award (a public school initiative designed to encourage physical fitness, referred to today as The President's Challenge). I remember the intensity of running that dash around the school, thinking there was no way in heck I was going to blow it no matter how out of breath I was or even if I was ready to drop. And with this fierce tenacity, in fact, is how I approached just about everything.

On a business front, I was quite the enterprising little urchin. At five, I went door-to-door selling Christmas cards. Later on, I sold handmade crafts from a wagon on the sidewalk in front of my house, where the businesspeople had no choice but to walk by each night on their way home from the train station down the street. I even briefly dabbled in one of those multilevel marketing product lines with my little friend from around the block. I didn't shy away from a good business opportunity, despite that most of them were short-lived.

I was certainly on the right track, despite family discourse that oftentimes gets in the way of a child's accomplishments; there were so many options open to me in terms of what I could do with my life. I even recall my mother once telling me that my teachers said I was "gifted" but added that she had hesitated to tell me (and didn't do so until years later) for fear I would get a "big head."

Early on, I enjoyed school immensely. I didn't see it as a chore but rather as an adventure. Elementary school went off without a hitch; it was just about as fun, interesting, and carefree as it should be. Middle school started out very much the same way—but soon took an ugly turn. Sometime during seventh grade, I met with unexpected and certainly undeserved bullying that, in retrospect, had a much greater effect on me than I realized until much later on in life.

Personally, I am, without a doubt, a non-violence kinda gal— was then and still am. I didn't grow up fist-fighting, pulling hair, or committing any other such vile acts, nor did I know anyone who did that sort of thing … until the "the bridge," that is. The Verrazano Narrows Bridge, the longest suspension bridge of its time in 1964, provided for an influx of Brooklynites that changed the peaceful landscape of our hometown for good.

The first bully I encountered was Roseanne. With an attitude as nasty as her physical attributes and a mouthful of braces to boot, she was perceived as a force to be reckoned with. Roseanne didn't live in my neighborhood, but we took the same bus to school each day. I had no idea what her problem was—we barely knew each other— but she sure had it in for me. One fine day, Roseanne decided to launch a terror campaign that involved telling me she was going to kick my ass, and enlisting the help of others to get the word out when she wasn't around to do so herself. This went on, day in and day out, for quite some time. She made a point of threatening me every time she saw me. Naturally, when she alighted from the bus each day, my insides tightened into a knot. I was petrified but never ratted on her. Rather, I toughed it out (as we all pretty much did back in the day) and went about my business, until the harassment stopped as unexpectedly as it had begun. Roseanne never did attempt any physical violence (thank goodness)—but she didn't have to. The idea was enough.

No sooner did Roseanne fade into the past that a second round of terror befell me the following year. By now it was eighth grade and I was getting bored with being the little Goody Two-shoes teacher's pet. I had taken up with a different crowd, kids with whom I could assert my independence by goofing off—that is, cutting out of class, getting high, and chasing boys.

One day, my newfound "friends" decided they were going to call me out for what they apparently considered the unpardonable sin of no longer liking the boy from our group I had casually dated—"dated" meaning I liked him, he liked me, and we called ourselves boyfriend and girlfriend. They staged an obscenity campaign that included yelling "tramp" and "whore" (which they, with their Brooklyn accents, pronounced *who-a*) at me every chance they got, which usually was in the middle of the school hallway between classes, when everyone could hear. Away from school, one of the boys in the group took to spitting on me every time he saw me. It was beyond repulsive. This torment went on for months but didn't stop me from going to school. In usual fashion, I toughed it out, albeit not an easy feat. I just couldn't fathom why anyone, let alone those in my social circle, would do such a thing. It was utterly devastating and left me with serious emotional scars.

When I entered high school, yet more bullying ensued—the worst bullying of all. Starting high school and being a teenager was difficult enough, but to have to look over my shoulder every day made it ever more challenging. This group of mean-spirited girls intercepted me in the school's courtyard every chance they got. Suffice it to say, I was afraid to walk around alone. They, too, screamed out vile epithets, and once again, I had no clue as to what I had done to deserve such treatment. I was merely a teenager, trying to get through school.

One day, the pack leader, Jackie, wanted to fight me in the middle of the courtyard. Just the thought of the two of us duking it out was unimaginable to me. I had never had a violent encounter of any kind in my entire life—and I certainly had no interest in taking up fist-fighting (over nothing) anytime soon. But one day, after being incessantly tormented and prodded to fight, I conceded, though I insisted we take it across the street, off school property, where no one could see.

There we were on a gravel dead-end road—me … and all of them. I was utterly horrified. At that time, in the late '70s, tube tops and big hoop earrings were all the rage. I was more freaked out by the prospect of having my tube top pulled down and my boobs exposed or getting my earlobes ripped than I was of getting a bloody lip. I removed my earrings and prayed my top would stay put. But no sooner did I prepare for battle than I began to cry. I couldn't fathom scratching, hair-pulling, punching, and kicking over … nothing. I didn't care if they made fun of me for crying either—it was better than the alternative. My reaction was genuine. And then, much to my astonishment, instead of getting berated by Jackie's posse, she apologized.

Still, I felt like a pariah. I was scared, lonely, and confused. Kids who are bullied often feel they are at fault, and it was no different for me—I felt like I'd done something wrong, even though I wasn't quite sure what that was. Again, I didn't report the bullying to anyone at school, nor did I get my parents involved. Back then, a kid would get more ribbing for being a tattletale than for backing down from a fist fight. Hence, I bowed to peer pressure and made it through that time physically unscathed, albeit a bit further worse for emotional wear.

Bullying can be enormously hurtful, of course, but at the same time, it also can teach valuable lessons. I firmly believe that being bullied becomes an integral part of who we are. It unquestionably has folded itself into me. It left an indelible mark on my psyche and, to some extent, shaped the way I deal with others. I took away three important lessons from my bullying experience I carry with me always: (1) I never resort to physical force except out of self-defense; (2) I try to carefully choose my battles and then give those I choose all I've got; and (3) I do everything in my power to refrain from ever behaving like the people who brutishly set out to hurt me.

Despite my strong resolve, I contemplated dropping out of school in freshman year, until a friend, several years older and obviously much wiser and whose opinion I valued highly, talked me out of it. I can still hear him telling me it would be a huge mistake, that I'd be sorry looking back in a few short years, knowing it would have been over. Boy, was he right!

Then, somewhere in the midst of my sophomore year, I had a major epiphany. The girl who had contemplated leaving high school not so long ago suddenly decided college was in her future. The prospect of starting a female-owned and operated auto repair business no longer held such intrigue. Instead, I set my sights on higher education, and off I went to announce the news to my high school grade advisor, who was noticeably shocked. Although I think he realized my potential all along, I surmise he never pushed the issue knowing that like a lot of rebellious teenagers, sooner or later I'd come around.

As time went on, I became increasingly more excited at the prospect of college, even though I never grew to like high school any better. Hence, when I was offered the opportunity to join the co-op program (where a student works and attends school on alternate weeks), I seized it. This was the perfect diversion. Not only did it give me a leg up on starting a career as well as put a few bucks in my pocket (even if it barely covered the cost of my tedious commute), it also got me out of Dodge.

In deciding where I was headed academically, I took a very pragmatic approach. My first passion was psychiatry, but that quickly went up in smoke when I realized it would take approximately twenty-two years of night school to become a psychiatrist. The thought of eight years—that is, a four-year degree pursued on a half-time basis—was daunting enough. Hence, I switched gears and set my sights on accountancy, a degree that would not only require less than a twenty-year commitment but also would provide a cornucopia of career opportunity.

But accountancy would never come to fruition.

I foolishly allowed a slew of naysayers to slowly but surely talk me out of it. "A CPA? You?" I heard over and over again that I was "not the accountant type"; that I just didn't fit the button-down, number crunching bill. After a while, I started to doubt myself and starting rethinking my calling. Computer science came to mind. It had all the attributes of the kind of practical career I was looking for, namely that it was a field pregnant with opportunity.

But computer science, too, would turn out to be just as shorted-lived when one ill-equipped professor managed to singlehandedly stomp out that fire before it ever even really started to burn. My very first computer science class turned out to be my last for no reason other than the incompetence of a professor more concerned with bragging about allowing his fiancé to make up our exams than he was about teaching us enough to pass them. The whole class bombed, forcing those of us for who computer science was a major to explore other pastures. Regrettably, I was too afraid to speak up to the school's administration until a couple years later when I had realized the magnitude of what had occurred. By then, they said, it was too late.

Left once again to figure out my path in life, I decided that business management tickled my fancy. This field of knowledge, I thought, was about as universal as it gets. Still with a scientific bent, it also allows for the kind of imaginativeness not necessarily known to be associated with accountancy and computer science. With this, I believed I couldn't go wrong.

Despite possibly finally having found my niche, I still had the worry of how I was going to pay for school. While I was eligible for low-interest student loans and got one or two miniscule grants that barely made a noticeable dent in the bill, I was flying by the seat of my pants every semester when I faced the nearly monumental task of scraping together enough money to cover the bill. Still, I was determined to get a college education, no matter what it took.

My stint at St. John's University lasted a whopping nine years, despite that it was not the college I necessarily *wanted* to attend as much as it was the college I *could* attend. Despite having the credentials to get into the school of my choice, logistics limited my prospects to those places close to home where I could work by day and attend school by night, which, as it turned out, was an incomparable experience—character-building in ways I couldn't have imagined at the time.

Early on, during the first year or so, I worked in Manhattan in the banking industry, performing monotonous administrative tasks. Much to my chagrin, there wasn't much an inexperienced female could do without an education, so I took whatever came along. After getting laid off one year later due to the economic downturn in the early '80s, I threw in the nine-to-five towel and became a bartender. In addition to only having to work two or three days a week to earn more than I did working full-time at the bank, it was also great fun. It was not, however, as certain family members repeatedly reminded me, a "real job."

I next tested the waters of retail management—one of the few ways an aspiring management major could get actual managerial experience—but soon landed back in the nine-to-five grind, this time on Wall Street. Wall Street, for me, though, wasn't about finance or glamour. No. If truth be known, I detested the whole Wall

Street scene despite going to great lengths to study for and pass the Series 7 (broker's licensing) exam. I was by no means looking to be a broker; rather, I wanted the extra cash that came with the credentials. Outside of that, my main focus was school. Getting good grades was of paramount importance; I didn't want a job getting in the way.

In January 1985, after five years of night school, I finally had my associate's degree in hand. I would have graduated a year sooner if not for the Reagan administration's misguided attempt to bail the country out of the Savings and Loan crisis, which meant that folks like me—independent working poor—had to earn less than $3,000 a year, *after* a full year of being independent from one's parental home, before being eligible for a loan. Not a hand-out, a loan. It was devastating. But loan or no loan, I was as determined as ever to finish college. And I did.

In May 1989, after nine years that seemed like an eternity, I was at last one step closer to the American dream, that is, *my* American dream: I'd earned a Bachelor of Science in business management. A goal that once seemed almost unattainable finally had come to fruition. That was an immensely important day—and a huge relief. I was finally on my way.

By then, I was just over a year into my tenure at New York City Transit, working as a budget analyst. My first day in the Department of Buses (or Surface Transit, as it was called then) was March 21, 1988, having left Wall Street only two days prior. I was pretty jazzed about setting forth on my journey as a public servant. This was more than a job for me; it was an adventure of sorts—a brand new world I enthusiastically welcomed after all the years spent helping others attain their goal of making money buying and selling stocks and bonds. Best of all, I worked right on Staten Island, only minutes from home.

My new office environment was a stark contrast to a brokerage house. The sleepy quietude of the Staten Island Division office at 357 St. Marks Place was very foreign to me—with the exception of the guy directly to my left, who made enough noise to make up for everyone else and smoked enough cigarettes to kill us all off in short order. Worse yet, I was a young, single woman amongst a bunch of "old guys", with whom I feared I had nothing in common.

I recall sitting at my desk the first week, wondering what the hell I'd gotten myself into. *Could this possibly be worse than Wall Street?* I thought. In time, however, things turned around and, before long, I began to develop an affection for the "old guys" with whom I spent my days as well as a growing appreciation for the public sector.

Not everything, however, would prove paradisiacal. The party turned out to be short-lived as my life was thrust into a complete tailspin. My naïveté about how things really worked, that is, the machinations of the world of government employment, would send me on the wildest, most devastating ride I never could have imagined in a million years.

CHAPTER 2

HIGH FLYING BIRD

MY CAREER WAS THE CENTERPIECE of my life; it (unfortunately) defined who I was. Growing up during the feminist revolution convinced me that marriage and kids were secondary to career. I foolishly bought into the notion that being a stay-at-home mom was for women who didn't know any better, that a woman's top priority should be her career, and that her degree of success therefrom was the ultimate definition of her existence. Between that and seeing my mother struggle as she did, I promised myself I wouldn't even think of settling down until I had a college degree and a flourishing career, however long that took. And now I was finally on my way.

Without question, March 1988 through January 1992 was the high point of my career. Not a long stretch, mind you, but one I'll forever cherish: a job I enjoyed in an industry I adored. I loved going to work every day. I could barely believe I had finally found my lot. Or perhaps it found me. But either way, no more dreaded Sunday nights!

Public transportation was a far cry from Wall Street—or any other industry I had known, for that matter. The organizational cultures were so completely divergent that it was shocking. Not that I was used to seeing women in positions of power, mind you, as Wall

Street, too, was by far a male-dominated industry. But New York City Transit (or New York City Transit Authority, as it was then called, or the TA, for short)—and Staten Island Division ("SID"), in particular—gave a whole new meaning to the term prehistoric.

Staten Island Division's management was a predominantly right-leaning, middle-aged, white male boys club, where the guys made no secret that they—"the men" (as they would refer to themselves)—would rather their kingdom stay that way. Not that there weren't *any* minorities among them. The negligible number of blacks, Hispanics, women, and other minorities that did manage to slip through the cracks via affirmative action (or occasionally by affiliation) were far and few between and otherwise strategically placed throughout the remainder of the organization to somehow give the impression that the TA was an arbiter of equality. If not for the affirmative action initiative, however, I can say with relative certainty that minorities, especially women in the case of SID, would have ceased to exist where "the men" were clearly unaccepting of change—mainly the kind that meant allowing those not of their ilk to infiltrate their cloistered world.

Where women were concerned, they could generally be found in the lowest paying jobs performing administrative duties. For those amongst the managerial ranks, they were almost never on the operations side of things where the "action" was. That was strictly male territory. The transit industry itself was not female-friendly up to that time, and New York City Transit was no exception. There existed a boys club atmosphere wrought with antiquated mind-sets, where women typed, fetched coffee, answered phones, and occasionally cleaned up lunch or other office mess. I didn't have a clue as to the pervasiveness of this backward culture when I "signed up".

Staten Island Division was one of the five "Divisions" of (what was then called) Surface Transit. Surface, along with (what was then called) Rapid Transit (otherwise known as the subway), were the two transportation departments that comprised the New York City Transit Authority (NYCTA). NYCTA (referred to herein as NYCT) is one of a family of transportation agencies under the parent organization (or Public Benefit Corporation as they now refer to it) known as the Metropolitan Transit Authority (MTA). Staten Island is unique in that it does not have a subway system, as do the other four boroughs, but instead is home to a single-line above-ground railway (then called Staten Island Rapid Transit Operating Authority or SIRTOA).

Staten Island Division (SID) employed around fifteen hundred people, the preponderance of which were bus operators, bus mechanics, line supervisors, and dispatchers located within the borough's two bus depots: Castleton and Yukon (a third has since been added). Within the Division's headquarters was a group of around fifteen employees including superintendents of both "transportation" and "maintenance", administrative managers, analysts, and clerks with whom I directly worked.

With the exception of one white woman who had moved on to another agency before I started, there had been no minority administrative managers at Division until a year or so after I started, when they filled the labor relations manager position with a black male. He became the "token" minority of our little family. On the operations side, there had never been a female manager—at least not quite yet—although there were those few strategically placed aforementioned minority males in each of the depots who had, no question, been the products of affirmative action.

Among the bus operator ranks, the female population was slowly growing. Although only a small percentage of all bus operators were female, one of them managed to make it (via exam) to dispatcher, a supervisory level position one rung above bus operator and one below entry level management (or in this case at that time "deputy superintendent"). This represented a major break in the glass ceiling that didn't go over well with "the men". Years later, she became the first female transportation deputy superintendent. This went over even worse. Being a "first," she was the target of a great deal of unwarranted negative fanfare, especially because she sued the TA after suffering a miscarriage while driving a bus—as the story goes—in the early stages of her pregnancy, against the advice of her physicians.

Generally, bus operators were assigned "light duty" if they could not perform their regularly assigned duties for any number of medical reasons, up to and including something as inconsequential as a stubbed finger. But not her. As a female bus operator, she was a pioneer who would "pay" for the audacity to tread where she clearly wasn't welcome.

Before I met her, all I knew was what I had heard through the grapevine—and there was a lot of loose talk about this so-called "troublemaker". The guys bad-mouthed her incessantly, making her out to be public enemy number one. The negative commentary included how she cheated on the supervisor's exam (as she achieved a perfect score) and how her cheating had something to do with her father (who had also worked for the TA as a dispatcher) and how all of that somehow equated to her religious beliefs. It wasn't until years later when I realized that things weren't necessarily as they had been portrayed. I got to know her a bit and learned over time that there may well have been a great deal of validity to her story, namely that she was treated unfairly only for having been female and nothing else. Meanwhile, I was ashamed of myself for ever listening to the gossip. It was a lesson learned—fortunately for me, in light of what lay ahead.

Initially, I didn't have any gender-related problems with my male coworkers, most of whom treated me like they did each other—at least to my face anyway. In the beginning, though, I suppose I was somewhat of a novelty too. I was single, attractive, bubbly, and intelligent. Okay, the intelligent part might not have gone over as well as the rest, but it seemed even that attribute could be tolerated so long as I wasn't stepping on anyone's toes. I think most of the guys saw me as a glorified clerk—or "secretary" as they would often refer to me—simply because they had no other concept of how to perceive a woman's role in the workplace.

No matter what they thought of me or women in the workplace in general, though, most of the guys I worked with—and most of those I encountered throughout the system—had their eye on one thing: retirement. A typical career, in their view, was seen as something of a prison sentence. If I heard "How many years you got?" once, I heard it a million times. I got so sick and tired of that question that after a while—well—let's just say some folks knew not to ask me anymore. But when they did, my answer was simple. I wasn't there for life. I had a college education, and my stint at the TA was simply a springboard to bigger and better things. I don't know if this caused resentment, but I didn't much concern myself with it. All I knew was that I was growing to love what I was doing and, as such, beginning to envision public service as something I wanted to be part of for a long time to come.

My glory days at SID were not, however, without their trials and tribulations. Once the novelty wore off, I was confronted with an incident here or there, presumably meant to put me in my place, not just for being female but for being the kind of female that I was.

The most painful experience, and one that changed the course of my life in a most profound way, centered around a scholarship program designed to give employees like me (non-managerial "professional/technical") a chance to attend a graduate school he or she might otherwise never have a chance to attend. Each year, NYCT awarded two full graduate scholarships, called mayoral scholarships, to, presumably, the most deserving applicants. As SID's training coordinator and one who was actively in the market for a graduate school, I had the inside track on exactly who was in the running and what my chances were of being awarded one of the two scholarships. When I found out from the guy in charge of the program—a guy with whom I communicated frequently—that there were no other applicants, I thought I'd struck gold. A full scholarship to New York University—I could barely believe something so great could even happen to me.

The criteria were fairly straightforward. In addition to other basic requirements, interested applicants had to enlist a sponsor who was a member of management, someone, that is, who would vouch for his character, work ethic, and such. Our soon-to-be general manager, George, then assistant general manager in charge of SIRTOA, whose office was in the same building, was the perfect person to tap. I had known George for years, we had a superb relationship, and it was clear he thought the world of me. Not only did he immediately agree to be my sponsor, but he was exuberant about it. So far, so good.

Then, one day, totally out of the blue, in the midst of sailing along the way to a coveted college scholarship, I was called into my boss's office. Bill, our assistant general manager—a twenty-something, white male only a couple of years my senior and usually a fairly decent guy—showed his true colors. Granted, Bill had a definite streak of chauvinism that occasionally reared its ugly head (which accounted for all of my not-so-great experiences over the first few otherwise glorious years). Outside of these limited instances that could easily have been chalked up to poor judgment, he was a pretty cool guy. But not on this particular day. As soon as I entered his office, I knew right off something was up—and it wasn't good.

The consistently fluid and ever-articulate Bill stumbled over his words in what began to look like an awkward attempt at diplomacy. "Stop beating around the bush," I said, "and just spit it out." He clumsily went on to tell me that I wasn't eligible for the scholarship—nor was anyone in my position. The program, he insisted, was reserved for management. As the Division's training coordinator, I knew this was untrue.

Stunned, I went on to make a case that obviously fell on deaf ears. Wherever the conversation was going, it was clear Bill was on a mission to deliver news that would prove to alter the course of my life in ways of which even I was yet to feel the negative repercussions. To this day, I don't know for sure what exactly went down that day. I can only venture to guess, based upon his past, albeit infrequent, incidents of "bad judgment", that he did not want to see me, a woman, achieve a higher level of education than he had, and perhaps, toward that end, might have harbored concerns of someday finding himself answering to *me*.

The whole thing proved a crushing disappointment, not just for what occurred but for *how* it occurred. If it had happened today, Bill might have come to regret his actions. But then, I was green. I hadn't quite honed the skill of argument, nor did I possess the confidence to more fiercely challenge him. Instead, I walked away, utterly devastated, and let it eat my insides out for a long time. I sometimes still wonder how things would have turned out had Bill exercised some integrity in his handling of what could have and should have been a no-brainer. Would I have stayed clear of the harm that ultimately befell me had he not cavalierly thrown this roadblock down on my path to success? Unfortunately, I'll never know.

There were a few other times when Bill felt the need to put me in my place that tainted my glory days at Division. While the scholarship ordeal was the most impacting, it was by far not life-threatening such as was the time when he thought it was cute to place me in a potentially fatally dangerous situation to teach me a lesson. At the very least, it represented a blatant lack of concern for me, not only as a woman but as a human being.

Back then, employees were required to take a driving test

in order to operate TA patrol cars—a process borne out of—as well as complicated by—bureaucracy. Obtaining a driving permit required a trip to the South Bronx, the not-so-inviting epicenter of the Manhattan and Bronx Surface Transit Operating Authority (MABSTOA), the (now antiquated) entity under which myself and certain other NYCTA employees were governed, wherein an employee with a current and valid driver's license would need to physically demonstrate an ability he already clearly possessed. The South Bronx, however, is frankly not a place for a young white woman in a marked car—or any car, for that matter. She might as well be driving around with a neon sign reading, "Rape me and leave me for dead." As such, it was arranged that I would hop a ride with a couple of coworkers headed up there on other business.

On the day I was scheduled to go, I was required to be at work at 6 a.m., two or so hours earlier than normal. As very bad timing would have it, my alarm failed to sound because, I later discovered, I had inadvertently moved the dial slightly off the radio station when setting it the night before. I woke up at my usual time instead. In a total panic, I immediately called the office, even though I knew my ride was long gone, and explained what had happened. I got there as soon as I could, mortified for what had occurred. I did not take slip-ups like this lightly, but considering the circumstances and my otherwise stellar employment history, wasn't much worried about repercussions. I would just reschedule the driving test for another time.

Nothing doing. Bill decided that rather than allow me the courtesy of male accompaniment the next time around, he would send me to the South Bronx alone on a date to be determined. Panic set in. He knew full well, as did everyone, that I was petrified of the South Bronx; even worse, he knew of the potential risks associated with his decision. When I confronted him, Bill told me point-blank that I was lying about having overslept. I was beside myself. I couldn't understand why he so vehemently refused to believe me when he had no reason to believe otherwise. I recall arguing back and forth to no productive end, until I walked away, deflated. I felt as though I had no rights and no recourse except to take matters into my own hands, which I did, by arranging a ride to the Bronx on my own.

Although this and the scholarship incidents were pretty lousy (and obviously meant to keep me in line), I didn't allow them to overshadow all the goodness. And despite that the work of a budget analyst wasn't exactly the stuff dream jobs are made of, it was a start. Joy that didn't come from the tasks at hand came from an atmosphere beaming with antics and laughter. It was unlike any other workplace I had ever known. Even our boss, Tom, took part in the fun, especially on Fridays, when we had "storytelling time." I vividly recall how he lit up like a kid on Christmas morning as the office comedian, Vic, regaled us with some of the craziest stories we'd ever heard.

Before long, we added another member to our little family. Carmine, an associate staff analyst from the central budget office in Brooklyn, was given a lateral transfer to Staten Island Division after approval was given for us to increase the budget staff by one. I already knew Carmine, at least as much as you can know someone through phone contact, as he was the central budget liaison to whom each borough's analysts would submit their monthly budget reports. I also knew of Carmine from years prior to working at the TA through a close friend who worked almost side by side with him for a long time. All I heard was what a screw-up he was and how he did very little aside from sell clothes out of the back of his car. Nevertheless, I decided to reserve judgment. As I had no firsthand negative dealings with him, I was intent to keep things neutral between us.

Carmine, however, didn't waste any time in living up to his reputation as a slacker. I began wondering why we had hired a guy who came with such baggage, and couldn't help but to just come out and ask. I was told by my immediate supervisor—one of the two men that conducted the interviews responsible for his induction into our little family—that after three rounds of interviews, Carmine was the best of a bunch of otherwise unsuitable candidates, and that in order to avoid the risk of losing the position, they "settled" for him.

Holy cow! They filled the position with someone they didn't even deem suitable, just to avoid the risk of losing it? No question, I was beginning to see how government really worked.

For the most part, Carmine spent his time doing whatever it was he was known for doing: organizing baseball cards (a collection he claimed to one day finance his daughters' college education as if to suggest this made it permissible to do during work hours), selling clothes, and working his other job as a janitor (where he would polish floors before arriving for his "real" job), and whatever else would make him a buck. Didn't matter that he came in exhausted every day after getting up at the crack of dawn to clean floors and that he had little energy left for his analytical duties. And it didn't matter either that he used company patrol cars to drive about Staten Island all day looking for baseball paraphernalia. The bottom line is that he was a seasoned bureaucrat who knew exactly what he could get away with—and did.

Between the maintenance of his baseball card collection, the energy expended performing his other job, and his overall lackadaisical work ethic, it didn't take long before I lost my patience. I was doing my work *and* his and for a lot less pay than him. Sometimes I got the feeling that he believed his tomfoolery to be justified because he already had his American dream—house, wife, kids, job he couldn't lose that paid for it all—and could do whatever he wanted. I think he expected me to look the other way. Well, I couldn't. I didn't fault him for working a second a job or doing whatever it took to do right by his family—I entirely respect that—but for when it got to be at my expense for as long as it did, my understanding waned.

Occasionally, I paid Bill a visit to let him know that I was not pleased with the arrangement: Carmine making ten grand more than me while I do his work and mine. He repeatedly told me that things would change, so I hung on, doing whatever it took to complete all tasks at hand, with or without my counterpart. But nothing ever changed—except my level of resentment. And to think I even went so far as to forfeit holidays with *my* family so that Carmine could be with his. Ugh. I guess it's true that no good deed goes unpunished.

After enough time had passed, when I was fairly certain that Bill was not going to do anything to turn things around, I decided to take a more proactive approach: I asked for a promotion. I figured I should at least be making as much as Carmine, especially if I was going to continue to do his work. Bill was very receptive to the idea but said that it wasn't going to happen right away—we'd have to include it in the following year's budget so as not to bring any undue attention to the request for a promotional position in the middle of the year. It seemed to make sense—in a bureaucratic sort of way, that is—so I didn't argue. I was just elated to get the heads up and went about my business confident it was only a matter of time.

In the interim of a far longer-than-expected wait, during which I was repeatedly told the paperwork was in the pipeline, I finally graduated college in May 1989. This was the proudest day of my life; a day that at one time had seemed so very far away. It was a bittersweet time, though. I was incredibly relieved to be done with school, but at the same time, sad to say good-bye to a place that felt like a second home. Still, I looked forward to a much-needed academic hiatus during which time I could decide where I would go from there, both in terms of education *and* career.

For the year following graduation, I took full advantage of kicking back and doing some of the things I'd hardly been able to squeeze in for the previous nine years. Namely, I hadn't really had all that much opportunity to socialize during a time when other young adults were "out there" finding themselves, much less without the burden of schoolwork on top of the responsibilities that come along with independent living. And so I had myself a ball, went out every chance I got, trying to make up for lost time, I suppose. Still, I had a career to consider and a decision to make about graduate school.

Even though the mayoral scholarship thing was dead in the water, I kept NYU in my sights, despite the staggering tuition. I knew that if I wanted it badly enough, I'd get it on my own. I'd paid my way through undergraduate school and certainly didn't need my employer—or the taxpayers—to foot the bill for my advanced education either.

Any of you who have been there know that the process of applying to college, especially graduate school, can be daunting. I was required to write three rather involved essays (into which I put my heart and soul); provide a number of professional references (one of which I got from our general manager, Tom); take the GSAT exam (into which I didn't really put my heart and soul); and pay a rather hefty application fee (that cost enough to cover a week's worth of groceries). Fortunately, however, I was told by the school that none of the entrance factors weighed as heavily as one's undergrad GPA, that that one factor alone could be determinative. Fortunately, that was my strongest selling point! Unfortunately, however, some things are just not meant to be. After all the effort put forth, I was not accepted into the program. I was seriously disappointed—again— but not sure what had gone wrong.

Once more in my life, both naivety and ignorance got the best of me. I was clueless as to the political intricacies of applying for school—and the truth about how some folks really operated. I thought I would apply and, depending on whether I measured up against the existing standards, I would be accepted or rejected. I also never questioned Tom's integrity; I foolishly assumed that if he agreed to vouch for me that he was doing it to help, not hinder, the process. Silly me. It wasn't until some time later that I came to learn that a successful applicant not only was one required to be the son or daughter of a pedigreed parent alumni or some other such affiliation, but that Tom had ulterior motives I never would have imagined.

As part of the application process, Tom was required to complete a questionnaire that he was asked not to share with me. Rather, he was instructed to mail it directly back to the school. Realizing that I was in the dark about his wrongdoing, after all, I'd never be the wiser as to what he had done otherwise, one of the secretarial staff made me privy to a copy of the questionnaire. The blood instantly drained from my body. I couldn't' believe my eyes. It wasn't all bad, mind you, but enough negativity concerning my character that such a school would easily have the perfect excuse to pass me by—and did. First he made sure I didn't get a scholarship for which the taxpayers would foot the bill—but now to foil me from getting an education for which I would pay myself? It just didn't make any sense. Again, I was seeing how things really worked, how if someone doesn't want you to have something even if it's for no reason other than one's gender, and he has enough influence over you, you will likely not get it and probably never know why.

I was crushed but wasn't about to give up on my dream. I quickly recalibrated, formulating a plan I considered to be more readily attainable. As I'd grown to adore the public sector by then, I decided that is where academia should take me. And so, I kicked Plan B into gear.

It wasn't long before my manager, Peter, brought to my attention a program offered at Bernard M. Baruch College in New York City that catered to folks like me—those with a career path who want to pursue a graduate education but unable to attend school during the day. For a mere seventy-two Saturdays, one could work toward an "executive master's" on a full-time basis. It was much more affordable than NYU, and although not cheap, it was nothing a good old-fashioned student loan couldn't cover. This was, after all, an investment in my future, and nothing was going to get in my way.

Back on the work front, the next year's budget cycle came… and went. Still, no promotion. Instead of answers, I was told, ad nauseam, that I was a much better employee than Carmine who would move up the ranks, while his bus had already pulled into the terminal. It was lip service that didn't get me anywhere. It certainly wasn't putting more money in my pocket. Wondering if I was being given "the business" after waiting so long for something that perhaps would never materialize, I decided to employ an alternate course of action: seek a promotion elsewhere. And so I did … and it worked like a charm.

Upon learning that he might lose his little workhorse, Bill somehow managed to close the deal: my promotion to associate staff analyst was finalized in September 1990. Not only was I now on par with my rather useless counterpart, Carmine, but also in a financial position sound enough to look toward homeownership. What's more, it was time to start graduate school. Finally, there I was up to my eyebrows in goodness! For the first time in my life, I felt like the American dream was within reach, waiting for me to embrace. From where I stood, things could not have been any better. I was truly on top of the world.

Meanwhile, back at the ranch, the entire SID administration was preparing for an exodus. Our general manager Tom, assistant general manager Bill, and budget manager Peter (my immediate supervisor) were heading for greener pastures—Tom and Bill left in September 1990, and Peter a few months later. I wished them well but was concerned about where this would leave me. I hadn't heard a word about who would be taking their spots but knew that whoever these persons were going to be could make or break things. So, when I found out that the new general manager was going to be George, the same George who graciously agreed to sponsor me for the mayoral scholarship, I was elated. This was like the cherry on the cake.

Then, as if things could even get any better, on January 15, 1991, I was called into Peter's office, where he was "acting" in Bill's behalf. Expecting the usual nonsense from Peter—such as reprinting a sheet of paper missing a period that nobody would ever notice, or some other ridiculousness for which he was famous—I got the absolute shock of my life. He announced that George had chosen me to take over his (Peter's) position as manager of Budget and Personnel. I couldn't believe it. Talk about being pleasantly blindsided. And a *second* promotion in only three months too. This was the break I had been waiting for. It appeared my hard work actually paid off, and I was over the moon with joy.

Everyone, however, was not as happy about my success as I was.

Carmine was seething. The affable guy with whom I'd peacefully—albeit begrudgingly—shared so much for the previous couple of years turned instantly bitter. He would not look at me, or talk to me, or do anything I asked. In fact, he started handing back assignments to me, nastily telling me, "Do it yourself." He sat slumped over his desk, like a crash-car dummy, quietly doing whatever it was he usually did, namely obsessing over his baseball card collection. I knew I was in for a tough time.

Adding to the musical chairs mayhem, Bill's spot as assistant general manager had yet to be filled, and there were no viable prospects in sight—that is, until George had the brilliant idea of temporarily filling it with one of our resident deputy superintendents, Fred, a bus operator turned dispatcher who had only very recently been promoted to management. "Three weeks until I find a qualified candidate," George said, insisting that if he didn't quickly fill the spot with someone—anyone—we might lose it, a chance he refused to take, but one that I believed to be more a product of his paranoia.

Fred was a nice enough guy—a quiet, reserved type who spent most of his time at SID puttering around with our computer system from the work station at his desk. He seemed to fancy himself some type of IT guy but was really just a novice hacker wannabe. He had no managerial experience, but that was never a prerequisite in such a notoriously cronyism-driven system. In fact, I'm quite certain that Fred didn't even have an actual set of responsibilities as deputy superintendent. He just quietly tinkered at his desk until summoned otherwise, perhaps, to drive someplace to pick up or deliver a report or some other mundane thing. It wasn't unusual, however, for one of the guys inducted into the inner circle to be without an actual set of responsibilities. Whatever it is that was asked of you, you graciously accepted, as long as it got you one day closer to retirement.

Three weeks came and went; Fred did not. George seemed in no hurry to do as he professed either. He appeared to be growing comfortable with Fred as his flunky, despite Fred's blatant lack of managerial prowess. But apparently, Fred didn't need any. Fred was a quick study in how to get by riding someone's coattails, and he managed to keep his head above water by riding mine! I showed him everything I knew, held his hand for months showing him the ropes, and then completed all the tasks for him. George knew Fred had no applicable skills, but as long as Fred remained loyal, George was okay with him—the presumptive appearance of loyalty was the main thing one really needed to project to be in George's good graces. Nevertheless, George continuously reassured me that Fred's stint was temporary, and I trusted him implicitly.

George and I always had what I considered a very cordial professional relationship. I felt very comfortable talking to him and believed we shared a mutual respect for one another. On many occasions, I sat with him in his office, chatting, about this and that, while he openly conducted business as though my being there was a way for him to demonstrate his trust in me—and perhaps a show of his machismo too. While it was obvious that George appreciated my vocational abilities, I sensed that he might also have liked having me around for reasons outside of that, although he never made any outwardly inappropriate gestures to that effect. Nevertheless, things between us were good, and unless he did something so foolish, they would stay that way.

Over time, however, George's true colors began to show. The face he had once put on for us prior to his big promotion was quickly changing. Mild-mannered, grandfatherly George was slowly unfolding into a passive/aggressive Mussolini. I soon realized that his kind, soft-spoken, affable manner was nothing more than a front for his insatiable need for control. He ultimately showed himself to be a manipulative, egotistical old coot, who fancied himself the godfather of Staten Island—and the timing couldn't have been worse.

No sooner did George settle into his role as our new general manager than the MTA found itself facing another of its innumerable financial crises. In keeping with the new mandates, working overtime was strictly prohibited and all promotions, pending and otherwise, were frozen until further notice. We happened to have had ten promotions pending at the time—one being mine. I'd already been counting on the extra cash to buy my first place, but now the wait would have to be just a bit longer.

George promised us all—eight male superintendent types and myself along with George's secretary, Nancy, that as far as he was concerned, our promotions were permanent, that although they might be delayed, the freeze would have no bearing on them, no matter how long it lasted. We were all assured that it was only a matter of time.

Next thing we know, George decided that he didn't want to wait to promote one of the eight men, Jim, a deputy superintendent for whom he had big plans. Certainly, that was his prerogative— except for one thing. He expected me to carry out his forbidden mission as though it was just another day at the office, to pretend as if no mandate had been handed down restricting us from taking such a step. And *that* was not something I was willing to do.

At the time, I took my responsibility as a public servant quite seriously. To me, it was an honor and a privilege to serve the public and to do so with a brand of dignity and dedication unmatched by anything I had ever undertaken. It might sound idealistic, but I *was* idealistic. Nothing was going to sway me to do anything I didn't believe to be above-board. Sadly, though, I would come to learn that things did not work that way in the real world, and especially in George's world, that by not being "a loyal servant" of a particular kind, namely one not willing to surrender her integrity without question, I would pay the ultimate price.

CHAPTER 3

AND THE HOUSE FELL DOWN

ALMOST ONE YEAR TO THE DAY of getting promoted to management in January 1991, things took a ghastly turn. What started out as something that appeared to be nothing more than an uneventful stalemate between George and me slowly transformed into a perfect storm of events that would have him doing a complete one-eighty and thrusting me into an emotional whirlwind I will not soon forget.

I surmised that George's affection for me first began to wane when I shied away from what he apparently viewed as not only my professional duty but also my personal obligation to him to process Jim's promotion. At that time, I had been a manager for only a couple months and wasn't about to do anything I perceived as contrary to organizational policy—not for him or anyone. But as ultimately became evident, George had no tolerance for subordinates who were not on board with him, funny-business or not. In retrospect, it is clear that his definition of loyalty was not mine. In putting the organization over him, I was demonstrating disloyalty in the highest degree, and George was prepared to show me what that meant to him.

While things were brewing between George and me, Carmine was busy with plans of his own. He never did accept being passed over for the promotion and wasn't letting it go. He incessantly and secretly complained to Fred (I later learned) that he believed he should have been chosen for the position because he had been there longer. I suspect he also felt his gender was a factor in his favor: he was a man with a mortgage, a wife, and two kids. Fred, a staunch civil service guy, knew nothing of a merit-based system of reward, nor did he recognize the value of anyone who wasn't one of his bus operator brethren. I suspect he easily agreed with Carmine's point of view. In Fred's and Carmine's worlds—and the world of civil service—one's tenure (and in this case, gender) took precedence over all else.

I suspect that Fred and Carmine didn't have a hard time getting George over to their side. After all, George was already questioning whether he had made a prudent choice in selecting me for Peter's spot. No doubt they used this as leverage to paint me as an ungrateful servant, well knowing how nonplussed George was by the whole Jim thing.

Of course, it certainly wasn't my business to dictate to George whom he should promote, but it was my business to operate above-board, the responsibility, in my humble opinion, of any individual within whom public trust is bestowed. But naiveté, and the idealism that went with it, had always been my Achilles' heel. I was now beginning to see that honesty simply didn't matter and, in fact, could prove to cause more harm than good. Still, I couldn't go along with something I knew was so totally wrong. If that is what was expected of me, perhaps they did choose the wrong person for the job.

As far as Jim was concerned, admittedly, there was a part of me that just didn't like him—although that didn't influence my decision to steer clear of processing his promotion. Jim was a scoundrel, a brown-nosing yes-man with a penchant for revenge. Let's just say that Jim's legacy was that "he would sell his grandmother" to get what he wanted.

Not surprisingly, Jim's impending promotion stirred a great deal of controversy. Not only was he a scoundrel, but he wasn't even a qualified one. But nobody made much of a stink about it outside of the grumbling amongst each other. God forbid his colleagues speak out against him for fear of finding themselves in our own version of Siberia: the South Bronx. That is where all bad operations managers went when they demonstrated independent thinking or had, by some other means, fallen out of grace.

One of our comrades, though, wasn't deterred. Wayne, Jim's former partner from their days as SID's quality control team, was a top-notch maintenance guy and all-around good soul that wanted that job as much as anyone else. And if anyone deserved it, it was Wayne. He was hard working, dedicated, innovative, reliable, and everything else you'd ever want from an employee. Wayne was also not afraid of George. Oh, and did I mention he was black? That alone gave him a snowball's chance in hell of not only being passed over for that promotion, but *any* promotion. But that didn't stop Wayne from at least trying.

One day Wayne paid George a visit to apprise him of his interest in the position. George attentively heard him out in his usual grandfatherly way ... and then handed Wayne a stack of job postings, all of which were lower-paying, less prestigious positions located far away from SID. George told Wayne he'd be great for one of those jobs instead, and offered to give Wayne a letter of recommendation. Wayne was livid—and rightly so. George's trying to push Wayne out with feigned praise and a stack of prospects was tantamount to skirting a discrimination suit and nothing more.

As much as it pained me, and as much as I would have loved to see Wayne get that promotion, the ball was in my court to see Jim reach the finish line. Meanwhile, all I could think about was how I could eloquently recuse myself from the whole ugly thing. I mean, how does one tell his boss "no" without looking bad? At some point, I finally got up the nerve to delicately let George know that promoting Jim went squarely against policy (as if he didn't know) and, as such, implied I had no intention to move forward with processing the paperwork. George didn't react, though, and I walked away, assuring myself that everything was okay between us, convinced that was the end of it. No doubt it was then that I sealed my fate.

All the while, unbeknownst to me, George had his little elves toiling away in the workshop with the goal of making his dream a reality. Fred and Carmine had before them this golden opportunity to show George that it was them, not me, who should be running the show, to prove to him that it was in fact "the men" he could trust to carry out his mission.

From the confines of my lonely cubicle, I sensed that things weren't going very smoothly for my colleagues. George and his dynamic duo were having a heck of a time getting the promotion wrapped up; in fact, the paperwork went back and forth from Staten Island to Brooklyn so many times it darn near caught fire. And if not for all the hullabaloo, I might not have ever known what was going on behind my back. But I did. And from what I witnessed, I was convinced I had made the right decision, even if I was forced to stand alone.

George never once intimated to me that he was upset with my stance. Rather, he acted like it was business as usual … well, kind of anyway. Over the course of the remainder of the year, he proceeded to gradually push through the remaining promotions, except his secretary's and mine. I was kept completely out of the loop too, even as George continually reassured me that everything was copasetic, and most importantly, that Fred's days were numbered.

When I'd ask why my promotion was not moving forward with the others, he told me over and over again that until he found a permanent replacement for Fred, he simply couldn't finalize my promotion because, he reasoned, that individual would need to be part of the process. For one, this made no sense since I had already been working as Manager of Budget and Personnel for nearly a year, and two, it was contrary to his earlier reassurances that all pending promotions were, are far as he was concerned, final, despite the freeze. But what was I to do? I just kept telling myself that everything was all right, even when I knew darn well it wasn't.

As for George's secretary, I discovered that some very sinister machinations were brewing behind the scenes. It turns out, Nancy's promise of a promotion was but a carrot dangled to elicit her cooperation—as the office spy! And she bit. In return for her loyal service, she would receive a promotion that, thus far, she had failed to see materialize. But this didn't stop her from merrily working undercover, spending a great deal of her time tracking my every move. She engaged me in chats and made note of everything I said. She listened in on my phone conversations and monitored my computer usage, including printing out the pages of homework I had been given express permission to stay after-hours to complete for my lack of having a home computer.

You could just imagine my surprise when one day I went to retrieve a homework assignment that went mysteriously missing. I worked four days, for five hours a day, busting my hump after a hard day's work in a desolate building in not the greatest of neighborhoods where I had to go to my car unaccompanied in the dark, only to find that someone had taken it upon himself to delete the work I had endeavored so feverishly to complete. At the time, I had no idea I was being spied on and was utterly taken aback by this entirely heartless and unkind deed. I just didn't know what to make of it. Fortunately, my very compassionate professor allowed me time to do the assignment over, but that didn't erase how I'd been betrayed.

Years later at trial, I learned that many of the conversations I had with Nancy, whether personal or professional in nature, or even some of the jokes I made aloud in the office, were notated and later taken out of context in an attempt to discredit me. I was stunned when the TA's counsel began throwing around things that had been said in a purely innocent manner to insinuate I was an undeserving slacker. I recall one incident in particular where I laughingly joked to Nancy that my phone beeper was for "personal use only". Clearly said in jest, she made a point to add it to the list she had apparently been working hard to produce in exchange for her promotion. But I never suspected a thing. As far as I knew, Nancy was the same old Nancy I had come to know and like—hard working, personable, and all-around nice.

As the year progressed, while Nancy believed herself to be in George's good graces, she and I both were being hung out to dry. Adding insult to injury, we often were expected to work overtime for free. Just because there was a ban on overtime pay didn't mean there wasn't work to do—and we did it. While Carmine was off scoping out baseball paraphernalia and attending bat signing events and Fred covering for his whereabouts, my workload doubled. I did whatever I deemed necessary to complete the day's assignments, occasionally asking the clerical staff to pitch in. Although I'm sure it was not proper to do so, at the time, it seemed the only way to keep up.

Things proceeded to get exceedingly more onerous, however, when I was left to my own devices during budget season. Of all the tasks with which I was entrusted as budget manager, this was *the* single most important. Preparing the Division's operating budget was a labor-intensive, circuitous process—not particularly difficult, mind you, but a process blown way out proportion by clueless bureaucrats who obviously never had the concept of efficiency in mind when they devised it. Nevertheless, there were deadlines to meet. My head would be on the chopping block otherwise.

Then, as if juggling this massive undertaking alone wasn't enough, the air conditioning went on the fritz. Picture it: a hot and sticky July in a building with a western afternoon exposure and no air conditioning. There I was alone, racing around like a lunatic feverishly trying to get the budget done on time—in business attire. When I approached him to lodge a complaint, rather than remedy the situation, the landlord attributed my intolerance to the extreme heat to my gender. After a polite attempt to point out the error of his ignorant thesis, I tried to appeal to him to repair the unit to no avail.

As the heat had reached dangerous levels on most of those days, I rightfully could have gone home. But I didn't. Instead, I stripped down to my athletic bra to keep from passing out. For one, it was after-hours, and, second, it looked more like a tank top than a bra. Simply put, I did what I had to do to get things done—on time—shirtless and all.

I managed somehow to get through budget season unscathed, mostly due to the patience and understanding of my colleagues in the other boroughs who knew something was up when they realized I was working alone. But just as things were coming to a close, I received another blow to the gut that nearly sent me into orbit.

The pinnacle of my disgust came one day while fielding a call at Nancy's desk, when, while flipping through the paychecks she often left sitting until which time she got around to handing them out, I noticed something odd about Carmine's check: it was for a lot more than it should have been. I immediately grabbed the pay register to investigate further, never expecting to find what I did. Much to my shock and outrage, I discovered that Carmine had been earning overtime all year long—several thousand dollars—*during a strict overtime ban.*

My immediate reaction was that it had to be a mistake. But after a few seconds of reflection, I realized I had been taken—again. Turns out that not only was he raking in a boatload of overtime pay throughout the first half of the year while I made one sacrifice after the next, but he was also getting paid for time he didn't work at all! To say I was furious is an understatement. After I regained my composure, it occurred to me that perhaps I had caught Carmine in something that George knew nothing about and which might finally persuade him to do what he'd been promising to do the previous six months: get rid of Fred.

The first chance I got, I met with George to discuss what I had found. He seemed genuinely surprised and concerned, although not as upset as one would expect under the circumstances. In his calm-and-collected signature style, he leaned in toward me, as though we were engaged in a top secret, clandestine rendezvous of some sort, and whispered, "Continue your investigation…but keep it quiet." He continued on for a bit until, I'm guessing, he believed he had convinced me he somehow cared. I left his office, satisfied he would take appropriate corrective measures once I had presented him with the evidence he requested.

But even this would prove to be as fishy as everything else going on around there. By the time I went to fetch the timecards, without which I could prove nothing, they were gone. I couldn't find them anywhere, and no one knew anything of their whereabouts either. It was at that point I knew I was being played, that this was something over which I had no control or the power to change.

As anticipated, nothing ever came of the whole ordeal. It went away like magic—unlike the hole I had dug myself into by then.

But things at the office continued to get progressively stranger as the months went on. And as they did, I began to realize that something just as odd was brewing with my physical being as well, something I'd never experienced before. I was feeling extraordinarily fatigued to where, at times, I suddenly could barely stand up; my legs would just about buckle under me. I took to wheeling myself around in my office chair and, on occasion, staying in it most of the day. I was rarely ill and had no physical issues I knew of, so this condition left me dumbstruck—and pretty scared too.

I went for a full blood workup, something I had managed to avoid my entire life, and it showed nothing but that I couldn't have been healthier. While that was welcome news, it made my predicament all the more perplexing. I wondered if my mind was telling my body something more than I was willing to openly acknowledge. Perhaps I simply had a sixth sense of what lay ahead.

By September '91, with a milestone birthday on the horizon and this weird, unexplained physical weakness I couldn't get to the bottom of, I decided it was time for an overhaul. It's not that I was out of shape per se but more that I wanted to achieve a higher level of physical fitness in the face of hitting the big, scary 3-0. Then, just by pure chance, one night while out with a friend, I ran into a guy I vaguely knew from around Staten Island, who happened to weight train at the gym. After chatting for a while, he offered to train me to which I enthusiastically accepted. Before I knew it, I was well on my way to a whole new me. I put in five hard sessions a week pumping iron—no excuses—and loved it. I barely had time to breathe, but I never felt better. And it's a good thing, too, that I had invested so much in getting myself to this new height of fitness, because life as I knew it was about to take a sharp left hand turn off a cliff.

It was now coming up on December 1991 and had been nearly a year since I was told my promotion would be made official. But rather than anything happening on that front, George called me into his office to make a rather unusual request. "I know it's a real shit job," he began his sales pitch "but I want you to head up our annual charity fund drive...starting tomorrow." Such an assignment was an unorthodox one for someone in my position—so I was immediately suspicious. However, much to George's apparent surprise, a reaction he tried his best to temper, I graciously accepted *and* signed myself up as the first donor. I wasn't quite sure what was going on but decided to go with the flow. I looked at it as an opportunity to get out of an otherwise unhealthy environment for a while and to do something worthwhile too.

The following day, I headed out on my new venture with a renewed attitude, when no sooner did I arrive at the depot than things began to go south. As it turned out, I quickly realized, I wasn't so much hawking charity donations as I was hawking myself! The guys didn't really give a hoot about helping the less fortunate; they were more concerned about their own perverted gratification. Some of them acted as though they'd been prisoners under lockdown for twenty years. It was quite unnerving, to say the least.

But hey, I'm not *that* soft. I thought, *Heck, I can do this. I deal with this sort of thing all the time. Okay, well, not necessarily at work. But still. I'm not gonna let these Neanderthals throw me for a loop.* I decided to remain calm and professional in the hope that things would get better the next day. The last thing I wanted to do was fail.

But nothing changed. In fact, it got worse. Much worse. As the unwanted comments and propositions escalated, so did the fierce headaches and sleepless nights. The sexual harassment, coupled with the frustration of not being able to get anything accomplished, was beginning to take a serious toll. I continued with the assignment for as long as I could, but ultimately, I knew it was time to pull the plug. The question was how would George take the news?

When I went to see George, I learned he was away from the office for a couple weeks. I rather took this as a blessing, though, and sent him a letter explaining what had transpired, hoping that if I put it in writing, it would have a greater impact. In the letter, I pleaded with George to release me from the assignment. I explained to him that as much as I tried, the rampant sexual harassment was proving problematic; it stood in the way of conducting a successful campaign. Although I wanted nothing more than to achieve and exceed his goals, I concluded that there was no way that could happen under the circumstances.

To my utter astonishment, George released me without any fanfare; in fact, he acted like his usual concerned self—and boy, was I was relieved. In retrospect, I wondered if perhaps he feared legal backlash over having knowingly placed me in such a potentially hostile environment and what the consequences would be if he did nothing to remedy it. There again, perhaps he had simply gotten rid of me long enough to do whatever it was he was cooking up back at the ranch.

Once back at Division headquarters, I sensed a stinging chill in the air. The eight-hundred-pound gorilla was hard to ignore. I wasn't foolish as to think things would've gotten better while I was away, yet I knew something was terribly wrong. My workload by this time had dwindled to almost nothing, none of my colleagues from the other boroughs were calling, and my coworkers were giving me the cold shoulder. I held my breath and prayed it was just a blip. But it wasn't.

On January 13, 1992, only two days shy of my one-year promotion anniversary, everything changed.

Upon my arrival that day, I was called into Fred's office. At first, I thought nothing much of it, assuming it was most likely another inane assignment or some other such thing. But as I entered the room, I knew something was up. Fred, obviously immensely nervous, proceeded to mumble the unthinkable. "You've been in the job for one year," he said. "We tried you out. Now we're gonna try Carmine out."

What? *Tried me out?* What in the name of God was he talking about? *Tried me out?*

I began to freak, my mind going a million miles an hour in every direction imaginable. I didn't know what to think, what to say, what to do, or how to be. A tsunami of emotions I had never felt before poured over me. It was unbearable—like being suffocated. Despite how badly things had become, this was not something I ever expected. I mean, if they wanted me gone, why wait a year to tell me something as ridiculous as "We tried you out"? I knew this was really bad—and it wasn't going away any time soon.

The emotional overload began to morph into shock. Part of me snapped into lockdown mode while the other part continued to swirl out of control. It's a difficult state to explain except to perhaps liken it to getting electrocuted: for the moments when the current physically paralyzes you, you remain acutely aware of what is going on yet can't do a thing about it. After you've somehow gotten separated from the current (assuming this occurs), you almost don't know what hit you; you're dazed and confused and desperately in need of assistance. All I wanted was to conjure up enough mental strength to unzip my skin and run.

Panic and doom quickly set in. I knew what had just happened but didn't want to believe it. George, the man hell-bent on loyalty, had betrayed me. It soon became apparent that he'd only been keeping up a front while trying to mastermind a way to take me down. And to add insult to injury, after an entire year, rather than at least trying to offer a plausible explanation for demoting me, all he could manage to come up with was using Fred to tell me they'd "tried me out." It was truly unbelievable.

In the few short minutes I spent in Fred's office, he didn't say too much else, not that I recall anyway. I think my senses took leave of me after the first sentence. All I could hear were sounds echoing in my head, like I was totally trapped inside of it. I knew the end of the line had come. Nothing I said or did was going to make a difference then—and things certainly weren't going to change overnight. I exited Fred's office threatening legal action. It was all I could think to do.

"Do what you have to do," Fred replied.

It was obvious that carrying out this mission was not something Fred was comfortable with. He, like George, generally avoided confrontation at all costs. But he wanted his buddy Carmine by his side and was obviously willing to do whatever it took to get him there. As merely a mouthpiece for George and someone utterly devoid of any knowledge of modern workplace legislation, I don't think Fred was much aware of the potential repercussions he could've faced for his actions—or perhaps he knew and simply didn't care. After all, he came from a world where the employee was forever under the watchful eye of the Herculean union, where women were non-existent or, at least, inconsequential, and where wrongful acts generally were met without repercussion. Here, he had George to protect him. Perhaps he believed that's all he needed to remain above the fray.

Nevertheless, I didn't give a hoot about Fred; he would have to deal with what came as the result of his blind devotion to George. All I knew and really cared about at that time was that my career—my world—had just gone up in smoke. Being relegated to my former position as analyst was akin to being fired—and then some. I felt humiliated beyond description.

Most of what happened during the remainder of that day is a blur. I recall sitting in the conference room with my friend, confidant, and SID's labor relations manager, Stoney, who rushed to my aid as soon as he heard what had occurred. He held my hand, trying to comfort me, but I was inconsolable. Nothing made any sense, no matter what he said. I had spent fourteen years working and almost as long putting myself though college to get to where I was, only to lose everything in a matter of seconds. And while I realized it wasn't the opportunity of a lifetime, it was definitely the springboard to my future. Now it was gone.

Although I'm not sure how I got home that day, once back in my apartment, I felt as though I had just lost a loved one. I was in shock and disbelief, although it still hadn't fully sunk in. The only saving grace for me was my four-legged "babies": Alex, Tony, and Phoebe. Without them, I don't know what I would have done. My three furry saviors got me through the night (and many nights thereafter).

The days that followed, I cannot recall much of. I surmise I pushed most of it into my subconscious for good. But I do know that I died a million times over while thinking about having to return to work the next day, to now be a subordinate to someone who was my subordinate only the day prior, and the same person who had just conspired to ruin me. How was I going to get through that? The thought of it was unbearable, but I knew I had no choice. Breaking every bone in my body would no doubt have proven less painful.

The next day was beyond surreal. It was as though having been gang-raped and left for dead … and then, while barely conscious, having to not only face the perpetrators the next day but to interact with them as if nothing happened. I was mortified. I wished I didn't have to go into work that day (or any other day) but I had to … and they knew it. Living hand-to-mouth, something everyone in a small office environment is bound to know whether or not you want them to, made me a very vulnerable target. Hence, I was now theirs for the taking.

Carmine and Fred took immediate and full advantage of the situation. As I sat outside the office I'd occupied only the day before, I watched the work pile up on my desk, assignment after assignment. Not once did Fred or Carmine so much as make eye contact with me when they came by; they just proceeded to drop papers on my desk as if they were competing for a prize. I didn't know what to do. It was obvious they were laying the groundwork for the finale. But worse than that, I didn't know how to deal with the humiliation—it was so overwhelming, I can't find the words to express it.

With nowhere to turn except to the guy behind the whole mess, I made an appointment to speak to George, who had until then stayed holed up in his office. During our meeting, he flatly told me, "You hate the organization, you hate the department, you hate the people, and you hate the job."

I was flabbergasted. Was that how he interpreted the actions of an individual who rolled up her sleeves to work alone in intense, cruel heat to get the budget completed; who worked innumerable hours of overtime for no pay; who acknowledged everyone's birthday, retirement, and other special occasions with homemade cakes and such; who willingly (at least tried) to chair the charity fund drive; who took the time to help anyone who needed it no matter what was on her plate; who planned the yearly holiday parties that everyone lauded as great successes; who participated in the March of Dimes walk-a-thons when no one else in the office could be bothered; who donated more from her paycheck than anyone in the entire borough from the first time she was asked; who helped countless coworkers with résumés they were otherwise clueless to write themselves; and who headed the coffee club, a thankless job for which she was always under fire? Who was he kidding? I was the quintessential office cheerleader!

George's comments were the line in the sand. I knew where I stood, and I knew I stood totally alone.

Meanwhile, my inbox proceeded to overflow with assignments I couldn't possibly complete on time, and things in general continued to deteriorate. Nothing was normal about going to work anymore. I was an outcast, ostracized by my coworkers who knew full well that associating with me was now off limits; it was the equivalent of choosing a side they did not want to get on. What's more, Fred was officially promoted to assistant general manager in January 1992. So much for three weeks.

Fred, George, and Carmine each had achieved his goal, and together, as the administrative body of SID, there was no stopping them—they had carte blanche to inflict emotional harm on me, which they seized the opportunity to do every day. There wasn't a day that went by where they didn't take the time to stick it to me even if it was so much as secretly removing my name from a list to send the message I didn't exist. As petty as that was, it still hurt. That anyone would take the time to inflict emotional pain every chance he got, hurts. I'm not sure if this was an attempt to drive me out or that they simply enjoyed watching me suffer, but regardless, it was reprehensibly cruel.

Carmine, now the new but entirely inept Manager of Budget and Personnel, didn't waste any time preying on my impotence. He immediately took to "borrowing" my ideas, presenting my accomplishments as his own. He would cockily scamper over to Fred's or George's office as though he had just invented the wheel to proudly show them what he had done, never once giving me credit for anything. But that was Carmine. He had no ideas of his own— and obviously no shame. It didn't matter, though. For him, it wasn't about achievement; it was about collecting a paycheck, whether or not he did anything to earn it.

Despite the insufferable conditions, I continued to press on, doing everything humanly possible to maintain my sanity while completing one assignment after the next. I felt like I was being forced to the edge of a plank where I precariously hung over the dangerous waters below. I had no choice but to be complicit. But the amount of work was way more than one person could ever possibly handle, and, I assumed, their way of building a record against me for insubordination, especially in light of the flimsy, irresponsible way in which they carried out the demotion. In the end, it was all about control. They now had me where they wanted me and had to buy time while figuring out what to do next.

My suspicions were right. It didn't take long before I was subjected to one disciplinary action after the next for failure to timely complete assignments (in addition to other extraneous nonsense). I railed against the pressure, but it was taking a devastating toll. After the initial shock of what I had been subjected to had subsided, I had no time whatsoever to grieve or heal. I was expected to function as if nothing had happened while being reprimanded and written up for fictitious infractions, with no fair or impartial way of defending myself. I was coming unglued.

It had come to a point where I was unable to sleep at night as I agonized over what I would face the next day. I made yet another appointment to speak with George for lack of any other way to stop the madness. I knew I had to at least try to put an end to the abhorrent treatment I was receiving from Fred and Carmine before I cracked. But on the day of our appointment, George was nowhere to be found. After rescheduling for another day, again, he failed to show.

After persistently chasing him for weeks, I finally wore George down. We spoke alone in his office where I characterized Fred and Carmine's behavior as abusive and asked that he put an end to it. George balked. He suggested that the four of us have a meeting later that afternoon, to "get everything out in the open." I reluctantly agreed.

Anxious but ready to get down to business, I walked into what would've otherwise looked like a surprise party, if not for the circumstances. The conference room was filled to capacity. Everyone was there. *What a piece of work*, I thought. *A pathetic coward.*

Before a packed house, George used the opportunity to reiterate SID's chain of command—his passive-aggressive way of telling everyone that I was now powerless. He went on to say that it was Carmine to who I would, from thereon in, directly report. Again, I felt humiliated beyond description. I thought I would die where I stood. Then, immediately after the meeting came to a close, I was issued a written warning for lateness and failure to follow instruction—right there in front of whoever happened to still be in the room. Could things get any worse?

Stoney intervened to help me appeal the charges, thank God, because I had no idea what to do. His role as labor relations manager, however, put him in a very tricky position. There he was counseling me, while it would've behooved him to remain neutral. It was no secret that George was somewhat of a racist and this was *not* going to help Stoney soften his stance. Stepping out on my behalf was tantamount to career suicide. But I don't think Stoney cared much about what George—or anyone—was thinking. He knew what he had just witnessed was wrong and was going to do what he could to remedy it.

On the day of the so-called appeal that Stoney graciously arranged—which was to take place in George's office, no less—I found no Stoney, no impartial setting—no nothing. Except for

George. Yes, George. The very same individual who had brought me up on bogus charges in the first place finagled a "hearing" in his office. Just him and me. Need I tell you the outcome?

On March 13, 1992, a week later, I was called into Fred's office and served with a three-day suspension for a laundry list of illegitimate, inconsequential violations, the most serious of which was lateness. Not any kind of blatant, egregious lateness that would call for discipline, but rather a sprinkling of one, two and three minute incidents that no one else would even be so much as looked at for. One top of that, Fred outright refused to put the charges in writing, a practice that was unheard of. Stoney argued feverishly with Fred and his henchmen to comply, but they refused. He did, however, argue for and get them to allow me to use vacation time to cover the lost wages.

The practice of making up their own rules as they went along eventually became commonplace for George, Fred and Carmine. If they found a reason to throw up a roadblock for anything I did, they made a new rule. For instance, I had unexpectedly been presented with an opportunity to go away to the Caribbean for a week (and God knows I needed it!). It was not uncommon for one of the administrative staff to request and be granted a week's vacation on a moment's notice. Suddenly, when I needed the time off, it was no longer acceptable practice and a whole new division-wide policy to that effect mysteriously surfaced the following day. This kind of thing went on regularly. It was utterly emotionally exhausting—it's still exhausting just thinking about it, some twenty years later!

The repressively punitive environment in which I was forced to function proceeded to take a serious toll, sinking me farther into an emotional funk. Putting on a face every day and pushing down my feelings was a monumental task that did nothing but exacerbate my festering anger, frustration, disgust, and humiliation. By day, I dragged myself into the office, wanting to die. At night, it was especially rough being alone with my thoughts, especially the thought of not knowing what I was about to face the next day. That alone usually kept me up to all hours.

Eventually, after seeing the clock strike two, three, four AM, night upon night, I starting drinking myself to sleep. Although I had never drunk at home before, short of suicide, there was no other way I knew of to stop the pain. And I wanted the pain to stop. I needed to disappear into the darkness. I would have done almost anything to disappear into darkness.

Over time, as the cruelty escalated, my restraint occasionally failed me. Every now and then, I broke down right at my desk, crying hysterically. I was like a pot of boiling water with a tight lid, waiting to explode. Fortunately, I was able to save the worst emotional episodes for home. There, in the privacy of my little clamshell, I had frequent, more turbulent breakdowns, over which I didn't have to feel embarrassed. Nevertheless, I went to work every day, where I continued to do my best to pretend I was okay. I knew that a slip-up of any kind would likely be the impetus of further, more heinous repercussions. Hence, there was no room for mistakes.

Before long, I was on auto-pilot as I marched in and out of work like a wooden soldier, blocking out the world as best I could. I often went straight to bed upon arriving home from work. Then, sometime around 9 p.m., I'd pull myself out of bed and go to the gym for a rigorous two-hour workout. While I admit that the endorphin surge went a long way toward making me feel human again, if only for a short time, there was yet another day waiting to get me. And get me, they did.

Most of the time, no sooner did I get off the elevator, that I took refuge in the ladies room. I had no choice but to run there to wait for the profuse, stress-induced, rectal bleeding to cease. It often was so bad that it kept me prisoner to that tiny, dank bathroom for upwards of twenty minutes. When I saw my doctor about it, she confirmed it was not a physical issue that she could remedy as it was the product of what I was being forced to endure. Hence, I had no choice but to deal with it for as long as the harassment persisted—and for as long as I was being harassed, it did.

And then even my bathroom habits became a target. The fact that I made a beeline for the ladies room most mornings where, ironically, I then had the audacity to spend time on the clock waiting for the bleeding that they caused to stop, was yet another opportunity to bring disciplinary charges against me. Toward that end, Fred summoned Carmine to monitor the time I entered and exited the ladies room throughout the day, every day.

Some mornings, though, it wasn't even easy to quickly get to the bathroom as George had arranged for one of my colleagues, and one he was aware I'd had a friendship with up to then, to stand guard at the elevator every morning to ensure I signed in at my designated arrival time. This dastardly endeavor—I came to call "the red line project"—often tended to erupt into some kind of controversy or other for my complete lack of tolerance to such egregious overreach.

At the stroke of 8:30—and only 8:30, a time specific to me—my now former friend and turncoat colleague would draw a bright red line across the sign-in sheet to indicate I was late. I wasn't given as much as a thirty-second grace period. If it was 8:31, I was officially late. This went on day in and day out. Some mornings I would walk in and just blow my stack. You could've heard a pin drop after that.

Then one morning, they took it to the next level. I seriously thought I'd stumbled into the Twilight Zone. No sooner had I walked away from the sign-in sheet at the front desk, I was called back by the "sign-in czar". When I got to where he was standing, he began to take me to task for my signature being "too big". I'd always thought a signature was, by its very nature, reflective of one's individuality. Well, not mine. Apparently, even my signature was in violation of our office rules. I was told that because it took up too much space—on a sheet that could accommodate fifty employees in an office of fifteen—I had to scale it down. *Holy shit*, I thought. *If this isn't grounds for immediate termination, I don't know what could be.* Naturally, I refused to comply as this stunt went just way beyond the pail.

Then one morning, many months after enduring the Red Line Project day in and day out, and in light of all of the other petty antics with which I was simultaneously forced to deal, I lost it. I walked off the elevator, saw the red line, and called Fred a "fat fuck." Not to his face, mind you, but as his office was only a few feet from there, I know he heard it. In fact, I'm certain the whole office had to have heard it. Funny thing is that if not for the TA's counsel making an issue of this incident at trial, I would not have even recalled it, as bad as it might sound. It's not that this type of rhetoric was commonplace, even in the face of my nearing a nervous breakdown. It's just that after being bombarded with such depraved indifference for months, it just came out. The incident then (not so surprisingly) got lost in the veritable shit storm of cruelty. Recalling it was like trying to count every snowflake in a blizzard: utterly and completely impossible. Interestingly, Fred failed to find it offensive enough to do anything about it until preparing his testimony for trial some years later because, I surmise, he was suffering from a guilty conscience.

The Red Line Project eventually culminated into the disciplinary action it was put in place to justify. Once I was red-lined a certain number of times—a number I was not entitled to know—I was brought up on charges, action that cut into my pay, and, therefore, into my survival.

It was obvious the disciplinary action would continue, and unless I took severe measures to put a stop to it, I would end up out on the street. Moreover, even though I might have managed to stay employed, I was allowing harm to come to myself in the process. I felt lost, worthless, and betrayed. It wasn't just my career that was in shambles either, but my whole life too. I knew I had to take action; I just had no idea where to begin.

I turned to Stoney, who by then was also in the crosshairs of George's sights. While the last thing I wanted to do was exacerbate his problems with our boss, I was desperate. But Stoney was a man of great integrity who didn't walk in lockstep with the crowd. He rose to the occasion to extend himself where he saw injustice, regardless of the potential consequences.

The very first thing Stoney told me was to exhaust all of my legal remedies in the order of which they are available, in order words, file internally before proceeding to the next level (if it even goes that far). The courts, he explained, might look askance at someone unwilling to try to reach a more immediate resolution. Since I was unsuccessful in my attempts to reason with George, the next logical step would be to file an internal Equal Employment Opportunity (EEO) complaint, which I did in April 1992, three months after the whole mess began.

Stoney was very reassuring and believed "the system" would work in our favor. I had no reason to doubt him. I was entirely confident that once the EEO department completed its investigation and realized what had occurred, they'd fix it. *After all*, I thought, *that's what they're there to do. Right?* Perhaps … but not before things got much worse.

Shortly after filing my discrimination complaint with our EEO department and before I'd gotten so much as an acknowledgment from them, I got slapped with a two-week suspension—the equivalent of an entire paycheck. I couldn't afford to lose one hour of pay, never mind two weeks' worth.

Once again, Stoney had accompanied me to the conference room where a seriously cotton-mouthed Fred rattled off a laundry list of alleged charges from a tattered piece of scrap paper. It was painfully obvious that he was a man so out of his element, that under different circumstances, I might have almost felt sorry for him. He looked as though he was awaiting execution; his hands visibly trembling, his skin pale, and his words barely audible. The pièce de résistance on his list of charges: "excessive bathroom time."

When Stoney asked that the charges be given in writing, Fred responded, "She doesn't get any", a response much like he had gotten in the past. I suppose I should have expected that. After all, putting the charges in writing was to provide me with evidence, evidence even someone as inexperienced as Fred realized to be sufficient to prove wrongdoing on his part.

As soon as Fred finished delivering the news, I immediately marched to George's office to discuss this travesty of justice. I didn't expect much, but I had to at least show him I was not going to stand for being treated so reprehensibly without putting up a fight. Losing two weeks pay would mean financial devastation. I had to do *something*.

This time, George gave me a choice. He said that I didn't have to take the suspension. Instead, I could take a transfer to one of our bus garages *the next day*, or I could take the suspension *and then* report to the bus garage upon my return. "Castleton Depot desperately needs an analyst," he said. "Your skills will be put to better use there." I could not believe my ears.

That's a choice? Needs an analyst? I thought. *Castleton needs an analyst like frogs need silverware!* But it didn't matter. This was blatant retaliation for having filed an EEO charge, everybody knew it, and there was nothing I could do that was going to change things. I was so overcome with grief, I just about lost my mind right then and there.

And so, there I was, master's degree just about in hand, staring down the barrel of a filthy, smelly, noisy bus garage, full to the brim with what I perceived to be Neanderthals. It was about all I could stand. What should have been a glorious time in my life was overshadowed by the cruelty of a few evil men who spent the majority of their time—and your tax dollars—conspiring to inflict as much emotional pain on me as they could manage to get away with.

Ironically, at the time all of this was going down, our new senior vice president, Ron, was also one of my graduate professors. What are the chances of that? I'm not sure why, but I never approached him about what was going on (although I believe he had to have known). Perhaps I was afraid I'd tell him, and he'd do nothing. Then what? Then, I'd have to sit there week after week, looking at him in class, knowing he was just as bad as the others? Or perhaps I just didn't want to bring the horrors of work to school. My Saturdays at Baruch were like a sanctuary, a place where I could forget the horrors of work. Whatever the case, I let it go. Then, not too long after the class wrapped up for the semester, Ron met a humiliating fate when he directed a lewd, sexually explicit remark toward his female underling during a video conference. The incident got splashed across the front page of the *New York Daily News*, Ron was terminated, and his underling got his job. Although I still wonder if I made the right decision, I like to think I chose that battle wisely. Maybe Ron was just one of the good old boys who would have jumped to George's side.

Whatever the case, whether or not rubbing elbows with the senior VP would have made an iota of difference, I was left with no immediate recourse and bade farewell to 357 St. Marks Place. As much as it was a relief to no longer have to look at the beasts who had wrung the joy out my life, I was about to embark on a journey I couldn't imagine being any better than the one that had just run its course.

CHAPTER 4

GOOD-BYE YELLOW BRICK ROAD

ALTHOUGH WELL ACQUAINTED WITH Castleton's brass—guys with whom I had worked side by side for years—I felt like a complete stranger. As soon as I entered the building, I wanted to die where I stood. I was no longer the energetic, enthusiastic ball of fire my colleagues knew from the Division but a messy-haired, wrinkled-clothes, bare-faced zombie stomped out by the forces of evil. One part of me was filled with humiliation, embarrassment, and raw emotion; the other part of me was devoid of feeling—totally numb and unwilling to live. I wanted to turn around and go home—but I knew I couldn't.

Day one started off badly. No sooner did I arrive than I began crying; in fact, I cried all day. I felt as though I had been transported to an alternate universe. *What am I doing here?* I couldn't stop thinking.

Ed, the superintendent to whom I was instructed to report and with whom I had one time worked side by side at SID, was clueless. He was a nice guy, but he was also as out of touch as he was nice. Ed's scope was, let's say, a bit narrow. He wasn't much aware of anything beyond the boundaries of his daily routine

There I stood before Ed, crying uncontrollably while he never so much as tried to console me. He'd had no training for how to cope with a crying female employee and probably never expected to have to do so. If it wasn't in the rule book, it didn't exist. Hence, I guess you could say I wasn't really a "crying female," just an employee who happened to be crying.

The next thing I know, Ed's telling me he didn't understand why I was sent there and that he had no idea what to do with me. *No idea what to do with me?* I thought incredulously. As if things weren't already bad enough, now I was the equivalent of a wayward shipment.

That didn't stop him from barking orders at me, though. He said that if he wanted to "use" me to lift boxes (simultaneously pointing to a stack of dusty old boxes in the corner), he could. I absolutely could not believe what I was hearing. This dim-witted dinosaur was standing there telling me that he could "use" me as he saw fit, including as some kind of stock boy? I stood my ground, however, regardless of my distress, and informed him, in no uncertain terms, that it would be a cold day in hell before he ordered me to lift boxes or any other such task unrelated to those of an analyst. And that was the end of that.

It didn't take long before Ed's barking faded to inaudible noise. My ability to sense my surroundings left me. My mind was entirely transported elsewhere, and all I could think about was getting out of there. Nothing else mattered.

Short of just picking up and walking out, however—which was a luxury I didn't have—the only thing to do was call the EEO department. After all, if not for having filed a complaint with them,

I'd likely not have been there in the first place. *Surely they'll be able to help me in some way,* I convinced myself. Using the germ-infested pay phone located smack the middle of the bus operators' hub—I called my EEO rep. I explained to him what was going on while struggling to maintain my composure amidst a bustling crowd of complete strangers. Sensing my desperation, he listened intently, but said there was nothing he could do to help. He was about as useless as tits on a bull.

With nowhere else to turn, I eventually sauntered back to Ed, where the next order of business was to find a place for me to sit. But there were no vacant desks—or even a spot for one in the office.

Ed directed me to the desk of a vacationing coworker and handed me a pencil and paper. *A pencil and paper?* This was 1992, not 1892! But computers—albeit around for many years—were not exactly part of the Castleton landscape. It was like being transported back in a time. If it wasn't happening to me, I'm not sure I'd have believed it. I'd busted my ass for eleven years putting myself through college … to end up in a place where there was nothing for me to do and nowhere for me to go.

I was forced to "desk hop" day after day, week after week. It amazed me that in such a huge building, there was not so much as a 4 x 4 space to call my own. With scads of taxpayer dollars wasted on failed projects and exorbitant salaries and other things that would make blood shoot out of your eyes, not even a lousy desk was to be found. Adding insult to injury, there was no ladies restroom either. Yes, *no* ladies restroom—in 1992. If that doesn't sum up the antiquity of Castleton, I don't know what possibly could.

The male managers (a term that's redundant, when you consider there were no other kind) had an expansive restroom that went from one side of the building to the other. It was so big that regardless of where they sat, none of them had to take more than a few steps to get there. In fact, I don't think I'd be so off the mark in asserting that they probably wouldn't even have had to get out of their chairs to "go". Women, on the other hand—me and our administrative assistant, Jackie—were expected to use the dank, beaten-up makeshift female bus operator's locker room (located way at the back of the building). I refused and made my discontent known.

Fortunately, I found a spacious ladies room downstairs in Maintenance. Not exactly something off the pages of *Architectural Digest*—it was a converted supply room with chipped paint and rusty iron-mesh window guards—but it was better than what was upstairs. If nothing else, it provided the occasional solace I so desperately needed.

Acclimating to depot life, however, included many more frustrating dilemmas than where I was allowed to pee. Overall, working in an almost entirely male environment was quite challenging; in fact, I imagine it was much like being thrust into a men's prison (and was somewhat reminiscent of the charity funds drive days). Although I went to work every day looking disheveled (as the depression had already gotten the best of me, and I didn't much care what I looked like), I still was the victim of endless unwanted and most definitely unprovoked sexually charged behavior.

While this sort of thing was fairly rampant, there were a number of incidents, in particular, that made me quite uncomfortable. Not that they were necessarily intentional; rather, they were the purely bone-headed acts of guys who very much lacked workplace etiquette. Being a girl from a blue-collar family and quite frankly having a soft spot for those who make a living with their hands, I tried to be patient with their ways. But it wasn't easy. There were times when I was so offended by what I encountered, I wanted to scream.

One of the most disturbing scenarios involved a food concession run by two bus operators. Buying from them was the most convenient way to get a reasonably priced, home-cooked lunch, which, being health conscious, I much preferred. The two guys treated me well but were deeply unaware of their obligation to conduct business within the parameters of a modern-day workplace.

One day I walked into the concession to find sexually offensive programming playing on the TV. The TV was situated in a way that gave the guys an unobstructed view of the back end of any female who happened along. I wore baggy, wrinkled clothing to work, so there was nothing really screaming, "Hey, look at my ass," but they looked anyway. And even if I didn't know for certain that they were staring at my rear end, it was still very unsettling to stand with my back to an audience of presumably hormonally revved up members of the opposite sex.

I didn't waste any time politely mentioning to the guys that their choice of programming (that I considered soft porn) wasn't exactly appropriate for the workplace. In response, they laughed it off, telling me to lighten up—in other words, get over it. I didn't appreciate their comments, and although the last thing I wanted was another battle on my hands, this was too much for me—especially in my delicate state of mind. I approached Ed about it, hoping that he'd at least let the guys know their behavior was out of bounds. I don't know if anything at the concession ever changed (or if Ed even viewed it as inappropriate in the first place) because I chose to stop frequenting the concession and had the guys deliver the food to my desk instead.

Fortunately, if I wanted to leave for lunch, I could, despite that it cut my time short. My apartment was a five-minute drive away from the depot, but adding the time it took to walk to the parking lot and the time it takes to go from one place to another, it left me with about half the time to relax than I would have had otherwise. Moreover, it was a struggle to put forth that much effort every day in the mental state I was in. When death seems a welcome change to life, going through the motions to travel back and forth for lunch is a monumental challenge. There were times, though, that the occasional jaunt back home to eat and see my "babies" was a necessary diversion and the only therapy I could afford at a time when I had no mental health benefits. After a while, I began to return home on a regular basis and spend as long there as I could. It had gotten to where I simply didn't care any longer whether Ed knew or if he took action against me for it. Emotionally, I was a wreck and on my way to becoming a physical wreck too. I'm pretty sure no one could tell from my outward appearance that I was beginning to fall prey to a whole host of ailments—but it was becoming painfully obvious to me.

The physical ailments first began to plague me when this whole, ugly mess went down, but it took a while before I realized that all of them were stress-induced. So when my vision suddenly began to blur the week after the demotion, I was perplexed. At first and for a while thereafter, I thought I had something in my eye. *It's too sudden to be anything else,* I thought. I'd repeatedly blink to clear it, but it wouldn't go away. After it persisted and never cleared up, I surmised it to be the result of emotional trauma, although I'll never know for sure. Certainly the timing is hardly coincidental.

Then there was the nausea. I was nauseated all the time—every day. It wasn't so severe as to prevent me from functioning but enough that I knew it was there. I actually thought I must have cancer or some other such heinous disease. After all, why would anyone be nauseated all the time? But after a while, I realized it was brought on by the stress, and once I did, I accepted it as the new norm.

Then there was the profuse hemorrhoidal bleeding—or rather, the extreme constipation that exacerbated the hemorrhoids that caused the bleeding that continued right on into the depot days. Despite working out five days a week, eating an impeccably healthy diet, and drinking buckets of water, by this time, I'd experienced many bouts of not being able to "go" for long periods—including once for a whole month. It was pure hell.

Even in my sleep, I couldn't catch a break. Every night I dreamed in vivid Technicolor, all night long. I had nightmares so realistic that I sometimes had trouble separating reality from fiction. I often woke up, sweat-soaked and screaming, "Leave me alone!" It was just awful. One night I woke up gasping for air and was scared out of my wits. I later learned that it was a type of sleep apnea, a breathing interruption brought on by extreme stress.

I began to fret and decided I needed to see a doctor—again—as I was experiencing more ailments at that time than I had collectively experienced in my life. Unfortunately, I heard the same thing over and over: "Nothing is wrong with you." Nothing that could be seen anyway. The doctors couldn't see the back pain; they couldn't see the nausea; they couldn't see the nightmares; and they couldn't see the anxiety. But that didn't mean they weren't there.

Although I managed to barely hold myself together—the stress was taking its toll. My depression worsened. It was even getting hard to drag my weary self out of my car and into the gym—instead I'd sit in the car and cry. I didn't want to live, much less work out. But I did it; I peeled myself up with every last scintilla of my being and went.

Back at work, I still had Ed and the "depot follies" to contend with. Ed didn't harass me, per se, but his neurosis made him an annoying worrywart of sorts whose insecurities spilled over onto those under his tutelage. He was scared and didn't want to be the fall guy for anything, especially not for defending a toxic female such as me.

In all fairness to him, Ed, at one time, also had his share of problems with the boys of SID when he got squeezed out of his position and was replaced by one of George's buddies. They brought him to the Division only to turn around and claim they had to "eliminate" the position. And then, by some miracle—*voila*—the position was back on the budget and ready to be filled. His situation was very different from mine, however. Although Ed's pride may well have been hurt, and rightfully so, his wallet wasn't. And that was all that really mattered to him at the end of the day. By then, he was close to retirement, knew to the nickel how much he had in his "bank", and wasn't about to let anything stand in the way—especially not some wayward female ex-manager who was dumped at his feet.

For Ed and most of his counterparts, as I eluded to earlier, women in the workplace were a fairly new phenomena. Without a section in the rule book clearly titled "Women and How to Handle Them," these guys were lost. Seeing females as equals—especially in management—just wasn't in their repertoire. When I'd talk about my predicament, I'd often hear comments like, "There are plenty of secretarial jobs out there," or something equally ridiculous, which, I assume, was meant to make me feel better.

I think the incident that best sums up how backward Ed and his cronies were was when I unexpectedly got my period. Now, normally this wouldn't be a big deal. But there again, Castleton wasn't normal. As I had bled through the long, light-blue skirt I'd worn that day, I simply wanted to go home to change my clothes and get tampons. As the depot wasn't located in a neighborhood with friendly convenience stores but rather in a gritty area with nothing much else besides a topless bar a few doors down, home was my only option. But no, that would have been too easy. Ed forbade me from leaving, forcing me to turn my skirt around and strategically hold in front of me for the remainder of the day in a desperate attempt to hide the stains while I prayed the bleeding would cease. Surely, this was God awful, but it wasn't an outright attempt on Ed's part to humiliate me. It's just that he was so scared of retribution that he dared not do anything for me that could be perceived as taking sides.

Of course, the next logical thing was to ask Ed to purchase sanitary products for the depot, in order to avoid the possibility of ever facing such a horrifying dilemma again. On the other hand, why would we buy sanitary products when we didn't even have a ladies room to put them in? Nevertheless, Ed's response was nothing

I could have ever imagined. Rather than the simple yes I expected, he told me that sanitary products (namely the tampons I requested) were "not a necessity." Of course they were "not a necessity"—for "the men"! I truly could not believe the exchange we were having.

I had about given up on Ed—surely if he sincerely believed tampons were a luxury item, there was no point in talking to him about female-related stuff—until something of a miracle occurred, that is. Castleton was about to get its first honest-to-goodness ladies restroom. I can't say for sure if it was due to my incessant complaining, but …the timing was undeniably curious. Jackie and I stood in utter amazement as we watched the construction underway; it was a day for Castleton's record books. And to think I might have been the impetus behind this historic event—I felt like a pioneer!

Not too long after the unveiling of the bathroom, the whole office got a makeover. I finally got my own desk and computer too—another, albeit small, miracle. But while the aesthetic changes were welcomed and long overdue, it was the relationship I developed with two of my coworkers that kept me sane.

Obie and Jackie were two of the kindest, most caring coworkers one could ever hope to have. Jackie, with whom I commiserated every day, was our office's administrative assistant. She definitely had a lot going for her and should have been working somewhere where her talents were appreciated. And Obie was a sweetheart of a man. His bright smile and gregarious personality proved to be just what Jackie and I needed to get through each miserable day.

Obie, as the story went, was one of the (few) black males who would not have been promoted to management but for the advent of affirmative action. He was every bit as competent as any of his colleagues and deserved to be where he was, regardless of a program designed to further the professional interests of minorities. But in Staten Island Division, there was always an excuse as to why a minority somehow was promoted to the level of his "superior" white male counterparts.

Jackie, Obie, and I had a lot in common. We were all seen as not really belonging—the common denominator, I believe, behind the strong bond we developed. We understood each other, shared a lot of laughs, and brought each other up from the doldrums.

But workplace friendships, too, proved problematic for the powers that be. Perhaps they saw our friendship as reminiscent of the days when minorities staged their rebellion against the white man— that there was potential power in our number—and had to put a wedge between us. Or perhaps this was yet another way in which to beat the joy out of me. Whatever the case, the office renovation provided the ideal opportunity for Ed and his cronies to segregate me from Jackie and Obie—the only thing in that cruddy old place that brought me any happiness. No sooner were the renovations complete that I was told I was moving to the opposite end of the building where Ed and I would share an office, just the two of us, alone *and* right next to our new boss's office—as far away as they could get me from Jackie and Obie without putting me in another building.

Now Ed was breathing down my neck eight-plus hours a day. He had an annoying habit of micromanaging stuff that had little to do with anything but his neurosis. For instance, one day he accused me of "doing my nails" on the job, after I pulled out a file to smooth a jagged edge, a task that took all of a few seconds to complete. He certainly wouldn't have accused a man of "doing his nails" under the same circumstances. (Heck, one of the guys could've whipped out his feet and done a full blown pedicure on Ed's desk, and it wouldn't have mattered.)

Another time, I was reprimanded for "having a camera on the job." I'd taken up photography to keep myself from focusing on all the negativity, and purchased a second-hand camera from a nearby photo shop during my lunch break that I placed on my desk upon my return. Ed marched over to me like the rule-book police and informed me that having a camera on the property was contrary to agency policy. I would have thought it was a joke but for all of the other equally ridiculous nonsense with which I dealt. "Cameras are not allowed in the depot," he intoned, "for fear of theft of technology." I couldn't help but laugh in his face. To whom did he think I might give this information? The Germans? The Japanese? We might have been one the largest transportation systems in the world, but we certainly weren't one of the most technologically advanced. Nevertheless, my camera never saw the inside of that building again.

Then there was the time I got food poisoning. Wow, was that scary—not the food poisoning, the way I was treated! I had begun feeling sick one morning right after eating breakfast. My stomach got queasy after which point I became so dizzy I could barely see. I wrote it off as stress-related and continued to do my best to get my work done for the next few hours until a concerned coworker happened by, saw I wasn't well, and strongly suggested I go home. I tried to explain that I couldn't—I knew I'd be made to pay for it—

but he persisted. Eventually, I caved, and another coworker drove me home.

When I came to work the next day, Ed didn't ask how I was feeling. No, I was instead slapped with a three-day suspension for leaving work two hours early and placed on a "chronic sick list," which required the production of doctor's lines for all absences, including those related to my period. For one, I had never heard of a "chronic sick list," and two, I was not about to produce any kind of medical documentation for anything having to do with my period. I put my foot down and outright refused … but there was little I could do about the suspension. I knew I had no recourse. The only comfort I got came from some of my more caring coworkers, men with twenty or thirty years service who said that this was some of most outrageous treatment they had ever witnessed in their entire careers.

Emotional pain aside, the main issue for me was, once again, losing pay. I had already suffered enough humiliation for an entire lifetime, hence nothing they did could make that much worse. So once again, as had been the case many times in the past, I raised a stink that bought me a pass on the lost wages when I was given permission to charge the time to my vacation balance, but the disciplinary action remained.

This, however, was only the beginning.

It was a Friday not long after the first suspension when it happened again. This time, it was strategically planned for the day prior to my vacation, right at quitting time. Knowing I was about to be away for two weeks, there would be no time to respond before I left. I was served with a written reprimand for a list of alleged infractions I never knew I committed. Thinking it had to be some kind of sick joke, I read the document and signed it under protest. To say I was blown away is an understatement.

I left that day, dragging what felt like a thousand-pound weight behind me. I was shaken and distraught, knowing that the first thing I'd have before me upon my return from vacation—if I came back to a job at all—was picking up where we left off.

When I returned from my two-week vacation, I was greeted back with yet another written reprimand only minutes after walking through the door. It was far beyond the scope of anything I could have ever imagined, even if I *had* done something wrong. There was no time to cry or reflect … or heal, only to do whatever I could to try to save myself, once again, from extinction.

I had learned, over time, to immediately sign disciplinary actions "under protest"—to make sure they didn't try to pull a fast one—and later to follow up with a thorough, carefully crafted rebuttal, which I spent a great deal of time toiling over at home. This was an emotionally draining process in which I took no joy. I usually broke down in front of my computer and cried, asking "Why? Why?" It was the last thing I wanted to have to deal with after what I'd go through during the day, but it had to be done. I just couldn't afford to take any chances.

When I submitted each of my rebuttals, Ed and his cronies would gather around to read them like sharks in a feeding frenzy. They could not, however, get through them without a dictionary. It's funny how those who looked down at me and regarded me as inconsequential were incapable of reading a rebuttal to their own disciplinary actions. Too bad it didn't stop them from doing something so wrong in the first place.

Amidst being bombarded with disciplinary actions, camera warnings and other such harassment, two men from the EEO Department unexpectedly paid me a visit. The department head and his sidekick, the rep who'd left me hanging the day I called the EEO for help, appeared out of nowhere six months after I had filed my complaint. In my usual naivety, I thought they had finally gotten around to my case and were there to conclude their investigation. They referred to their visit as being for the purpose of "fact-finding". I was so relieved.

Disheveled-looking as I generally was at work during that time, and frankly embarrassed for the way I looked upon receiving guests, I anxiously sat with the two men in a small room. I recall a bright light shining in my eyes, like something out of a scene from a movie. The two men barraged me with questions for several hours, working me over like I'd been suspected of espionage. I fielded their questions with ease, but it became apparent that they didn't appreciate my bluntness. It was obvious they knew I spoke the truth, but their increasing agitation suggested they weren't there for the truth. I chalked it up to arrogance, although I was confused as to why the men, who had come all that way to the depot to vindicate me, would act in such a manner.

After a three-hour fishing expedition and no fish, they relented. I was emotionally spent; a cold sweat came over me that I can still feel as I write. In retrospect, I realize I never should have spoken to them without some sort of representation, though in reality, it wouldn't have mattered. They weren't there to elicit facts but rather to get words they could twist into a response. It was an ambush. Whatever I said was going to be used against me, regardless. It was their job to protect our employer—and themselves.

It should come as no surprise that in December 1992, a couple of months after chatting with my EEO colleagues and eight grueling months after filing my complaint, I was dealt a crushing blow. I remember how nervous I was as I scrambled into the ladies room with Jackie to read the letter. My heart sank—I felt as if the blood drained from my body. I wanted to vomit. The TA would not be made to take one scintilla of responsibility for their wrongful actions. The EEO claimed that a lack of evidence that any law had been broken was behind their findings. It was an insulting slap in the face, simply beyond comprehension. *Could this really be happening?* I wondered.

I didn't know what to do or where to turn; once again, I was in shock, once again, left to my own devices, feeling emotionally hollowed out, despondent. But that would not stop me from doing whatever it took to make things right. I wanted justice—and walking away simply was *not* an option.

Now, nearly a year after being transferred to the depot and seeing that the people I believed to be designated to help me were actually there to help my employer, I realized this process wasn't going to be easy, that the truth didn't matter nearly as much as my employer keeping itself out of harm's way, and that getting them to pay for what they'd done would take a lot more than filing an internal complaint. *Fear not*, I thought, trying desperately to remain focused without completely falling to pieces. I kept repeating to myself what Stoney told me when this whole thing began: "Stay focused on the path to your goal. Don't allow anything to detract from that. They're going to throw stuff at you to get you to lose focus, to anger you, in order to elicit a response they can then turn around and use against you. You must not allow that to happen." With that in mind, I knew that I must confer with him, regroup, and with his help, take my gripe to the next level.

By now, Stoney was embroiled in his own hell with George. He, too, had begun the EEO process and was ready to take it up a notch. For him, standing up to the white man meant a ticket out— lawyer or not. I don't think George saw Stoney so much as a lawyer who happened to be black as he did a black man who happened to be a lawyer. All I know is that it took some real nuggets to harass the Division's labor relations manager.

Both Stoney and I were very idealistic. He continued to believe in "the system" and assured me we'd get justice, if we just stayed the course. I followed his lead. I had high hopes that as long as I had him by my side—and because we were now "in it" together—it wouldn't be long before everything was right again.

CHAPTER 5

IF IT WASN'T FOR BAD

IN APRIL 1993, YET ANOTHER breakthrough befell Castleton: the first black assistant general manager. This came as quite a surprise to everyone. This was without a doubt, huge.

Andy, our illustrious new boss—a bus operator who worked his way up the ranks—was the first black man to ever hold this position—the highest position ever held by a black man—in SID. Stoney and I were thrilled, although a bit suspicious. I didn't believe in coincidences—at least not under circumstances like these.

Andy brought with him his buddy, George, also a black man, as his second in command. I thought, *George and the boys of Division have to be shitting their pants to go such lengths. Two black managers at that level in Staten Island Division in such a short span? Unheard of.*

Andy and his buddy George did not get involved in my ordeal, at least not right away. In fact, we got off to what appeared to be a smashing start.

During the same time, Stoney and I took a field trip to the Equal Employment Opportunity Commission at the World Trade Center in New York City to file our federal discrimination charges. I walked in there, certain this was the last stop on the crazy train and that they would be the answer to our prayers; after all, *they* had nothing to do with the TA.

Our mission was a success; we left with a sound sense of assuredness that the EEOC would make things right again. The presumably dedicated individuals with whom we dealt guaranteed that it would take no longer than six months to investigate and respond. And although six additional months seemed like an eternity, I was convinced it was a small price to pay for justice.

Soon after filing my formal EEOC charge, the retaliation machine got fired up once more. Although I had never received a performance evaluation in five years, nor was an evaluation something an analyst was subject to, I was about to get one. But not because George or Fred or Carmine masterminded the plan; it was unwittingly the brainchild of one of our two new analysts.

Anita, SID's newest addition, told me that it was she who had pushed for the evaluation because she had been evaluated in her previous position in Brooklyn Division. *Oh, great*, I thought. I knew she had no idea that what she just asked for would be used to inflict harm on me, and I didn't say a word either. I kept quiet about my dilemma up to then and believed it best to continue to do so. But I knew what was soon coming down the pike for me. The boys of SID weren't going to pass up an opportunity like this to escalate their reign of terror.

Anita, now performing the tasks I once performed back at Division, was a very academically intelligent woman, but not a very street-wise one. And Pat, my new analyst counterpart in Yukon depot, wasn't very far behind. Both Pat and Anita came to SID with high hopes. Both were excited and enthusiastic—and in another world as to what they had just stepped into. And I wasn't going to be the one to tell them, either. The last thing I wanted was to come off as an aggrieved employee fishing for allies. Sometimes people just have to find out for themselves—and it didn't take long before they did.

I got along quite well with Anita (and Pat), although as time went on, it became obvious that there was a cultural divide between us such that I didn't think she could relate to where I was coming from in my fight for justice, especially that she had not yet experienced the wrath of Fred and Carmine. Pat, who worked at Yukon Depot located on the other side of Staten Island, was physically far from Division but not far enough to be out of harm's way. It came as no surprise when she began expressing her frustrations to me about the dynamic duo, and it wasn't long before Anita was doing the same. It was only then that I began to let the cat out of the bag. I don't think it really sunk in at first, but it seemed to bring us closer together. I guess misery really does love company.

In no time, Pat and Anita escalated to incessant, daily complaining about how reprehensibly they were being treated, especially Anita, who was under the direct supervision of Carmine. Things got so bad that Anita was forced to lock her file cabinet at night to try to keep Carmine from stealing her work. But that didn't stop him. Carmine, who was at that time filling in for Fred, who had suffered a heart attack, would systematically steal Anita's files at night, only to turn around the following day and pass off her work as his own. Carmine had his eye on Fred's position and obviously was willing to do anything to accomplish his goal. Anita, of course, kept quiet for fear of retribution, and nothing changed.

Anita and Pat soon became filled with regret for having migrated to SID. Neither of them, however, had the guts to do anything to try to remedy the situation. Carmine and Fred weren't out to get either of them. It wasn't like that. It was a simple matter of their clumsily attempting to manage a department they had no business overseeing in the first place. And now, Anita and Pat were the new recipients of Fred and Carmine's ineptitude, a situation with which they did not quite know how to deal. Instead, they turned to me—not that I minded. It was important to remain loyal to my colleagues no matter what, even if it added to my already bubbling over pot of stress.

Pat and Anita's performance evaluations went okay, to the extent that the process wasn't used to harass them. As I expected, however, mine was another story altogether. Fred, a person with whom I'd had no contact whatsoever for the period in question, was the person delegated to conduct my evaluation. But he was far too cowardly to face me—or heaven forbid let me know he was behind it. Instead, he handed it off to Andy, who passed it on to Ed, who was directed to deliver the news.

The evaluation had no mention of any accomplishments; rather, it predominantly focused on attendance. There was no thought involved, just counting days and determining whether I had failed to live up to the standard they had not, up to then, let me in on. And as it turns out, I exceeded my quota—again. In fact, Fred took it upon himself to decide I had been absent so many times that it warranted another reprimand—a written reprimand *and* a performance evaluation at the same time. Now *that's* efficiency!

In usual form, I whipped up one of my stinging rebuttals. If nothing else, I hoped it would serve to help make my case—whenever that day would come. I didn't bother approaching Andy either. We seemed to have a good rapport that I didn't want to risk tarnishing, and as he'd kept out of harm's way up to then, I didn't see the point.

For a few months following the evaluation, things were pretty quiet—not good, just quiet. It was like being taken off an open flame and put on a warming tray. The end result is the same; it just takes a bit longer to get cooked.

And then, the quiet broke—big time. Eighteen painstaking months after filing my discrimination charge—not the six months I was promised, but rather three times that—the EEOC reached a conclusion in their investigation. In all of their infinite governmental wisdom, these faceless bureaucrats concluded that my employer had done no wrong. I was completely astonished and totally dumbfounded. This was pure insanity.

Apparently, I did not yet truly grasp the underpinnings of government. It was bad enough that when I followed up umpteen times over the course of a year and a half that felt like an eternity, I'd get the same old song and dance—backlog this, understaffed that. But to get kicked between the eyes with this was more than I could bear.

All I had done seemed for naught. How was I ever going to be able to put a stop to the madness? And what was going to happen to me, now that my employer had chalked up another victory? I didn't have time to waste. After conferring with my guru, I prepared to forge ahead with the next logical step: filing suit.

Meanwhile, things were slowly creeping into decline with Andy—the one person with any authority over me with whom I had not become embattled. Although Andy and I got along, things with him were starting to become strained. For instance, he had an annoyingly infantile habit of perpetually tracking me around the office yelling my name to where it could be heard by all. I wasn't thrilled, but at least he acknowledged my efforts; he wasn't shy about letting me know how much he appreciated that I was able to do things for him that others could not.

In terms of his vocational abilities, Andy was not the most qualified manager I have ever encountered. He knew how to get by on the backs of others (as he did with me), but his academic prowess was seriously lacking. This was the impetus behind him tracking me around, and after a while, the amount of things he depended on me for started to grate on my nerves, even though I continued to do everything asked of me and work for him as hard I would have anyone else. Then, as the saying goes, all good things must come to an end. Things took a turn for the worst when Andy got involved in my second performance evaluation, exposing himself for the disloyal and dimwitted man he was.

Initially, the whole thing went off without a hitch. Frankly, I was amazed. Andy bestowed the responsibility on Ed to conduct the evaluation, and Ed took it upon himself to *try* to be as fair as possible. He gave me a decent review. Not great. Not what it should have been. But decent—and I was incredibly relieved. I didn't care so much what they thought of me or my performance as much as

I wanted peace. And always the optimist, I thought I had finally gotten it. In fact, I actually thought that Andy—a minority who could relate to what I was going through and therefore perhaps compelled to help—was somehow instrumental in orchestrating a kind of standoff to keep me out of harm's way until I finally got my day in court.

I couldn't have been more off the mark. As it turned out, the review Ed showed me wasn't at all the one I ended up with—not by a long shot. Ed revealed to me that Andy "revised" the evaluation, although I don't know if the changes were Andy's idea or those of the Division's gruesome threesome. Andy, like Fred before him, didn't face me like a real man; he remained safely hidden behind Ed— something with which Ed was obviously uncomfortable, especially after our being together in the same office for a year and his seeing firsthand what I was made of. As such, Ed knew that giving me an evaluation that did not fairly portray my efforts was plain wrong.

The review was abysmal. I was characterized as "marginal," a rating that would probably have gotten most folks fired in the real world. It shouldn't have been a surprise, but foolishly, I expected more. I'd worked hard, endlessly going above and beyond the scope of my responsibilities—and under strained and unusual circumstances, no less. But again, I'd fallen prey to my hopeless idealism.

Being rated "marginal," while grossly inappropriate and hurtful, wasn't the worst of it, however. That almost seemed complimentary in comparison to what came next. With the exception of the usual attack on attendance (that was getting really old at this point), the remainder of the evaluation was something else.

First, I was referred to as "disobedient" for "slipping papers under Andy's door." While an evaluation should be based on the quantity and quality of the work one does in relation to preset goals—mine clearly was not. Not even remotely close.

I was so incensed that I approached Andy for an explanation. *What in the world could slipping papers under his door have to do with anything?* I wanted to know. He explained that upon entering his office in the morning, on two occasions, he had stepped on papers that I had slipped under the door the night before. Apparently, the resulting footprint on the papers rubbed him the wrong way. He went on to say that these were acts of "disobedience" because I was warned not to do it after the first time but did so again anyway. He then proceeded to physically demonstrate how he would step on the papers, as if to somehow justify his sentiments. Rather than being grateful that I'd stayed late to complete his inane projects night after night, so that he'd be certain to have them first thing in the morning—and accepting that slipping them under his door kept them safe—he had decided to look past that to a footprint of his own making and reflect this in my review.

Next and probably the most off-the-wall thing about my evaluation that is still utterly mind boggling except for when you consider the source, I was rated "marginal" for "leaving dirty dishes in the sink." And you *cannot* imagine my reaction to this. After I got past the initial shock, I went ballistic—I was so infuriated that I almost lost consciousness! Andy might as well have instructed me to come to work in a miniskirt.

Ed explained to me that Andy was compelled to include this in my evaluation because someone had spoken to me on a couple of occasions about leaving dishes in our community sink, and as I allegedly had failed to correct my erroneous ways, I was, once again, "disobedient." He went on to explain that there were times when I left my lunch dish and coffee mug in the sink overnight and that I should have washed them before leaving for the day. I explained to Ed that whenever I did leave dishes in the sink, it was only because I was busy completing Andy's assignments, assignments that he repeatedly told me "nobody else could handle," and that he always seemed to need right away. I washed the dishes upon my return the next day.

So, let's see: I busted my ass day after day, working through lunch and past quitting time, mentally diminished and grossly underpaid, performing tasks that Andy's handsomely compensated managerial staff should have been handling but couldn't, and this is what I got as thanks for my undying dedication. *Holy shit*, I thought. *Talk about a dagger through the eye.*

I signed my evaluation, as I had so often in the past, "under protest." And as usual, I got right down to business, formulating one of my (now) signature rebuttals. *Paper trail. Paper trail.* It would have been easier to just tell them off and get it out of my system, but I had to respond to just about everything in writing. (Thank goodness we had enough dictionaries to go around; Ed and his cronies would have had a heck of a time getting through *that* rebuttal without them.)

So now, Andy, the same man who once told me I was one of the nicest, most generous people he had ever known (which begs the question: *How in the world does he treat the people he thinks little of?*), was now on board with George and the boys, and he was not about to miss a beat. He broke through the barrier and was clearly enjoying his new role as supreme dictator. Not that he was a grounded individual to begin with; his disconnection from reality was his trademark, as evidenced by the evaluation. And before long, I regularly ended up at the receiving end of his lunacy.

For instance, Andy's philosophy was such that if a person was not physically moving about in some way, such as driving a bus, I suppose, he was not working. He would obsessively pace back and forth past my office door to see what I was doing, and if I happened to be thinking (i.e., not moving about but rather quietly trying to contemplate a complicated spreadsheet formula), I was accused of "not working." I tried to explain to Ed, the perennial bearer of Andy's complaints, that there were times when I was thinking and that thinking didn't require me to move around. I don't know what Ed told him—or if he said anything at all—but this went on ad infinitum.

Another notable incident was when Andy arranged for me to be "loaned out" to our central budget department in East New York, Brooklyn as a way, I surmise, to express his disapproval for my having stood up to him during the evaluation process. The story was that the budget department was short-handed and needed "volunteers" from around the system. Of course I didn't volunteer, but I did agree to go, under the condition that I would be given a company car, travel expenses, and weekend overtime. I didn't really want to travel to such an unsafe place (which East New York notoriously is), but it was a chance to get away from the chaos and make some extra cash too. Besides, at the rate I was being suspended, I needed all the overtime I could get.

They gave me the car and opportunity to work weekends (which behooved them to do) but not the travel expenses. I suppose asking for cash was pushing the envelope. Of course, none of "the men" ever had to put his hand in his pocket for a toll. But I was not them. Nevertheless, I was almost happy to be going to a place I loathed.

So, off to East New York I went, where I worked eight long weeks—Monday through Friday there and weekends in the depot, where I toiled away in blessed solitude. I often wondered *Could more fun could be had by anyone?*

East New York turned out to be a decent experience after all, in light of how horrified I was to travel there. I made the acquaintance of many nice people *and* was further enlightened as to the machinations of government. The analysts I worked with (all minorities) were college educated, most with graduate educations, working their fingers to the bone and making piddly salaries compared to some of the old white guys who sat around, day after day, doing nothing but breathing. In fact, one guy spent his days sitting out in the middle of a huge office, reading the paper, evidently just waiting for retirement. It didn't seem to bother him that he was without so much as a meaningful task all day long. He had no shame whatsoever but rather a sense of pride for getting over on his employer.

I returned to Castleton after a two month hiatus, ready to pick up where I left off. I had no expectations of anything being any better and, in fact, figured that the only reason I was sent away in the first place—aside from the retaliation I already knew it to be—was to give George, Fred, Andy, and whoever else was now in on it time to conspire against me. However, much to my surprise, a day after settling back in, there was a major announcement that nearly restored my faith in humanity. George was done. Finished. Kaput. Through. I was flabbergasted, as was everyone with whom I worked.

We learned that George was "retiring" after an incident regarding a financial debacle that went down during his tenure as rail boss. I make no claim to know exactly what happened, but I wonder if it was due, at least in part, to his reckless disregard for the minority employees he mistreated and all others he so callously manipulated for so many years. Perhaps my stand was the straw that broke the camel's back. Regardless, it was karma, unfolding right before my eyes. While I never wish bad things on anyone or revel in their misery, when I learned George was through, I was happy and relieved.

Surprisingly, many of my colleagues did not (or perhaps could not) see George's departure as punitive. My guess is that it was merely denial, that it could just as easily have been them. I heard so many excuses as to what might have occurred that I wanted to hurl. "He's got plenty of money." "He got a good deal." "He has another business." "He's set for life." I didn't buy any of it for a second.

I had gotten to know George fairly well and knew that he thrived on being the "godfather." He wanted to be at the top of the heap, looking down on all of his loyal servants. He was a vital man who, as far as I could tell, was not ready to retire, so I imagined that he was humiliated and furious that he was stripped of his authority. He might have loved money, but it was power that really did it for him. But George was not by any stretch of the imagination put through what he put me through. Rather, the way they get rid of guys like George is to say they're "retiring"—to spare them the ultimate humiliation of being terminated.

Next thing we knew, George was gone. No fanfare. No retirement party. Nothing. Just gone.

Our new GM came in as quietly as George left. Kevin was a white-collar administrative type who presented as a decent guy. I assumed he knew about me before he ever set foot on Staten Island, but if he did, he kept it to himself. Nevertheless, trying to remain optimistic, I saw Kevin's presence as a door to opportunity—perhaps a potential fresh start that might serve to put all of the nonsense of the previous few years to rest.

My dealings with Kevin were infrequent, though perfectly cordial. My guess is that he intentionally stayed as far away from the matter as possible, and I really couldn't blame him for that. If it happened today, however, I would have told him that he was the boss now, and it was his responsibility to make things right, like it or not. But I wasn't quite savvy or emotionally stable enough to do that at the time.

What was immediately evident with the changing of the guard, though, and much to my delight, was that the individuals who'd previously thought they were the keepers of the kingdom now saw things from a very different perspective. Their smug grins were quickly replaced by looks of trepidation. Their protector was gone, and they now had a new kind of boss—one more of my ilk.

Andy, however, didn't seem fazed by the change, but Andy was in a class by himself. He thought that the system would not fail him, that the color of his skin would keep him safely under the cloak of the organization upon which he had counted since graduating high school, and that he could merrily go on doing whatever it was he did—without ever missing a beat.

CHAPTER 6

THE TRAIL WE BLAZE

AFTER HAVING BEEN AT CASTLETON for a while, I began working in the depot's maintenance department as well. What started as a purported act of generosity on Ed's behalf, culminated into a huge thorn in his—and Andy's—sides. For me, this otherwise grimy, polluted place eventually became a peaceful retreat—well, as peaceful as life could be at Castleton Depot.

One day, Ed decided to send me downstairs to do data entry—it was as though he was loaning a buddy his lawnmower. (*"Of course you can use her. Just make sure you return her as soon as you're through, gassed up and clean."*) To say I was not a happy camper is far from an understatement. As if things weren't already bad enough, I was to be further humiliated by having to perform the tasks of an entry level clerk. But from where Ed and his colleagues stood, it didn't matter if a woman had a graduate education; it only mattered that she was a woman—and data entry (and dishwashing) is what women did.

Suffice it to say that the data entry thing was *the* last straw. There's a time and place to throw down the remainder of one's chips—and this was it. Heck, I wasn't opposed to doing whatever it took to get the job done—I'd proven that time and time again. Back at Division, I'd scrubbed walls and hauled boxes, getting the office ship-shape to impress some federal transportation oversight agency that was supposed to pass through. But the data entry thing just hit a major nerve. I had to draw the line somewhere. I was being used and abused—and I refused to take it anymore.

Admittedly, I gave in a few times as I felt bad letting down the guys—guys I had known for years and liked immensely. And so, every now and again, I sat there punching keys, whining and complaining and bitching and moaning about it every second, but at the same time, realizing how much I actually liked being there, even if my skills were going to complete waste. As time went on, I began dabbling in more challenging, more exciting tasks. Before long, as hard as it was to believe under the circumstances, I not only enjoyed work again, but had become indispensable to the department.

But even this otherwise bright spot got muddled by petty nonsense when a war ensued between Jim, my new "boss", and Ed, as they argued over who would "have me" and for how long. This went on every day, all day. Was I Transportation's property or Maintenance's? How much of the day would each of them get? I'd been rated "marginal" and treated like dirt up to then, and now, I suddenly was being fought over like the last gulp of water on a desert island.

Maintenance was a good fit for me. If I had to be in a bus garage at all, that was the place where I could contribute the most—because I was comfortable with the one thing that really mattered: the people. The Maintenance guys were a very different breed from their Transportation brethren. Maybe I'm just partial, coming from a family of mechanically inclined men, but those guys were a breath of fresh air amid the exhaust fumes! They were far more respectful, and they seemed to truly appreciate me for more than my appearance. Why would I want to go back upstairs?

The Maintenance operation itself, however, was another story. I'd never seen such a disorganized and antiquated operation like that in my life—it made me wonder how in the world they even got the buses out the doors every day. But I didn't mind. I viewed this, like I tried to view most things, as an opportunity to do something positive. I looked forward to helping bring this ragtag operation into the twenty-first century.

Among the archeological treasures I found was a collection of moldy ledger books, where all of the historical data were logged on a daily basis and stored for future reference. Holy fossil, Batman! It was like something out of the Dark Ages. I thought the Transportation department was out of touch with modernity, with the absence of computers and a ladies room, but this took the cake.

I chuckled as I climbed atop a towering, decrepit monstrosity of a desk to reach the shelves housing the department's logbooks, tossing them off one at a time on to the floor below. I then packed up those moldy old ledgers and sent them to storage. The department head, Jim, was great about the whole thing. Rather than consider me as a toxic employee he dare not get next to, for fear of retribution, he was smart enough to realize he finally had someone there who would tackle the inevitable, and he wasn't about to throw that away.

Before long, I had managed to help get that oddly inviting place over the threshold of modern technology. Computers were suddenly more than just big scary desk ornaments. It amused me to see grown men quiver with fear over the thought of using a PC. Whenever I had the chance, I taught my reluctant-but-willing dino colleagues the basics. I saw them go from petrified to electrified! Seeing their unbridled enthusiasm for getting past that scary place was worth every second. Knowing I was making a difference for them by helping pave the way for a new era in Maintenance was priceless.

It wasn't long before I became to the "go-to guy" of Castleton Maintenance. Over time, the little office tucked away in the back—with it's barred windows and mice I refused to trap—became my new home. For the first time in many years, I felt a sense of pride instead of humiliation. I almost didn't mind coming to work. Almost. And although there wasn't a snowball's chance in hell that I would ever get promoted—for obvious reasons—I found myself functioning seamlessly alongside my colleagues.

I was now performing an array of significantly more challenging tasks—and enjoying it. I had real responsibility once again. I was counted on to make important decisions regarding bus maintenance, scheduling, and other day-to-day operations. Something I was doing made a difference. It wasn't a bad gig for the time being and, in fact, it was an impressive addition to my résumé.

Unfortunately, working downstairs didn't mean I could relinquish the monotonous tasks I had been performing upstairs. In due time, I was working two jobs for the price of one—and a drop in the bucket compared to any of my male colleagues. It was frustrating and unfair, but I was just thankful for being able to get away from Andy and the trials and tribulations of Transportation.

He, however, was not feeling quite the same.

As with any rare glimmer of goodness throughout my bus garage odyssey, this sanity-saving diversion, too, would not be without its ugly. Andy might not have had me under his thumb for a while, but he was determined to have me back. The steam was readily building in that six foot something pot while I was out of reach—and the lid was just about to fly off.

Some months after I began working downstairs, I also began to sign-in there. To me, it made sense (not to mention the beating it saved my back). It was where I spent most of my day, if not the entire day. But for Andy, this was a huge problem, a control obstacle of sorts. He could no longer zip around yelling my name every time he needed something. To remedy his problem, Andy instructed Ed to demand that I sign in and out upstairs in the morning, again when I took lunch, again upon my return from lunch, and finally when I left for the day. So although I was no longer working upstairs, I was being told to go up and down like a yo-yo all day, when I just as easily could have signed in where I sat.

At first, I resisted. I told Ed that there were many reasons I should sign-in downstairs, not the least of which was my physical limitations. Moreover, no one else was required to sign in and out for lunch. But Andy didn't want to hear any justifications; he simply wanted me to do as he ordered. When he quickly realized I was not going to comply, he went so far as to have my name removed from the sign-in sheet as if somehow this was going to divert me back upstairs. It didn't. I added my name back and signed in.

Eventually, I humored Ed in an attempt to temper the chaos and went up and down the stairs, all the while my own steam building. Finally, one day I just put my foot down and refused to play yo-yo any longer. I had to take yet another stand. Obviously, this did not go over well with Andy, who took it upon himself to sit at my desk and wait for me to arrive, like an angry father whose daughter disobeyed him by staying out all night. Sometimes he would wait for me, and other times I would hear from the guys that he was "looking for me." If I wasn't there at the stroke of eight, I was officially late. And just as had occurred so many times before, I was eventually brought up on disciplinary charges. My newfound contentment was way too much for the boys to tolerate, and they weren't going to rest until they put an end to it.

All of this petty nonsense was emotionally and physically draining. I merely wanted to go to work, do my job, and go home. I was so damn sick and tired of the extraneous hullabaloo that I didn't know what to do with myself anymore. It caused a great deal of mental anguish—and that was bad enough—but to be forced to endure physical pain simply because an over-the-top control freak wanted to keep track of me, was, once more, something I was unwilling to tolerate.

On my next trip to the chiropractor, where I faithfully went three times a week, I asked for a letter describing my condition and limitations. My doctor was only too glad to arm me with the documentation I needed, a line I was confident that nobody would dare cross. But for Andy, there was no line too bold to cross. He had no respect for my physical condition, and my attempt to document it only proved to escalate his harassment to new heights.

One morning, this tall, dark, rather mean-looking man, came barreling into the Maintenance office like storm trooper. I knew he was there for me as soon as I caught sight of him. He proceeded to sound off like a madman in front of everyone, scolding me for failing to sign in upstairs. I politely explained to him that I had a condition that made it especially painful to go up and down the stairs and reminded him that I had recently submitted medical certification to that effect. He nastily barked, "If you have a problem, go home!" When I asked him who was going to pay my bills if I went home, he said, "That's your problem."

This cat-and-mouse game continued, eventually leading to more disciplinary action. Andy was infuriated by my unwillingness to obey him, and he was not about to stand idly by. By this time, he didn't really need any coaxing either; he had become somewhat of a one-man show. Fortunately, while he often got carried away, he was incapable of cooking up the more sophisticated plans, the kind intended to finish me off. That was still very much within Fred's and Carmine's purview, now that George was gone. The question became whether the new general manager, Kevin, would remain in the fray while they continued their unfettered reign of terror.

In 1995, as bad timing would have it for me, the MTA was, as it had many times since its establishment, facing the prospect of getting its financial house in order. The newly elected governor, George Pataki, took an ax to the state's budget, targeting the infamously mismanaged mass transit giant for drastic and immediate spending cuts. And if you know anything about the fastest way to cut spending, you know where this is going.

My demise began under the guise of a system-wide employee evaluation campaign designed to scale back the number of workers in various titles. Among those in the crosshairs were all eighty or so budget analysts who would be rated on a predetermined scale, with the lowest-scoring on the list getting laid off.

As is often the case in government, the most vulnerable employees are held up as the sacrificial lambs. Analysts were the

TA's lambs. We had no union, no management association, nothing. We were easy targets with no recourse for a charade that was to trick the taxpayers into believing the TA did its part to get New York back on track.

Analysts represented the smallest, most grossly underpaid (but generally most highly educated) group of employees. Kicking us to the curb was but a drop in the bucket, if that. But perception is everything. If it looked good in print, that's all that mattered.

Under normal circumstances, I wouldn't have given this silly and futile exercise a second thought, except for that I could see the train barreling down the tracks. And I was tied to the tracks with Andy, the reckless conductor, making a brakeless beeline right toward me. Yes, Andy, the man responsible for relentlessly harassing the crap out of me and creating about as hostile an environment as I had endured up to that time was the one designated to conduct my evaluation. *Haven't they done **enough** damage already?* I thought. *Maybe Ed was right after all. Maybe they* could *do whatever they wanted with me.*

Or could they?

I decided this time was going to be different; I was going to be proactive. I refused to just sit there, waiting for the anvil to drop on my head—again. Heck, I couldn't *afford* to wait for that!

I penned a letter to one of the higher ups in Surface Transit named Pat, a woman who I never had any personal dealings with, but had known of for years. She was one of the "she-men," as I call them—the type who rise through the ranks because they're non-threatening, in a masculine sort of way.

I informed her that I was being mercilessly harassed and that the person who was leading the charge was to evaluate me. As such,

I surely would lose my job if he was allowed to go forward. I pleaded with her to do something. But she did nothing. I never heard a word. I foolishly thought that once she knew what was going on, she'd be compelled to do something, especially as a woman who might have experienced discrimination herself. Not a chance.

The evaluation process moved forward as scheduled. I finished last on the list. Last. It was ludicrous. Next thing I knew, I was out the door—no send off, no nothing. I was jobless—and paralyzed with grief.

Fortunately, I was sharing a summer house on Long Beach Island, New Jersey, with a couple of buddies that year. I packed up what I needed, brought my four-legged babies to my mother's, and headed down for an unexpected, indefinite vacation. I wasn't about to wallow in pity. I had been through the wringer and desperately needed a break. It's certainly not the kind of break I had in mind, but it was a much-needed one nonetheless. Outside of that, I had not a clue what I was going to do.

Within a short time, I met the man who would become my husband. Talk about finally catching a break! It was unbelievably, incredibly nice to have such a distraction. We had a glorious and memorable time together, but the pain never really went away; it was merely masked by the temporary high of a new relationship.

Then, two weeks later, just when I thought I'd never see the inside of the walls of the TA again, I received the most curious call from my dear friend and colleague, Joe. Joe, a very highly regarded member of management and someone who I'd known for ages prior to working for the TA, apparently liked a good challenge. He said he saw my name on a re-hire list and wanted me to come work for him in East New York, Brooklyn, *the* last place I ever wanted to end up. I was elated and flattered—and nauseated all at once.

I thought the world of Joe, but realized that by accepting his offer, I'd have to go to work in a war zone, not to mention that I'd be pulling him into an ugly situation that could very well prove a detriment to his career. One thing I learned for sure at the TA is that you could be a hero today and a zero tomorrow, no matter how well-liked you were. But Joe didn't seem fazed. I, on the other hand, was petrified. Should I risk my personal safety for a job that might do us both in? On the other hand, I'd get back to work a lot sooner than expected *and* put my skills to good use for someone I respected immensely. Joe was very persuasive; he just wouldn't take no for an answer—and I didn't want to let him down.

Before the deal was sealed, however, things took an unexpected turn. As soon as the boys back at SID learned Joe had scooped me up, they wanted me back! Initially, I was absolutely floored—but also keenly aware of what they were up to. It made me think of the kid who tosses aside a toy with which he's grown tired and only wants it back when another kid takes interest in it—then how valuable that toy suddenly becomes. In this case, the toy was no longer theirs to keep.

CHAPTER 7

THE BITCH IS BACK

EAST NEW YORK SURELY WASN'T where I wanted to be, but it was all I had. I admit that I was scared for my life and, at the very least, concerned about my general safety. Armed with a cell phone and mace, I braced for my tour of duty in hell.

East New York is a true "hood," not like they're portrayed in music videos either. This is a place where the stores are aptly named for the products they sell. The store that sells donuts is called "Donuts," the store that sells food is "Food," and so on. Unless you fit in, stay out. The worst part of what I faced each day was parking on the street and walking to the building—a building, by the way, with no security! Anybody could walk in off the street without thinking twice. I didn't know of any incidents having occurred inside the building other than a few stories about missing personal effects, but on the outside, it wasn't unheard of for innocent civilians to be taken down by ricocheting stray bullets.

Fortunately, I managed to avoid conflict, except for the time I got rear-ended on the way home after working overtime. I actually had the audacity (or perhaps stupidity) to get out of my car alone in the dark but miraculously lived to tell about it. The guy turned out to be a med student who took care of the repairs without incident. Things didn't go nearly as smoothly, however, back at 1 Jamaica Avenue.

Many of my male colleagues parked inside the building, and I believed I should be able to do the same. And I did. But that didn't go over well with some of the other employees with whom I didn't work directly but who worked in that building and had their own ideas about the parking hierarchy. They seemed to think that because they had seniority or held what they viewed as more important positions or knew somebody, where they parked took precedence. This was not a perk for me but rather a safety issue from which I was unwilling to back down. One day I got into a scuffle with one of the "regulars", when he began to lambast me for parking there. It was obvious he viewed me as disposable, a lowly woman who had no place inside. Every time he saw me, we got into it again. This went on every morning for a long time. But I wasn't about to take orders from him—this was a matter of life or death. He, nor the very limited parking spaces, was enough to drive me out. Eventually, I lost that battle, but was given an alternate place to park, an outdoor, fenced-in area where some of my coworkers parked and were able to escort me in and out each day.

My two years on the inside were equally turbulent although not quite as bad as the environment from which I'd just been banished. If not for Joe, however, I would have fallen prey to the same relentless daily torment I'd dealt with for the four years prior. Because of his physical presence—and only because of it—did things not escalate into a free-for-all. As soon as Joe was off or away on business, mayhem ensued, mostly in the form of pettiness from his second in command, Paul. Paul was so incensed by my being there (getting between him and Joe) that he would do anything to stir the pot to the degree he believed he could get away with it. He wasted no time and missed no opportunity to make otherwise simple, straightforward situations complicated.

The day I crossed the threshold of 1 Jamaica Ave and planted myself at my desk, it was blatantly obvious that everyone had already been apprised of my legal woes as well as my friendship with Joe—and they felt threatened. The rumors began to fly about the place, filling up everyone's time with idle gossip. I felt like Tippy Hedren in the Hitchcock movie *The Birds*, when she was trying to duck into a phone booth to escape the birds that would inevitably peck her to death.

From day one, I was not Teresa; I was "Joe's girlfriend." The ignorance had already taken hold of some of my new coworkers, who, for whatever each of their reasons, chose to see me not as an analyst, not as an employee, but merely a mistress. Joe occasionally took the blabbermouths to the woodshed for stirring the pot, which did serve to temper their tongues somewhat, but only when he was physically there.

Regardless of what was going on, however, I focused on my work and tried to pay no mind to the scuttlebutt—after all, words are just words. But when things escalated to where my phone wire was cut, that was another story altogether. While I admit that something like this wouldn't have been such a big deal under other circumstances (although I'm not sure what constitutes acceptable circumstances), I didn't take too kindly to it, especially because it left my unsuspecting mother panic-stricken when I didn't answer my phone all day.

I suppose, in the grander scheme of things, having a phone wire cut was the least of what I dealt with over the years. It paled in comparison to my being rated "marginal" for leaving dirty dishes in the sink, being suspended immediately before and after vacation, or being made to walk around a bus garage full of men wearing a menstrual blood-stained skirt. Being in a new environment, though, I wanted nothing more than to have to deal with nothing of the kind.

Not everyone knew of my history with our employer, of course, and some of those who did reacted favorably. They would tell me how glad they were that someone was "finally" doing something about the blatant discrimination they'd all witnessed at some point or other. That really made me feel good, like it wasn't about me but for everyone similarly situated.

Upper management, however, was not quite as exuberant as some of my coworkers.

Lars was Joe's boss and, of course, mine too. He was fairly new there so I wasn't sure how much he knew, but gathered he knew nothing. Before long, he seemed to think I was the greatest thing since the wheel, much the way George did in the early days. He was quite pleased with my performance and didn't hesitate to frequently let me know. And as it turned out, Lars actually grew up with my father. I thought, *Well, if all else fails, perhaps the "it's who you know" theory will work in my favor.*

Under Lars, everything seemed to be coming together—things looked to have taken a turn for the better. I really thought that I would be able to start over and return to the career path I so badly wanted to be on and sorely missed.

It didn't take long, however, before Lars learned of my lawsuit—and he wasn't exactly cheering me on. He went from nice to nasty overnight. I don't know what he expected. I certainly wasn't going to make a point of telling him I was suing our employer. I just held my breath and hoped for the best. But Lars wasn't about to let go that I had declared war on the place that buttered his bread. I knew the love affair was over when one day he scolded me in front of the entire office.

I had been cajoled into heading up our annual charity drive (yes, another one), but after careful consideration, decided it was not something I could take on at that time. I knew what the job entailed, and was not equipped to handle it amid all else that was brewing in the background. I was comfortable contributing an additional percentage of my pay to keep with the spirit of giving. But that was as far as I was willing to go.

I feared, however, that begging off wouldn't go over well, and it most certainly didn't. Lars seemed to be waiting for me to "screw up" so he could pounce on me for my "disloyalty"; this made for a golden opportunity for him to do so. I was told later that Lars had said, "When twenty camel jockeys say the camel is no good, it's time to get a new camel." Guess the "it's who you know" thing didn't quite work out for me the way I had hoped.

Fortunately, Lars wasn't there too long, and just as when George left, I was thrilled. I prayed for another fresh start—perhaps a guy (or gal) with an open mind, someone secure enough to look beyond the litigation. The slate was again clean; I was getting yet another chance to try to turn this thing around once and for all. I had nothing to lose that I hadn't already lost—except my job.

Enter John. I'd never met him, but his reputation preceded him. One of the ladies with whom I'd worked at SID used to tell one crazy story after the next about him. I never imagined he'd be my boss, but there he was. He was, by all accounts, known to be an off-the-charts pseudo-transit-guru, sometimes—perhaps affectionately—referred to as Quasimodo for his uncanny resemblance to this character. And he was now running the show.

John was described as a lunatic prone to vituperative outbursts, tossing furniture about the office, and literally bouncing off walls, going feet over head, and a cornucopia of other grossly inappropriate behavior. He never was reprimanded for it. Rather, he was lauded as a genius—a man a cut above the rest. In fact, this was not his first go-round at the TA. He returned after having taken a hiatus to work his magic on a neighboring public transit system. But I didn't care what he'd done in the past. My sights were set on the present, on picking up the pieces and moving on. I tried to get to know John as though I had heard nothing about him.

John also knew nothing of my legal action and, like Lars, was immediately impressed by my abilities. He, too, made no secret about how he felt. Still, I made certain not to get ahead of myself, but remained cautiously optimistic. I had been lifted up and let down too many times before. I knew that John was a loose cannon that could blow at a moment's notice. I just had to pray that he'd somehow remain ignorant of my past—or not give a crap about it. That was, however, a bit unrealistic even for me. And sure enough, not all that long after he joined us, John, too, did a one-eighty. I truly believe that if not for Joe, I would have been tossed out, lawsuit or not.

All of these setbacks did nothing to alleviate my depression. I hid it well on the outside, but on the inside, I suffered; I was beginning to shut down. There were so many times I could barely keep my eyes open at work and was forced to take a nap in the ladies room. If I hadn't, I'd have fallen asleep right at my desk.

But I pressed on. I didn't want to let Joe down—well, that and pride. Pride and loyalty matter to me, and to that end, I gave every assignment my best effort regardless of how badly things were going. Most of the time, I got punished for my unwavering positive attitude. But now and then it paid off, this time, in quite an ironic way.

One day, Joe asked me to compose a letter regarding a technical matter I knew absolutely nothing about. Not only did I doubt my ability to produce a first-rate product, but I wasn't happy about having to write the letter in the first place. Apparently, a few of my highly paid colleagues had taken a stab at the same letter—unsuccessfully. I did the best I could and thought nothing more of it.

Soon after, John popped into the office and shouted out in his raucous signature style, "Now *this* is a letter! This is how a letter *should* be written!" And on and on he went. I was beaming. It wasn't as much for having written the letter as it was because John had no idea I'd written it—not until *after* his exuberant proclamation, that is. I just sat at my desk, quietly busying myself, while he sounded off. And then he asked who wrote it. And my response went over like a lead balloon. Time to rearrange the furniture …

That incident sealed the deal for me. I know it ticked John off to know that the person he could've counted on to do his grunt work was the same one he felt he had no choice but to despise. He said of me, "She's not to be trusted."

Still, his opinion—that I was not to be trusted—sure as heck wasn't going to stop me when the next opportunity presented itself. Although I was truly hanging by a thread by now, I wasn't giving up. So when a job posting came out for superintendent, I wasn't thinking anything but promotion! Of course, it would be a tough sell, getting it past John, but that wasn't enough to make me go away.

Becoming the first female maintenance superintendent was an exciting prospect. I loved going out in the field, something I occasionally got to do, and wanted more. I thought this was where the "charity work" I'd done in Castleton (working as an unofficial, underpaid superintendent) might actually pay off. I'd amassed knowledge over those few years that went a long way toward building a meaningful new foundation, which I was eager to put into action.

And so, I applied—along with a slew of other folks, for the handful of newly created positions. Approximately 120 people interviewed for this coveted job, just about all of whom were male, and most of whom had a lot more hands-on experience than me. Still, I had a lot going for me that made up for the experience I lacked. I was psyched. Was this *finally* the new beginning for which I had waited so long?

The first-round interview went about as great as an interview could. Upon exiting the room where the interviews were conducted, one of the panelists followed behind and stopped me right outside the door to tell me how impressed he was. He absolutely gushed for a few minutes, stopping short, it seemed, of giving me the job on the spot. I had to do everything in my power not to jump up and down for joy, but I maintained the utmost professionalism, thanked him, and left work that day walking on air.

A few days later, I found out I'd aced the interview, placing second out of some 120 prospective candidates. It was amazing—more than I could have hoped for. I wondered if I possibly could have beaten the nearly unbeatable odds and broken through a seemingly hopeless situation. If so, it was a miracle. This was really huge.

But even this prospective new lease on my career would be met with great resistance. Apparently, I had placed "too high" on the list and had to be moved down a few rungs. Although I found it hard to believe that something so ridiculous had to be done, Joe feared that he would be accused of somehow manipulating the results, not because his integrity had yet been called into question, but because our friendship might well cause that to occur. I went along with whatever he said. The last thing I wanted was for him to end up like me.

I was deflated but told myself it was just a number on a list. I simply wanted the dang job, and if I had to be number nine instead of number two, big deal. More than that, I didn't want someone I cared about to undergo an inquisition he didn't need to endure. My problem was not his problem. My loyalty to Joe was paramount. After bravely putting himself out there for me, the least I could do was go along with what he believed to be best for the both of us. Second place, ninth place—I didn't care.

Despite all the strategizing, certain folks decided that this was not going to happen, no matter what, and the wrangling went on for months. Things got ugly. Joe's colleagues gave him hell, one of whom went so far as to say "women don't belong here!" In fact, some suggested I should be removed from the list altogether. Eventually, Joe said that if I wasn't promoted, no one would be. He put his head on the chopping block for me as no one ever had. He put integrity over bullshit—not something often seen in government, or anywhere.

The in-fighting continued for months until finally, the promotions were put on hold. In fact, they stayed on hold. They never materialized for anyone. No letters, no calls, no nothing. The whole thing just fizzled out amid the turmoil. The powers that be waited for the job posting to expire (after six months), rather than face the consequences of not promoting me. The whole thing was shameful.

It wasn't too long after that when another superintendent position materialized. One would think by now I wouldn't— or shouldn't—bother. But I still had nothing to lose. I believe in miracles—and hoped this was going to be mine.

This time, though, my chances were automatically diminished as there were only two positions available. The two successful candidates would team up to administer training throughout Surface Transit. As luck would have it, this was yet another skill I had previously developed, again, during my stint at Castleton.

Just before my "transfer" to East New York, I had conducted a hazardous waste training class in the depot. Not exactly an exciting subject, but the experience was great. Things were going along fine, until some crybaby union guy complained that I was taking overtime pay away from his guys—not because anyone was particularly qualified or even interested, but merely because I wasn't one of their brethren. The union reps raised a huge stink and before I knew it, the rug was yanked out from under me. I was so bummed, but equally glad for the extra cash and invaluable experience—experience I could now put to good use.

When I arrived for my interview, I got the shock of my life. The panelists weren't the usual cast of characters. Not hardly. Rather, they were two female "behavioralists" from the City University of New York (CUNY), brought in for the express purpose of conducting the interviews. Certainly seemed suspicious, but I liked it. If this didn't level the playing field, nothing would. No list fixing. No expired postings. No screaming matches. At the time, I didn't really care what their motives were. I only cared that the process be untainted by the pack of chauvinistic bureaucrats who were more concerned with the genitals I didn't have than the credentials I did.

Both women were vivacious, outgoing, and enthusiastic. I got a really good vibe. The three-hour interview went superbly. I believe they would have given me the job right then but for not having the authority to do so. The tide seemed to finally have turned. Again, I had restored confidence in being able to undo the damage and move forward ... although I admit the whole thing didn't really pass the smell test.

Just as the time prior, I landed right at the top of the list—this time I came in first out of some sixty or so interviewees. I was elated beyond belief. I held my breath and hoped for the best. Then one day while out in the field on a bus inspection, I was approached by a vaguely familiar-looking guy who began congratulating me on getting the job. I looked at him curiously and said, "Thanks, but I haven't yet heard anything."

"I know you and I are the successful candidates," he insisted. "We're going to be partners."

Half of me wanted to celebrate. The other half was not convinced. I felt a guarded sense of relief but didn't want to count my chickens quite yet. Still, either this was happening or nothing ever would.

Next thing I knew, the in-fighting ensued once again. Joe was as frustrated as I was, maybe even more so. He got so fed up with his colleagues that he threatened to quit if I didn't get promoted—he put up quite a fuss. And that is where I had to slam on the brakes. Under no circumstances would I allow him to go to that extreme for me, especially when the job wasn't going to materialize anyway. The fact that he even defended my honor that way was enough. At the end of the day, Joe had more to lose than I ever could. It was over for me. I had hit the wall. The boys had won, and it wasn't worth his committing career suicide over.

And so, that would turn out to be the last interview of my career at New York City Transit. The only thing left to do was to hang on for dear life as my trial drew near.

CHAPTER 8

IT SAYS SOMETHING FOR THE LEGAL BOYS

IT WAS NOW 1997, five long years into the perpetual nightmare from which I still hadn't woken. I had railed against the abuse for as long as I could, but the beastly bureaucrats had managed to wring the normal out of my life and the joy out of my soul. The wounds were raw, because there'd been no time—and no way, for that matter—to heal. And here, with my trial only months away, I was about to board the next emotional roller coaster.

I was a mess and knew my life had changed for the worse, but I was too far gone to take an objective look at what I'd become. There'd be a lot of work to do, and I knew it wasn't going to happen overnight. So when I learned that I would have mental health coverage beginning January of that year, I couldn't have been more relieved. To me, this was not merely good news; it was a gift from God.

Meanwhile, as if I had any more space on my emotional hard drive, I had to prepare myself to face those who had caused me irreparable harm. I counted on my attorney, Tom, to soften what would be an ugly showdown, but I wasn't so sure he was up to the challenge. I had my doubts all along about Tom's integrity, doubts I conveniently compartmentalized during a time when I was incapable of taking on more controversy. I'd chosen him at random, because in 1994, when there was no Internet, I had no idea where to begin to look for legal representation. So I didn't look; I found my lawyer the good old-fashioned way: word of mouth. One of my colleagues at Division knew of him through a friend whose case he'd won. That sounded good enough to me. Looking for answers at a time of desperation left me very little wiggle room. Then again, as far as I knew, a lawyer was a lawyer; they were all pretty much the same.

When I first met with Tom, he did the usual lawyer shtick, such that he didn't dare intimate I had a strong case, even though he knew right off I did. Lawyers are businesspeople. Their primary motivation is a paycheck, not justice. In fact, justice is probably the farthest thing from the average attorney's mind. This was certainly true for Tom. He might have been sympathetic on the outside, but on the inside, his mental calculator was working some serious overtime.

What I learned far too late in the game, and long after everything was a done deal, was that my case was a "Title VII 101", if you will. Title VII cases are those, such as mine, relating to workplace discrimination. When an aggrieved employee steps forward with as much evidence as I did, it's obvious, short of blatant incompetency on the part of one's counsel (or a bad judge), that it's a slam-dunk. Tom was a seasoned attorney who knew better than to show his cards. The only way he could be sure to have me on the hook, was—well—to bait me. Toward that end, Tom authoritatively announced that his standard was to be "at least 50 percent sure" of winning before agreeing to take on a case.

It didn't take much for an attorney like Tom, who knew employment law by rote, to size up a client who reeked of desperation, with a basic bag of Title VII woes in tow. The trick was to placate me for as long as it took to win my trust, and then—*wham!*—turn the tables before I knew what hit me. And so before I knew it, Tom was trying to decide if he wanted to represent me, not the other way around. Lawyers count on a client's vulnerability. A desperate client with blind trust is always the best client. To that end, I was a model client.

Of course, the free consultation didn't do anything to dissuade me. It is a surefire way to rope in new clients who have fallen prey to situations of seriously damaging emotional proportions, especially for cases where a client has no viable means of support due to the circumstances surrounding his/her workplace discrimination case. Had Tom charged a consultation fee, I likely would have gone elsewhere, but free was good and all I could afford. This is also where "free" ended. Tom waited until just the right moment—just before I got up to leave—to tell me that while he believed I had a case, he needed one thousand dollars to "review" the flurry of paperwork he had before him. I was taken aback. I didn't have a thousand dollars on hand, but I agreed to pay him.

Tom knew my financial situation—I (foolishly) gave him full disclosure. I thought he needed to know that I lived hand-to-mouth, with no assets to speak of. I (foolishly) thought he was a "nice guy," sympathetic to my plight, who was just as concerned about getting justice for me as I was about getting justice for myself. I told him that I would have to take out a pension loan—a long, unnecessarily protracted process riddled with bureaucratic red tape—to pay him, but he didn't seem to care much. He knew I wasn't going anywhere anytime before he had me on the hook.

No sooner did I begin the daunting process of tapping into my pension fund than Tom asked for another two thousand dollars "to litigate." Here I thought I was being represented on contingency; at least, that is what he originally said. After mulling it over a few minutes, however, he must have figured if I was going through all the trouble of taking out a loan, he might as well get a little more while the opportunity presented itself—just in case.

At the time, my pension fund represented all the money I had to my name from any source whatsoever. A whopping five or six grand seemed like a small fortune to me at that time. But that didn't stop Tom from trying to get as much of it as he could.

It made me very uneasy that I had exhausted a preponderance of the fund it had taken so many years to build up and that I was counting on to get me through old age. Still, I convinced myself that it was all in the name of justice. And besides, before long I would be back on course, earning a bigger paycheck and building a more sizable pension a lot faster than before.

But Tom had other ideas. Suddenly, three thousand wasn't enough. He wanted even more—to "cover costs", he said. Knowing what I had just gone through to pay him the first two retainers, I found it almost hard to fathom that he would attempt to put a person in my fragile state of mind through that process all over again; I thought he was supposed to be on my side. As usual, however, he knew just how to wrap the lousy gift in an attractive box. He assured me that, if victorious, I would get back every penny I'd paid him. How could I say no to that?

In retrospect, I see that there was a very specific method to Tom's madness. He made certain he had me where he wanted me by ensuring that after I drained my pension, I could not afford to hire another lawyer no matter whether he did right by me or not. And so, out of equal parts vulnerability and sheer ignorance, I was on my way to federal court with Tom. I had never been in a courtroom, never mind being on center stage. The prospect was scary but exciting. I trusted that Tom would do everything in his power to protect my interests (even in light of the fact that he had just bankrupted me).

Before Tom and I got down to laying out the actual strategy for my case, he asked me what I sought in terms of an award. I told him I wanted my job back and for the three men who harmed me to be punished. He explained that individuals could not be found liable under Title VII. The organization, if found guilty, would do with their ill-mannered employees as they saw fit. There is no personal liability for individual offenders in civil employment matters, unless it is an act that rises to a criminal level, such as sexual assault. This was disappointing. Money in lieu of justice? It just didn't seem fair. I wanted the perpetrators to pay for what they did to me and for things to go back to the way they were. But, I know now that as with many other aspects of this ordeal, I was being completely unrealistic.

I found myself scratching my head, trying to figure out just how much an employer should pay an aggrieved employee for callously and premeditatedly destroying not just her career but her life. I had no idea. How could I put a price tag on that? I know people do it all the time. But not me. All the money in the world could not erase the wrongs committed by my employer or fully heal the emotional wounds therefrom.

I also realized that going back to work at the TA, if there was even a chance of that happening, likely would not be a panacea. Being reinstated to my previous position (or even a comparable one in another location) might bring with it a host of problems, namely retaliation, which would then lead to further litigation. But Tom confidently assured me that if I experienced retaliation in the same or even another position, the federal court wouldn't tolerate it. "They frown highly upon such behavior and will take immediate, stringent corrective measures," he said. That sounded feasible to me.

Tom also presented other prospective remedies in lieu of or in addition to job reinstatement and money, such as letters of apology and other workplace accommodations. Letters of apology? Such letters wouldn't be worth the paper they were written on—it would mean nothing to me if they were *forced* to say they were sorry. Be that as it may, Tom and I agreed to leave the remedial aspect of things open for the time being.

As Tom proceeded to prepare my case, I worked the grind in East New York, continuing to do whatever necessary to make the best of a seemingly hopeless situation. It was at this time that I was desperately trying to get promoted to the position of superintendent. I kept Tom and his staff up to speed on a regular basis, throughout the time of the two failed attempts to get promoted, and was instructed to fax him all the pertinent documents, such as cover letters, résumés, and responses to the applications, if any, from the TA.

It was now early 1997; my day in court finally was within reach. The anxiety was building; my stomach was in perpetual knots. I went to work every day as if I was counting down to a prison release. All

I knew was that after five years of nonstop torment, I wanted to get on with it and that this couldn't happen a moment too soon.

The idea of being the focus of a legal proceeding was unnerving. My unwavering optimism didn't calm me much, and the thought of reliving the whole ordeal didn't help matters either. I was so wound up that I couldn't eat or sleep for weeks. I knew I'd once again come face-to-face with those who had turned my life upside down. Frankly, I didn't want to see them ever again.

The trial began on Monday, March 3, 1997. I spent the first few days giving testimony—first direct, then on cross. It felt weird sitting there in front of nine strangers to whom I had to reveal intimate details of my personal and professional life. I tried to block all that out and just focus on answering the questions without falling to pieces.

The TA's attorneys—two women—made the process more difficult than it needed to be with their shamelessly unprofessional behavior. Their antics were truly embarrassing, as they mimicked and mocked Tom right in front of the judge—and got away with it too. Tom and I both were stunned.

It was obvious that the TA chose women attorneys as a ploy to try to pull the wool over the jurors' eyes. It's a known common tactic to use female attorneys in a discrimination case brought by female litigants. It's meant to say to the jury, "Hey, look! We don't discriminate against women. We have female attorneys!" Of course, there are female attorneys just as there are females in most other positions. But that doesn't mean discrimination doesn't exist within the organization, especially ones as large as the MTA.

In contrast to our adversaries, Tom's performance in the courtroom was fairly admirable. By admirable I mean he took the high road, never fanning the flames of opposing counsel's incendiary behavior but rather focusing on demonstrating to the jury that his client had indeed been wronged, as that is what would score a victory with not only the jurors but with the judge too. He even kept a cool head during innumerable sidebars predominantly instigated by opposing counsel. Moreover, he conducted both his direct and cross examinations with the utmost of professionalism. I'll give him that.

The TA, on the other hand, had no interest in courtroom etiquette; they were instead focused on attempting to manipulate the judge. It was obvious from the second they opened their mouths that they would serve themselves poorly. As soon as they began their cross examination—the first impression the jury would get of them—they tripped themselves up terribly.

Referring to a monster-sized deposition on their desk, they attempted to paint me a bombastic liar, but even at that, they were incredibly clumsy. It appeared they thought that if they could give the impression of somehow catching me in a lie, they'd have the case in the bag.

But they failed miserably. After asking two questions concerning my school hours and the homework I did while on TA property (in my office after quitting time), they were forced to nix their strategy before it was too late. They quoted from the transcripts of one my many depositions, trying to suggest I had come to court with a whole new set of facts, but they quickly realized they couldn't say that I was lying simply because I phrased my words somewhat differently than in my depositions. The truth is the truth, and the truth simply does not change. Clearly annoyed, they shut the transcript and moved on. They never pulled out that thing again.

They then proceeded with a different line of questioning that seemed to be taking the case to a place that would be considered procedurally off limits. Tom instantaneously asked for a sidebar. The conversation wasn't quite audible from where I sat, but I didn't like what I perceived was going on. When the judge instructed the defense to limit their questioning to events before and up to November 1994, the date of my federal filing, I was perplexed. *What about everything after that? The promotions I didn't get? The retaliation? The hostile environment I was forced to work in for the nearly three years after begin tossed out of Castleton? What the heck was going on?*

As soon as I could get Tom alone, I asked him about the judge's ruling. His answer was shocking. He told me that I would have to file a second suit to bring those actions. He went on to say that that's the way it works; that since the first suit was already filed, there was no way to add the events after November 1994. This was the first I had ever heard of a second suit, and Tom conveyed the news as nonchalantly as if he was giving me the time. Because we were right there in the courtroom, where I had no choice but to remain calm, I did so. More than that, I was already filled to capacity with painful emotion and had only enough strength left to get through what was immediately before me. All the same, my mind was racing; I was seeing red but made certain to maintain a cohesive front with my attorney. I couldn't help thinking that either I'd been seriously misled by the individual whose services I'd enlisted to help me, or he simply didn't know what the hell he was doing. Either way, I got screwed.

Meanwhile, my mother and my then-boyfriend (now husband) sat nervously in the courtroom, day after day. Their presence gave me further incentive to continue to stay focused; to give clear, concise testimony that most accurately reflected the events that brought me there in the first place. It was such a blessing to have that kind of support, particularly because I knew the process was difficult for them as well, especially for my mother. She often had to take refuge in the hallway—she simply couldn't bear listening to the lies spewing forth from individuals whose only objective was to smear her daughter.

For me, it wasn't quite so shocking. I had grown accustomed to being attacked, even though it never got easier to hear. The scorching crescendo was the day when George, Fred, and Carmine testified back-to-back. It was bad enough to be in such close proximity to them, but listening to their testimony proved even worse.

True to form, George presented a pack of eloquent lies to the court. In fact, I don't think anything truthful came out of his mouth. Fred, on the other hand, seemed to be suffering from a very severe case of memory loss. I'd never heard "I don't know" so many times in such a short time span in my entire life.

Carmine was due to testify last. But not before there was a big hoopla over him, Fred, George having had lunch together that day. Despite being clearly instructed not to do so by the judge (which is fairly standard protocol), they went ahead and did so anyway—and got scolded. I guess some things just never change. Fortunately, they were not cunning enough to use the time they had spent together more wisely, as demonstrated by his stunning testimony.

Carmine apparently was too scared to get up there and perjure himself as his colleagues before him had done. He seemed fearful that his testimony would contradict theirs, so he decided to tell the truth. Little did he know that he probably could have lied like the dickens since neither of his cohorts had had an attack of conscience.

Carmine painted a vivid picture of a conspiracy that he and Fred—and later, George—devised, beginning almost immediately after I was promoted to manager. It evidently had been spurred by their desire to remove me and to give the position to Carmine, after he complained to Fred that he was a more "deserving" candidate. However it is he justified being more "deserving", I'm not sure, but I don't think even he could go out on a limb so far as to suggest it had anything to do with better job performance.

Carmine, however, did leave one small thing out of his testimony (that I admit I'm relieved he left out): he didn't mention his unrequited love for me or say that that was the reason behind his anger over losing out on the promotion. One day when Carmine and I went out to lunch together, he foolishly decided to bare his soul to me, telling me about his feelings toward me, how it was about "much more than the way you look." He even went so far as to try to kiss me. It was so uncomfortable; it was painful. I didn't know what to say to a man who purportedly was happily married, with two small children that he and his wife went to great lengths to have. But somehow I managed to gracefully dance around it by reminding him I was involved with someone. Our relationship after that was somewhat uneasy but no less friendly. Still, I never imagined there would be any fallout over what occurred at any time in the future, and I know now I was naïve for thinking that. Nevertheless, while hearing Carmine's testimony was immensely difficult, it was also much welcomed vindication. There was no longer any doubt about my account of what had occurred. The jury heard it; the judge heard it; everyone heard it. It was what I believe sealed the TA's fate.

The day the three amigos testified was the hardest day of the two week trial. I tried to hold back the tears, but couldn't. It was like trying to hold back floodwaters with window screen. As I began quietly sobbing uncontrollably, the TA's lawyers demanded, in the most arrogant tone, that the judge "stop the crying" because it was "disruptive." The judge complied and asked for "whoever" was crying to stop, as though she didn't know who it was.

Even Tom demonstrated gross insensitivity in regard to my crying. He counseled me not to. "It won't bode well with the jurors," he said. I was speechless—I'd had a sincere reaction to hearing some pretty horrible stuff that went on for a very long time, a reaction I believe just about any juror out there would understand. In fact, it's hard to fathom that any human being in general would expect me not to cry. But again, trusting Tom's judgment, I managed to somehow regain control of myself, as difficult as that was to do.

As the trial progressed, Tom proved more and more to be a hindrance, rather than a path to the kind of justice to which I believe I was entitled. In fact, once the fog cleared and I was able to step back and view his performance for what it really was, I found myself looking at a long list of missteps it was too late to change.

First, there was Tom's advice to exclude the sexual harassment from my complaint. "It could look like you're grabbing at straws, like you're too litigious," he claimed. (I didn't even know the meaning of the word "litigious" until he told me, let alone that I was.)

Second, he advised allowing the jury to decide the compensatory damages—a very bad idea when they didn't have all the facts. How could the jury determine a just award if they were precluded from knowing the degree to which the plaintiff actually suffered?

Third, his decision to forgo interviewing any of my witnesses (a strategy he repeatedly bragged about) was a bit risky for me, but it was a time-saver for him. Tom's reasoning was that the witnesses would appear to be more truthful if the jurors knew it was the first time he met them (rather than the witnesses having been prepped to testify, as is commonplace with trials).

Fourth and last was his failure to amend my complaint to include the additional acts of discrimination and retaliation—and then to lie to me about it. This seedy stunt was the truest reflection of his character. My guess is that once he knew he had enough evidence to cement a win, anything more merely cut into the time he had to devote to his next case.

Concern grew as I wondered what I had gotten myself into— my best interests never seemed to be my attorney's priority. Most troubling of all was the notion that I had to file a second lawsuit— something just didn't sound right about that. But I wanted to trust Tom—it was too painful to think that he had done me wrong.

I certainly had some reflecting to do, but before I could even think along those lines, I still had a trial to get through and a workplace to return to, neither of which I was looking forward to one iota.

At the end of the first week of trial, I went back to work (no court on Friday). I suppose I could have stayed home, but I wanted to do the right thing by Joe. I was torn between my illness and my allegiance to a friend. Nevertheless, there's no doubt in my mind that as the friend that he was, he would have totally understood if I stayed home.

I expected my coworkers to be curious about the proceedings—and they were. But there was now a new dimension to my presence that gave me a strange feeling about that whole day. I felt as though I had been marked—as if I wasn't already. Being the woman who finally stood up to an employer notorious for discriminatory dealings was already a burden unto itself. But now it was like I had become radioactive, as if my coworkers knew not to get too close to me for fear of some kind of retribution. All I knew by then was that I didn't need to deal with more of the same nonsense after sweating through a trial and five years of hell. I had reached the end of my rope.

And so, it was on that day, Friday, March 7, 1997, I made a life-changing decision, one I suppose should have been made sooner but for fear that I would end up living out of a cardboard box. One minute I was busy working, and the next, I was cleaning out my desk. I just didn't give a hoot anymore. *Win or lose*, I thought, *I'm outta here!* My supervisor, Paul, commented on my packing expedition. He asked if I was coming back, to which I replied, "Not if I can help it." Once those words came out, I felt like I had just freed myself from the tentacles of hell.

So that was it. Nine years of desperately trying to build a career at New York City Transit were behind me. It was so strange. On one hand, I would never be the victim of their heinous torment again, and on the other hand, it was the end of my career, as I knew it. I was only thirty-four.

Meantime, the remainder of the trial was still before me. I thought, *What's four more days? By the same time next week, my life will have changed for the better.* I could finally move on—life would finally be good again.

The trial concluded on Thursday, March 13, 1997. A jury of nine would now decide whether I'd proven my case. Talk about high anxiety—I think that was the longest few hours I had ever known. No matter how confident I was, there was always a chance the jury would surprise.

I faced the jury while the verdict was read. After only a short deliberation, they came back with favorable decisions on all counts of discrimination and retaliation. I was ecstatic beyond comprehension. I wanted to kiss each and every one of them! I wanted to kiss the whole world! I gave the jury a nod of gratitude and headed for home on a cloud.

After arriving back at my apartment, I felt like I hadn't been there in a long time even though I was there that very morning. I imagined it was how one might feel after being released from prison for a crime he didn't commit and being back home for the first time in years.

Nevertheless, it was all over. I was exhausted…but on top of the world. I couldn't wait to call everyone who was waiting to hear the news.

CHAPTER 9

DARK DIAMOND

EMERGING THE VICTOR OF a legal battle with one's employer is a big deal. It most definitely was for me. The dark, emotionally draining journey that consumed my entire being for the better part of seven years was over. I could now pick up the pieces and move on—or at least try.

But that is not how it works in the real world. The high of winning was short-lived. Once the dust settled, I was faced with the harsh reality that I had lost my career and been left with my sanity hanging on a thread.

The burden lifted off my shoulders by a stellar albeit spotty victory would soon be replaced by a whole new set of troubles. Unbeknownst to me, there were still many mountains to climb. While I thought I reached the top, I was really only a short way up the side.

It all started with a call from Tom, asking if I would do an interview for our local paper, the *Staten Island Advance*. He said they were interested in the story and wanted to do a piece on it. I had my reservations, but then I thought, *What's the point of going through such an ordeal if not to shed light on it for the benefit of others?* So in the spirit of enlightenment, I did the interview.

The next day, much to my utter astonishment, my story made the front page under the headline: "Discrimination Victim Reaps Hollow Reward."

I had no idea my saga was going to be splashed across the front page, nor did I ever think to ask. The most I expected was a little piece tucked somewhere in the back of the paper. Moreover, something about the whole thing made me very uneasy, aside from the fact that my personal business had now become public. I couldn't quite put my finger on it, but my gut instinct seemed to be at odds with my conscious thoughts.

Meanwhile, all of the loose ends of the trial had to be tied up. Tom would present his case to the judge for whatever fees, costs, awards, and the like to which he believed I was entitled, and my adversaries, in true form, would do what they could to put the kibosh on it all.

Tom and I had discussed the prospect of reinstatement versus front pay. Front pay allows for one to be paid in lieu of returning to work when the environment to which he would return is likely to be hostile or when the work he performs is specific to that particular industry such that employment elsewhere would be difficult if not impossible to find. Although the function of a budget manager isn't specific to NYCT, I pointed out to Tom that going back there likely would not be a good thing for me as evidenced by what transpired in East New York (something a seasoned attorney such as himself should have already known). He readily agreed with my take on things and said he would argue for front pay.

At that time, front pay wasn't yet commonplace, and because of that, it was a roll of the dice as to whether we'd succeed. If the judge was not agreeable to front pay, I reluctantly agreed to settle for being "made whole"—the conceptual goal of a Title VII action—by accepting a commensurate managerial position, despite that the mere thought of returning to such a hostile workplace made me shudder.

The TA dream team, however, had their own idea as to the meaning of injunctive relief. They apparently decided it would behoove them to attempt to persuade the judge to order me back to a job in brokerage, an industry I hadn't worked in for ten years (and that I wanted nothing to do with ever again). They actually went so far as to present a comprehensive soup to nuts statistical work-up, including availability and salary ranges of jobs they claimed to be well-suited to my qualifications. Not even Tom saw that coming. It was not only sheer gall on the part of folks thoroughly unwilling to concede their loss, but also an honest to goodness example of throwing everything at the wall to see what sticks. Thank goodness, nothing did.

After realizing they had to comply, at least to some extent, the TA's counsel pushed for a managerial position over front pay. It was obvious that they did not want to see me awarded a dime more than they already had to fork over. Moreover, they knew full well what I was being put through within the confines of 1 Jamaica Avenue and, as such, it would be the worst-case scenario for me to go back there—or anywhere else at the TA for that matter.

Tom made a lackluster plea on my behalf. While he indeed put forth my preference to be awarded front pay, he failed to say a word about the reprehensible treatment I received in East New York, namely that the harassment never ceased after being transferred out of Staten Island Division; that the circumstances surrounding my case were by then systemic; and that given the two, it could easily be inferred that the harassment would continue. Rather, he spent all of a few seconds on me and the balance of the hearing defending his fee application.

At this stage, Tom had no reason to extend himself any farther than he absolutely had to. He had pretty much all but secured his $86,000 purse. He stood there nickel and diming like a panhandler, while my ticket back to hell got written. He went item for item, page for page through his lengthy fee award submission, as though this was the last money he'd ever see. If only he had put that much time and effort into preparing my case.

Not surprisingly, the judge decided against us, in light of Tom's tepid courtroom presentation. Instead, she bestowed upon the defendants the honor of deciding my fate. Yes, the severely scorned entity that was just proven to have committed a host of Title VII violations against me, including a barrage of retaliation, was to determine what served best as restitution for their wrongdoings. This was an outrage. It defied all common sense and logic. Tom should have raised a stink. But he didn't.

My fate once again was in the hands of my adversaries, a privilege one would think they'd have jumped at for fear of the tables turning. But no. They dragged their feet and failed to cooperate. After several appearances before the judge over the following several months to attempt to enlist their cooperation in offering the job they were so incredibly eager for me to have, they finally came to the table with a job that didn't even exist—it was a soon-to-be created position—one in each of the five boroughs—they claimed needed to be filled as soon as possible. They couldn't say when that was or whether the position was on par with the one I had lost, but decided that Brooklyn was the place for me.

In all fairness, I can't blame the judge for her decision no matter how much it hurt me or how misguided it might have been. I blame Tom for that. Had Tom come forward to let the judge know that sending me to Brooklyn, a place where I had been harassed the two years prior, was not a prudent move, she likely would have then raised the question of why it is he didn't amend my complaint to include that period. Then, Tom would have had to answer to someone with influence over his future dealings, not just little old ignorant me. Hence, even though Tom knew that sending me back to the lion's den was cruel and wrong, he had no choice but to stay mum or else fess up the truth in open court.

Knowing what Tom was all about, I wanted to get away from him as soon as humanly possible. But there was the matter of an appeal to contend with before I bode him farewell. At first, I freaked when he told me there'd even be an appeal. But that was Tom. The mention of an appeal any time prior to when it inevitably occurred would have proved to be nothing more than another conversation he didn't want to waste time having. What was worse was that my adversaries made a motion to put a stay on my award, pending the appeal's outcome. That meant I wouldn't see a dime until the appeal was decided, thereby forcing me to continue to scrape by with no income whatsoever for the duration of an unspecified period of time.

So with no income and not a penny left to my name, there was only one way to go: Tom.

Tom's offer to represent me was reluctant—although it turned out his reluctance was all part of the act. He got me going by saying that appeals cost at least $20,000 to start, then left me to marinate in my fear for a few days. Once he believed I was so frightened I'd agree to anything, he went on to say that although he wasn't an appellate attorney, he would represent me anyway, "free of charge."

I was filled with both relief and trepidation, but agreed to the "offer," no matter how little experience Tom claimed to have. I knew virtually nothing about appeals except that I had to keep the TA from winning. After Tom scared the crap out of me, and again, had me just where he wanted me, I agreed to let him handle it. The only saving grace—and the only reason he was even interested in this alleged kind deed—was that his fee award was in jeopardy.

The next thing I knew, I was sitting in the Second Circuit Court of Appeals for the allotted ten-minute argument. I don't remember a word of it; I only remember being extremely anxious. In fact, I think I was having another out-of-body experience. Just the notion of being in such close proximity to the evil perpetrators of the destruction of my life was emotionally crippling. Frankly, I don't even know why I went. Maybe I knew in my gut that Tom was dishonest and that my being there would somehow serve to counter that.

By the time the appellate handed down a decision, a year had passed since the trial. And it was an incredibly long year at that. I thought that once the appeal was behind me, everything would go back to normal, that all the waiting would be worth it and that somehow, I'd pick up the pieces and move on to bigger and better things. But even this event proved to do little to restore my mental health—or my faith in the legal system.

The TA lost their appeal, sans one count of discrimination, no doubt, due to Tom's gross lack of concern for my interests. That one count represented a substantial financial loss that I couldn't afford to cavalierly dismiss as, by this time, my illness had gotten the better of me. But I had no choice. There was no further recourse I knew of. This was, in fact, the end of the line.

Overall, in spite of Tom's flagrant legal tactics, my federal victory was a positive one. It proved once and for all that my employer had indeed acted inappropriately under the law and that treating employees the way they did me would not be tolerated. And while I doubt that it penetrated the skulls of some—such as those who firmly believe a woman's place is in the kitchen—I'm fairly certain the message resonated with others. In fact, I later heard through the grapevine that women were being offered promotions to the same male-dominated position I twice failed to get in East New York. That alone made me believe it was all worth it.

In the end, I might have gotten a bit beaten up in ring, but I came out standing. And while I doubt if I made an enormous dent in righting the wrongs perpetrated against woman in the workplace, at least I made a small gash. All those gashes add up.

CHAPTER 10

LONG WAY FROM HAPPINESS

EVEN WITH THE TRIAL BEHIND ME and all the loose ends tied up, I found myself sinking to even lower depths than ever before. I had a big win under my belt—and a gaping hole in my life. I never expected to feel so empty, so lost, and so hopeless. I expected to be dancing in the streets, happily getting on with all of the many things I enjoyed. But instead, a dark cloud settled over my life, and it wasn't going away any time soon.

I sank to a level I didn't know existed; I was in a real emotional quagmire. If not for my strict physical fitness regimen (and all the Scott Peck books I faithfully read on the stationary bike), I would have not been able to counter the ill-effects of the stress. I looked better than ever on the outside, but I'm guessing a portrait of my insides would've been pretty ugly. Having been left to my own devices for the first five years took an almost irreversible toll.

Even with a support system of family and friends, it was a lonely and difficult existence, suffering from depression and anxiety. Sympathy and a bottle of pills just didn't make things right. For me, the process was one of grieving. I desperately tried to navigate through pain so unimaginable that I wasn't even able to share it with my best friend—being depressed, I simply didn't have the wherewithal to reach out to anyone. I often didn't care if I lived or died, never mind chatting about it with others. Besides, I came to learn over time that nobody I knew could relate to such immense pain being borne out of an uncommon set of circumstances like mine. They might have seen it as a bad situation or a professional inconvenience, perhaps from which I could pick up the pieces and move on, but in reality, it was the slow and painful death of my whole identity.

What I went through can be equated to the process normally associated with death. Grieving, after all, isn't reserved for losing a loved one. We grieve a whole host of things, and this was no exception. But still, it's probably hard for a lot of folks to imagine this applying to the loss of a livelihood. They seemed to think, "Okay, so you sued and won. Great. Everything's good then, right? You have lots of money and a new lease on life." They couldn't have been more wrong.

The plain truth is that I was ill prepared for dealing with the harsh realities of government employment and what came with it in my particular case. Even New York City street smarts didn't give me the know-how to navigate such stuff. I knew I was struggling, but I did not want to live a life of dysfunction. I just wanted to feel the way I did "before".

When I began talk therapy in January '97, I was blessed with a therapist I'll call Marion. God love her—she turned out to be a blessing. I didn't find out until later, though, just how fortunate I was. She was the consummate professional. On the flip side, she gave me a false sense of what the field of psychology was about, with her patience, insight, and wisdom. She listened intently, without interruption; she allowed me to vent the whole spectrum of problems I faced, whether or not they had anything to do with work; she let me learn from what I told her through self-reflection; and she never injected her personal business into our sessions. I don't know what I would have done without her.

Marion decided after a few months together, that talk therapy alone was not enough and recommended I get on medication. With limited choices, I blindly selected a doctor from a list of providers in my plan and came up with Dr. E. Unfortunately, he turned out to be a colossal disappointment.

His appointments were scheduled in strict assembly-line fashion, in five-minute intervals, making it imperative that he got each patient in and out the door posthaste. I was very leery of him, but I was also far too sick to start over once I realized what he was about. Even having to give my medical history again would have proven too much.

From the beginning, I was deliberately explicit about why I was there and what I was experiencing. I told him of the fallout from a legal battle with my employer and how it had impacted my life. I told him I was anxious, depressed, and constantly reliving the horrors of the past five years, both when awake and asleep. I told him that I always had been a fastidious groomer, but how I had lost interest in the routine I once knew. And I had become an aesthetic mess too. My fingernail and toenail beds were exposed from picking; my normally flawless skin was dotted with scabs and scars; and my teeth slowly were disappearing from grinding. I was a flat-out mess—and I was soon getting married.

Dr. E. took a family history, prescribed drugs, and sent me off on my merry way.

For what felt like the longest six months ever, I was put on an absolutely horrid medication used to treat obsessive-compulsive disorder. I was like a zombie. Sure I didn't obsess—I had no energy to obsess! Or do anything else for that matter! Finally, after complaining that I could no longer stand living in my own skin, I was taken off that horrendous drug (I should never have been on in the first place), and put on another, far more tolerable one.

I continued on with my five-minute quickie med consults with Dr. E. for two years, until one day when he callously humiliated me for being a few minutes late (yes, *that* again!). Getting my disheveled self to his office was a chore unto itself, but that didn't seem to matter. He proceeded to scold me right out there in the waiting room in front of all the other patients, while looking down at his watch. But this would pale in comparison to what came later on once he had become instrumental in my fight to secure Worker's Compensation benefits.

Once it became apparent that I could no longer function at work and had no clue whether I ever would be able to again, I filed for worker's compensation through the TA. I was (and am) a proud person, and I'd never depended on anyone for sustenance outside of childhood. But now I was incapacitated and seeking to live by a means other than the hard work that had always carried me through in the past. It was difficult enough to *not* work, but worse, for me, was collecting money for it. But I had no choice. I realized I had to learn to put my pride aside for the sake of survival.

What should have been a simple administrative matter became another full-blown, nasty battle I will not soon forget. NYCT, the same employer who paid claims for such things as stubbed fingers (something bus operators were notorious for at that time), decided they would not honor my worker's compensation application (called "controversion"), citing a preexisting condition. They claimed I had always had obsessive-compulsive disorder, even though it was something they failed to ever substantiate.

As Manager of Budget and Personnel and even before that time, I witnessed the filing of worker's compensation claims like it was for sport. Never did I recall a time when anyone was denied, let alone challenged, unless for some obviously egregious violation. Of course, the hourly workers had a fiercely protective union behind them; I did not. As such, I was left out there flappin' in the breeze, like a flag Scotch Taped to a flagpole in a tornado.

In the interim of settling the worker's comp issue (which I will get back to in the next chapter), there was the matter of disability insurance—my last and only resort for income at the time. Unlike applying for worker's comp, a process that can become an entangled mess, filing for disability benefits generally was a simple, straightforward one.

Wait—did I say simple and straightforward? Not a chance. I filed for disability because I had no income. I had no income because my employer put a serious emotional battering on me that rendered me unable to work. These are indisputable facts, and I was merely looking to collect benefits to which I was rightfully entitled and should have automatically received. The TA, however, didn't see it that way.

In order for one to begin collecting disability benefits, one's employer must submit information to the insurance company on his behalf. This was not something my employer had to go to any lengths to do, but rather they needed only to submit one page of basic information. Despite all we'd been through, namely that the trial was over, done and behind us, it never occurred to me that there'd be more to it than that. But rather than complying, rather than just acknowledging that meeting their obligation was inevitable, they prolonged the process for one whole year. The insurance company was dumbfounded but nevertheless forced to close my case—until *I* was able to enlist the TA's cooperation. I cried, I slept, I fell to pieces. I just wanted to die. I was too sick to brush my teeth, never mind fighting for disability benefits.

The TA finally conceded when they'd run out of excuses. My relentless persistence might have had something to do with it, too. But who knows for sure.

After emerging victorious from yet another hard-fought battle, I should have been jumping for joy. Not quite. By then, I was choking from debt to the point that whatever money I did finally receive was gone before I got it. Don't get me wrong—I most definitely breathed a sigh of relief; I finally had a "paycheck." But it was temporary. The battle was won, but the war still far from over.

A month later, in April 1998, I finally got married. I waited almost thirty-six years to tie the knot for the very first—and what I planned on being the only—time. What should have been a joyous time, however, was tainted by my employer's venom. On the outside, I put on a happy face for the world. On the inside was another story. The sadness of losing my career was something I wouldn't soon get over. And no amount of money, no wedding, not even a life partner would make up for it. Sadness followed me like The Plague, overshadowing everything that might otherwise have been good.

Eventually, I began to isolate. My depression got worse, and the meds weren't doing much to help. I slept a lot because I didn't want to feel the pain anymore. Sleeping was the closest thing to being dead. When awake, I often contemplated suicide but couldn't bear the thought of what that would do to my mother. And what about the rest of my family? Friends? Even my beloved "babies"? So I kept in the forefront of my mind the blessings bestowed upon my life by the good grace of God. I continued to conjure up the strength to go on, knowing it was the right thing to do, no matter how unbearable it was.

I realized that the process of healing, though, was going to be a long one if I was forced to continue to deal with the petty, mean-spirited backlash of which I'd already gotten a whopping dose. The therapy (and meds to a certain degree) certainly helped to keep me afloat, but I had yet begun to scratch the surface of the work that needed to be done to get back to myself again.

Immediately following the conclusion of the battle for disability, I had to shift focus to the battle for worker's compensation benefits. Time was of the essence as disability would last for only two years and one year had already passed. Although I applied for both benefits at the same time, and had already been hashing out the worker's comp issue for a year, it was time to turn up the heat—that is, until Tom, my now former attorney, threw in the monkey wrench when he decided that the $86,000 he got paid for representing me was not all he was entitled to. He wanted more.

When the time came for the TA to pay up on the federal award, they sent a group of checks directly to Tom for him to divvy up, although I admit I have no idea if this is standard practice. Tom, however, decided to take matters into his own hands when he withheld one of my three checks. In the envelope that should have contained them, were two checks and a contract in place of the third that he directed me to sign over to him. This, he contended, would cover the $4,000 in costs not reimbursed by the court. I was stunned.

I demanded my check be returned and refused to pay him another cent. We went back and forth several times. I refused to sign over my check to him, and he refused to return it to me.

I felt powerless. At the mercy of depression, the last thing I had energy for was wrangling with my attorney. But more than that, I felt entirely let down. Despite what I had already come to know about Tom, I didn't expect this. I still expected him to conduct himself in a manner befitting an individual entrusted to foster and uphold the law. Sadly, Tom just wasn't that kind of individual, especially where money was concerned.

The next thing I know, just when I thought I'd seen it all with him, Tom gave me the surprise of my life when he slapped me with a lawsuit for breach of contract. In it, he alleged that I had reneged on my promise to reimburse him for costs not paid by the defendants. This stunt just took the cake. Incensed and just as anxious to respond, I decided I better make absolute sure I had all my ducks in a row with the accounting first. Maybe I was wrong; maybe I did owe him money. Maybe I unwittingly signed a contract that had come back to bite me in the checkbook.

I dug out copies of old invoices and sat them alongside a copy of the final invoice Tom submitted to the court, and went over them, line by line, starting from day one. The first thing I noticed was that there was no credit for any part of the $5000 retainer I'd paid him—the one I'd been assured he would credit back to me, pending a win. Perhaps it was an innocent oversight, but that alone would have been reason enough to refuse to sign over my check.

But it got worse. There was yet a further, more disconcerting discrepancy that made a $5000 retainer look like chump change. The final invoice contained many entries for hours worked that were not included in any of the old invoices. They weren't all together at the end of the final invoice such that they would have represented the most recent transactions, but they were rather strewn throughout the document, even going back years. There was only one conclusion I could draw, especially in light of what Tom had shown of himself to me. I wasn't sure what to do about it, but felt strongly I had to do something.

With nowhere else to turn, I wrote a letter to the judge, expecting her to be as concerned—no, more concerned than—me. But I was clearly wrong. Whatever the reason, and I surmise it had something to do with choosing to dare not open a can of worms from which the court feared what would creep out, her silence was deafening.

Still believing that I was doing the right thing by bringing what appeared to be a sinister act into the light, I contacted the district attorney's office. I thought for sure that they'd *have to* act on it. But they wanted nothing to do with it either. That is when I came to know that this was a political hot potato that nobody from the legal community wanted to touch (and probably rarely, if ever, does).

I still, however, had one last weapon in my arsenal, not so much as to expose Tom, but more to defend myself against his allegation that I had reneged on our contract: I hired another attorney. The last thing I wanted to do, but the only means by which to stop Tom in his tracks. After coughing up a hefty retainer, and going back and forth to no meaningful avail, nothing ever came of Tom's suit—or mine. He probably thought better of devoting so much of his time to a flimsy case that might have backfired. And I certainly wasn't going to push the issue—as painful as it was to accept that the man entrusted with one of the most important matters of my life had done as much damage as those he was hired to expose.

My new attorney did eventually get my check back—but not the file that I had also requested he attempt to regain possession of, a file, no less, containing the athletic bra that I had worn that day way back when I toughed out budget season, alone, in the dead heat, and which I was required to hold up in front of me for the jurors at trial.

At some point, I took a ride to Tom's office to attempt to retrieve the file from him, but he refused to return it then just as he had several times prior, despite that the law was clearly on my side. My husband was about to go into the building to ask him to hand the file over when Tom came bursting outside and approached the car. He poked his head fully inside the window (of a car containing two small children, no less) excitedly repeating "But we won! But we won!" "Perhaps", I responded, "but I'm here to get my file back." Again, he made it clear that he had no intention of surrendering the file unless and until I paid him the $4,000. I quickly gathered we were going nowhere with that exchange and left. Tom never got his money. I never got my file—or bra.

CHAPTER 11

TINDERBOX

ONE VERY LOVELY DAY IN May 1999, very much out of the blue, I received a certified return receipt letter from my friends at NYCT. *What could this be?* I wondered. It had been a while since they'd been in touch. Why it was an "Intent to Terminate" letter. I was utterly perplexed. How could they "intend to terminate" me from a position awarded by the federal court?

The letter stated that if I didn't return to work within sixty days, I would relinquish my employment. *But I'm sick,* I thought. *Because of them. How can they do this?* I was convinced it was just another way to torment me; that they were bluffing. I didn't see any reason to call in the cavalry quite yet. I put the letter aside and forgot about it.

Then, in late July, only two months later, I received another certified letter. As promised, it was a "Letter of Termination." Could it be that my eleven-year run had really come to an end? As far as I could ascertain as that time, I was no longer employed by New York City Transit.

I knew full well this was an act of retaliation and recalled how Tom had assured me of the intolerance of the courts in regard to such behavior, and how if the TA ever did retaliate, I could readily seek recourse. But I wasn't sure about anything Tom had said anymore.

After the last go-round, I was very leery. I lost a tremendous amount of trust in the legal system and wasn't thrilled about the prospect of setting out on that course again. I also didn't want to waste money on another legal battle (if, in fact, it would come to that), especially considering how hard I fought for the limited money I did have. *Ugh. Just stuff me in a barrel and toss me over Niagara Falls already*, I thought miserably.

Fortunately, I had developed an attorney/client relationship with Mike, the same guy who I'd hired to ward off Tom. For the most part, I liked Mike—he was a straight-shooter and seemed to be plugged into the real world. He understood what my case was really about and how to effectively handle it, and proved this in his limited dealings with Tom.

Mike threatened the TA that we would take legal action for wrongful termination if they did not cease and desist. They didn't; they weren't going to budge. Mike went a few rounds with them, during which time I prayed there would be a swift end to the whole thing. Then my retainer ran out. And so did Mike. Okay, he didn't run, exactly, but he wasn't working for free.

I now had no idea what to do. I'd already sued and won. *Doesn't that mean anything?* I thought. *Am I supposed to sue again? Or what?* The only logical thing to do was to write a letter to the EEOC, asking how to proceed. After all, they're the so-called watchdog of the aggrieved worker.

After sending off a three-page letter containing a detailed summary of the whole ordeal, I was contacted by a case manager named Dorothy. The main purpose of my letter, I told her, was to find out whether I was required to file another EEOC charge. Instead of a straightforward answer, however, she gave me a bunch of mumbo-jumbo about having to check with their legal department. "I'll get back to you," Dorothy said. Of course, I trusted that she knew what she was talking about.

Ultimately, I had to chase after Dorothy for months. I spoke to her briefly once or twice and then waited. Although it was difficult to conjure up the mental strength to do so, I continued to call her when I could, leaving a series of messages to which I got no return calls. I finally began to panic. With a serious deadline looming, Dorothy was nowhere to be found.

The last time I tried her number, there was a recording saying she was off on a two-week vacation. In government terms, that meant all of Dorothy's responsibilities came to a screeching halt. Was she so busy prior to then that the common decency of a response was too much for her? Or perhaps she just didn't give a damn. She was, after all, a bureaucrat. Perhaps I simply expected too much.

I was terminated on July 28, 1999, and had three hundred days from that day to file a charge of discrimination—or so I thought. The statutory clock, as it is referred to, begins the day the act of discrimination occurs, and a new charge is required for each additional "discrete" act thereafter. (Note: There are *very* strict statutory guidelines regarding timeliness. Failing to comply is grounds for dismissing a charge, barring extraordinary circumstances.)

My three hundred day deadline, according to my calculations, was sometime toward the end of May. Dorothy received my letter in early February. I thought, *you're entitled to a vacation, Dorothy, but don't you think perhaps you should take a few minutes to tie up those loose ends before scampering off for two weeks while people's lives hang precariously in the balance?*

At that point, Dorothy was no longer someone I even wanted to deal with—I had lost all respect for her. She was useless to me. Instead, I decided to contact Dorothy's supervisor, Rosemary, who was utterly perplexed as to what was going on. She had no knowledge of my letter or why her subordinate gave me the information she did in the first place. She knew nothing of running a charge by their legal department. Rosemary was, however, sure that my time was running out and that she had to get my charge processed posthaste. And did. We made it just under the wire by a matter of days.

And so, once again, I played the waiting game. My past experiences with the EEOC practically assured me that it would take a while for them to conduct one of their signature investigations, so I let the process run its course. While the wait was nowhere as long as it was the first time, it was just as disappointing. Once again, the EEOC found no wrongdoing on the part of NYCT, despite our now indisputable legal history. Once again, I was about to enter the ring. Round 2! *Ding!*

With my Right to Sue letter in hand, I filed a federal complaint against NYCT in 2001. It was hard to believe I was about to engage in yet another legal conflict. Moreover, I was in this one alone. All I knew was what I'd picked up along the way—and that wasn't much. I wanted to hire an attorney but didn't have the funds. And even if I could find one on contingency, after dealing with Tom, I was a bit lawyer-shy anyway. My greatest concern was whether I could withstand the pressure of self-representation, a potentially gut-wrenching and tricky prospect.

In the end, I lost—but not because I didn't have a case … or an attorney. The decision, as it went, was predicated on a thoroughly asinine Supreme Court precedent. On top of that, the judge seemed to be trying to send the message that once you've had your shot at the big time—and I'd already had mine—you were through. She did have a legitimate legal basis for her opinion, mind you, but I had an equally legitimate argument to counter it.

Delaware State College v. Ricks, decided in December 1980 by a 5–4 vote, established that it is *intent*, rather than an act itself, that starts the statutory clock. So according to this convoluted thinking, when I received the TA's intent letter in May 1999, I was, at that time, already terminated, and it was incumbent upon me to file three hundred days from then rather than July. I'm not sure how I was supposed to know this; in fact, I'm fairly certain that no layperson in the land could know this, short of having once experienced it. Heck, the EEOC certainly didn't know this either. I do know, however, that such thinking completely defies all common sense and logic. Can you imagine someone being convicted of assault, simply for saying he *intended* to punch someone else? It's hard to wrap my mind around such backward thinking, but five Supreme Court justices apparently did.

No matter how ridiculous the precedent upon which she relied might be, the judge was well within her rights to shut me down—barring consideration of the EEOC's role in the matter. But therein lies the problem. Had it not been for the EEOC's screw-up—a screw-up to which they openly admitted in writing, the most compelling kind of evidence one could have short of the individual herself physically coming forward to tell the judge in person—none of this would have ever occurred. This is inarguably the "extraordinary circumstance" required by law to mitigate an untimely filing. That alone should have sufficed to keep my case alive. But the judge blatantly ignored this as though to send the message that she didn't want me back in her courtroom again.

In the remainder of her opinion—a very brief opinion consisting of a few sentences that appeared to have had almost no thought behind them—the judge asserted that although she appreciated my illness, if I was able to make it to worker's compensation hearings every few months then I should have been able to timely file an EEOC charge. Talk about a stretch. She also went on to say that I had failed provide the EEOC with a phone number where I could be reached (even though it was clearly displayed at the bottom of the three-page letter sent to Dorothy; Dorothy called me on a couple of occasions; and the calls were accounted for on the phone bills submitted as evidence.)

Unfair as it was, if I wanted to keep my complaint alive, I faced the daunting prospect of another appeal. It was that or walk away and lose all of my employment-related benefits and forfeit a job it took so much effort to win. No matter which path I chose, I was damned. And unlike the first appeal, this one wasn't going to come as easily. I no longer had counsel willing to throw its hat in the ring for free. If I was determined to get justice, I had to roll up my sleeves and do whatever it took to make that happen on my own.

With no means by which to pay for representation, the first order of business was making a motion for the appointment of counsel. If granted, a litigant is allowed to proceed *in forma pauperis* (IFP), which is Latin for "in the form of a pauper." While one need not be a homeless person living out of cardboard box to be granted an IFP status, he must meet certain financial requirements—requirements the court does not disclose.

Not surprisingly, the TA did not take too kindly to my IFP application. No sooner had I filed my motion papers than another conflict ensued wherein they proceeded to stage an all-out no-holds-barred campaign to have the court deny my request. They were clearly on a mission to take me down before I got off the ground. I gathered that they knew, as did I, that the lower court's decision wasn't exactly sound, leaving the door wide open for a reversal. There was a lot at stake. In the meantime, I had to answer to their attacks—attacks I had come to know as emotionally charged, mean-spirited, and hurtful dissertations, rather than legitimate legal arguments—without the benefit of counsel.

In their response, the TA attempted to paint me as a well-off suburbanite, living in the lap of New Jersey luxury, who could easily afford an appellate attorney—on a monthly disability check. Moreover, they asserted that as an "intelligent person" with "the ability to write," I did not need counsel anyway. *Gee, thanks for the vote of confidence*, I thought, *but I don't think so.*

I fought back with as much fervor as I could muster. I wasn't about to let them take anything more away from me than they already had. The struggle was long, bitter, and nasty, but in the end, their dirty dealings failed them. The Second Circuit Court of

Appeals granted my motion and appointed pro bono (free) counsel. I was immensely relieved and indescribably grateful, even though I was sickened by knowing that this was just the tip of the iceberg of yet another gut-wrenching ordeal.

My appointed counsel, a Seton Hall law professor, Jon, and two of his students, Ryan and Kevin, were a very driven and compassionate group of guys who always made me feel that they unquestionably had my best interests at heart. I admit that law students aren't exactly the portrait of a legal dream team, but these guys were very sharp considering the practical experience they lacked. They immediately grasped the essence of my case as it relates to Title VII, and, unlike Tom, they kept me in the loop at all times. Finally having an ally I felt I could trust was a humongous relief.

My new legal eagles put together what I believed to have been a very strong argument to reverse the lower court's decision. It was an argument based on a set of facts that comported with Supreme Court case precedent, and in terms of presenting a solid argument, it doesn't get any better than that. Short of the political undercurrents that can roll in and mercilessly collapse any sound argument in the blink of an eye, or a judge who doesn't much care what the Supreme Court thinks, I was convinced that the appellate would have no option but to reverse.

I remember the day I got the news. The e-mail subject line read "Bad Decision." My heart dropped; it felt as though the blood drained out of me. I was utterly stunned. I could not imagine what went wrong.

Standard of review. That is what went wrong. Without getting too immersed in legalese that is likely to make your head spin, there are two commonly applied standards of appellate review: de novo and abuse of discretion. This sounded like Swahili to me at the time too—until the guys explained it. Once I grasped the concept, I realized how it was possible to get such a bad decision even in the face of a nearly inarguable set of facts.

Simply put, a de novo review allows for a fresh look at one's case. In other words, the appellate ignores the lower court's decision altogether and treats the case as though it had never been before the court at all. The latter standard, abuse of discretion, only reviews the decision of the lower court to determine whether the judge abused her discretion in formulating her decision; in other words, it looks to ensure a judge properly applied the law. There is no "fresh look" but rather the presumption that all facts were appropriately construed by the lower court.

A de novo review is an appellant's friend; it allows for somewhat of a chance that he will succeed in having his decision overturned. Abuse of discretion is the appellant's arch enemy, and the standard under which my case was reviewed; it reduces his chances to near zero.

My guys fought feverishly to convince the court to apply the de novo standard, but in the end, because the lower court judge acted with prejudice, that is, she formulated an opinion at all, I wasn't entitled to that standard of review. Had she not done so (but rather dismissed on summary judgment which is where a judge decides one does not have a case as a matter of law and dismisses it), I would have automatically gotten a de novo review.

The point here is not to confuse you with legal intricacies, but rather to convey that this judge wanted me gone, and did whatever it took to accomplish her goal. By taking the time to write a few measly sentences, she knew she'd pretty much abolished my chances of having her decision overturned. Very slick indeed.

Nevertheless, I said a prayer and filed a motion for reconsideration and reconsideration *en banc* with the appellate, both last ditch, near-impossible attempts to have one's case reheard—but the decision remained unchanged. My last hope, if I even dared to go there, was to petition the Supreme Court. This, however, would be a monumental undertaking that a pro se might be deemed nuts to even consider. However, when you know you've been wronged, and you've been wronged in as many ways and for as long as I had been, *and* your survival depends on it, it makes the decision that much less difficult. After thoughtful but brief contemplation, I decided I was willing to exhaust every available remedy all the way to the top, even those I knew to be practically unattainable.

And so, I geared up to petition the Supreme Court of the United States of America. Never in a million years would I have even thought for a moment I'd ever face such a lofty—and perhaps foolhardy—endeavor. But there I was, ready to take the plunge.

CHAPTER 12

IF THE RIVER COULD BEND

MUCH TO MY WOEFUL CHAGRIN, and despite that we had already been through so much for so many years, a great deal of unfinished business with my former employer lay ahead, namely a substantial sum of money they owed me in the form of benefits for which they made me grovel more years than I care to count. There always seemed to be something before us to squabble about; nothing was ever easy. In fact, with every encounter came the anticipated, unnecessarily malevolent retaliation.

At times, I actually resorted to pleading with them to cease and desist; I wrote to them and begged them to just do the right thing. I'd tell them how sick I was, hoping they'd be able to put the past aside, but they had no intention of ever doing anything of the kind. After having cleaned their clocks once and rattling their cages with a second, albeit unsuccessful, complaint, they were fixed on a path of vengeance that wouldn't soon end. And as long as I continued to deal with them, even for the simplest of things, I knew life would continue to be unnecessarily difficult. And difficult it continued to be.

While apprehensively gearing up to take my sorely disappointing appellate defeat to the highest court in the land, yet another matter over which we could not seem to reach a civilized agreement had me rethinking my strategy in a big way. I did not have the time—or endurance—to juggle two conflicts at once. One was too much. I was now faced with the choice between trying to collect $80,000 or going forward with the Supreme Court, where, even in the highly unlikely event I did achieve success, there was no guarantee I'd be any better off financially any time soon, and, in fact, would likely go through another several years of hell before seeing a dime. It really came down to a practical matter of odds: little chance of advancing a Supreme Court petition versus somewhat of a chance to recover $80,000. This was a no-brainer.

This particular locking of the horns with my adversaries began a few years prior with my application for worker's compensation benefits in July '97, only months after their stinging federal court defeat. As I mentioned earlier, my quest for comp did not go well, in fact, it took six hard-fought, gut-wrenching years to finally "establish" my case. It was not until then, when I had finally established my case, that the TA came to owe me some $80,000 that they outright refused to pay. And all hell broke loose once more.

I was familiar with the New York State Worker's Compensation system insofar as my duties as budget manager went, but I'd never had the misfortune of having to collect. All I really knew was that it was easy for the union guys to collect, no matter how minor the injury. In addition to stubbed fingers, there was a running joke in one of the depots about a particular set of steps the guys would 'trip up' when they wanted to go out on comp, i.e., wanted a paid vacation. Then there was the guy who was out on comp for three years … with a *toothache*. Or how about the guy with the back injury who came to Division headquarters to pick-up his paychecks looking like he was training for Mr. Universe, proudly flaunting his new physique. So imagine my disgust at being challenged vehemently by an employer who went out of its way to intentionally (and successfully) inflict harm on me. In fact, I ended up sicker for having tried to collect worker's comp than I was before I began.

Still, I foolishly believed, as I had so many times before, that once I was able to present my case, this time before the comp board, my benefits would be paid without further ado. I was confident no judge could possibly question the severity or nature of my illness, especially in light of a federal victory that established "pain and suffering". I thought I'd go before the judge, present my evidence, and soon thereafter begin to collect. But that was about as far from what occurred as anything I possibly could have ever envisioned. What I mistakenly expected to be a relatively easy, straightforward matter turned into years of hell that I am loath to recount.

As I had done prior, I hired an attorney upon the recommendation of another. I knew nothing about this man, Jon, except that he'd done right by the person who referred him. Despite what I had just been put through by Tom, however, I wasn't much concerned because worker's compensation law is vastly different from other areas of law in that it is but an assembly line of cases, where clients (claimants) with work-related injuries seek to recover state-regulated weekly benefits from their employers at informal (often brief) hearings before an administrative judge. Clients don't pay worker's compensation attorneys up front either, making affordability a non-issue. That's good and bad—good because I was guaranteed an attorney; bad because there isn't a heck of a lot of incentive for attorneys, who get paid small, flat fees on a hearing-by-hearing basis, to get your case resolved in a timely manner.

When an employer "controverts" an employee's claim for benefits (refuses to pay, for any number of reasons) as they had done to mine, that puts the employer in the driver's seat. Not that it should. But it does. The New York State Workers Comp Board was (and presumably still is) entrenched in corruption, not to mention the layers of wasteful bureaucracy one might come to expect from such an entity. Although there have been a handful of reforms over the years to eliminate or at least minimize the rampant abuses that plague this bloated government agency, in no way have those changes prevented employers like NYCT from using whatever tactics they could manage to conjure up to prevent claimants from collecting, which is their ultimate goal.

Bolstering their advantageous position, NYCT is a "self-insured" employer, meaning that they are also the "insurance carrier". That means there is no middleman and therefore no impartiality whatsoever. This blatant conflict of interest enabled them to stick it to me all over again without a care in the world. Sans a shred of evidence to substantiate their position, they were able to assert and maintain that I had not suffered a work-related illness but rather that my claim was predicated on a pre-existing condition—basically that I had been sick from the beginning of my tenure with them (and theoretically for all the years prior, for that matter)—leaving me to prove and reprove, over and over again, that which I had proved right from the get-go.

Every few months, I attended another hearing (the same hearings the federal judge referred to in her opinion as the basis for deciding my illness was not serious enough to prevent me from filing a timely EEOC charge). Each trip in from New Jersey to Staten Island was like a long drive to the edge of a cliff. Each time, I tried to remain hopeful that I could somehow put on the brakes, but I usually went off the cliff. I was sent away empty-handed time after time, confounded and frustrated by the whole thing. I'd often self-mutilate, lose sleep, and obsess for days in anticipation of yet another round of fruitless tomfoolery. When I was there, I was a pathetic ball of anxiety.

After three or four hearings (the equivalent of more than a year), I expected we would have made at least some progress. But we never really did. Regardless of what transpired, I was repeatedly reassured by Jon that we had to tough it out until next time, for if we appealed any of the judge's decisions, it would be at least a year and a half for an appeal to come to fruition. *A year and half?* I would think. *There's no way I can go that long. I'm barely hanging on as it is.* And with that, I shut up and went along with what I was told, like a good little client—just as I had with Tom.

My hearings were always as concise as they were fruitless. Jon would speak his piece; the carrier would speak theirs; and the judge would make a decision on the spot. The result was transcribed, and another date was set for the continuation of unresolved issues. Carriers knew how to play the game, how to work the system. This was especially true for a carrier like the TA who had been down this road zillions of times and knew every trick in the book. Moreover, they were well acquainted with everyone, most importantly the judges and fellow (opposing) counsel who worked out of the same location where the hearings took place. This cozy physical arrangement certainly left a lot of room for these folks to lose their objectivity.

Jon obviously knew his way around the system very well—this, proving the greatest obstacle of all. At every hearing, I'd scratch my head in complete bewilderment, wondering why he still wasn't able to establish my case—even partially—when I had already proven it by several means. I was right there at every hearing, and I heard the same thing everyone else in the room heard, and yet I never had a clue what the heck had just happened—when it happened right there in front of me! It was like a sleight-of-hand magic trick. After each hearing, I'd ask Jon to explain what was going on. He'd throw me a few sensible sounding crumbs, scare me with the appeal nonsense, and shut me right up. With that, I'd leave, cry hysterically all the way home, and wait for next time.

I came to see after a while that not only was my employer motivated to drag out the whole thing, but so was my attorney. It's all part of the game. For the carrier, it postpones paying on the claim, and for the attorney it means another paycheck. Everybody wins—except the claimant.

Before I knew it, more years had gone by than any appeal possibly could have taken. Eventually, it got to where I'd sit in the waiting area wondering how many more trips I'd be taking back there rather than when it would all end. I recall overhearing other claimants kvetching aloud amongst each other about their cases and how long they'd been strung along. The more I heard the more freaked out I'd get that I, too, would be staring at those walls for just as long—even though I did have a few encouraging breakthroughs along the way, breakthroughs that my adversaries, not surprisingly, found a way to put a stop to posthaste.

The first time was about one year in when my case finally got "partially established" (that is where the judge temporarily awards a lesser amount of compensation on a limited basis). The idea is to then keep the carrier from countering the evidence that got you there—or just hope that they don't even try. Of course, it didn't take long before the TA came up with a plan. Suddenly, they had decided to send me for an independent medical exam (IME), something they could have (and should have) done at the time I filed my application. An IME is an alleged impartial process whereby an employer faced with paying on a comp claim requires a claimant to be examined by a doctor who is neither the claimant's doctor nor one working for the insurance carrier, for the purpose of determining whether and to what degree a workplace injury has occurred. IME's are generally administered as soon as a carrier has been notified of the claimant's injury.

In the case of workplace harassment, the stakes are even higher for a carrier. Illnesses or injuries borne out of discrimination claims are not regarded in the same fashion as those arising from normal, everyday illnesses or injuries in the sense that worker's compensation is deemed insufficient to make an aggrieved employee whole in the face of purposeful acts of malice. If an employer were to pay on the claim of an aggrieved employee under these exceptional circumstances, it would be tantamount to admitting guilt. Hence, it is this employer for whom the IME becomes one of the most critical weapons against liability.

Normally, I wouldn't have minded attending an IME—I had nothing to hide. But I knew I wasn't being summoned to attend for any other reason than for the carrier to put the kibosh on my temporary award until they could find a clever way to stave me off for good. It was evident that the process was an ill-motivated one, and therefore, I wanted nothing to do with it. But as a claimant, I had to attend or forfeit benefits altogether.

When I first received the letter instructing me to attend, I immediately knew I was in for a wild ride. Rather than being sent to a psychiatrist—or anyone in the field of psychology—I was directed to be examined by a cardiologist in New York City. *A cardiologist? I don't have heart problems! How the heck would a cardiologist know whether I had been made psychologically unwell by my employer?* It didn't matter. If I failed to show, I risked compromising my benefits. And so, with my husband along as a witness, I attended the exam.

The exam proved to be yet another of the many surreal experiences of my crazy journey during which not a word was spoken about my illness. Rather, I was subjected to what appeared to be a perfunctory cardiology exam—and the doctor's mandatory follow-up report reflected this. He'd taken the time to notate the size of my heart and a bunch of other useless, irrelevant information but never once made mention of the many conditions about which I'd complained. In the end, however, the doctor was obligated only to conclude that I didn't suffer a work-related illness, regardless of how he reached that conclusion, which he did. He got a pat on the back and an uninterrupted flow of patients, and *I* lost the measly pittance of benefits it had taken me a year to secure. Moreover, the whole process did nothing to improve my condition; in fact, it exacerbated it to new heights.

For months after that crushing disappointment, I anxiously pressed on, continuing to submit medical evidence and, in time, managed to once again partially establish my case. This was a tremendous relief, despite that the weekly benefit amount would barely made a dent in my finances. The main thing, however, was that I had gotten my foot back in the door and was that much closer to reaching a conclusion.

No sooner did I take this one significant step forward that I was pulled two steps back. I'd barely received my first check when I was again directed to attend an IME. This time, however, they managed to find a psychiatrist. I guess even the TA realized that a cardiologist was pushing the envelope a lick too far. They did, however, make certain to exact their signature retaliation by sending me to a location as far away from home as possible, something they were fully aware would cause a hardship. Nevertheless, with my husband by my side, I trekked back into New York City for what I feared was going to be a repeat of the time prior.

The examination proved to be seemingly routine—nothing out of the ordinary transpired. My illness was apparent, and the doctor's report accurately reflected this. I was shocked but pleased—I had finally gotten what I needed to move forward with my case, and that was all that mattered. But I wasn't out of the woods yet; I was scheduled to come back for a follow-up exam in three weeks. I wasn't at all pleased at the prospect of having to go all the way back there, especially under the strained circumstances, but I did.

Much to my complete and utter amazement, quite by a miracle about which I was not made aware, I had fully recovered from an emotional battering that only three weeks earlier was the underlying cause of an illness so severe, I was rendered indefinitely and totally unable to work. The report was strewn with a bunch of other senseless, self-serving hogwash obviously put forth only for the purpose of covering this quack's scheming backside. I was sure that there was only one explanation for what had occurred.

I was beside myself. The corruption was so blatant, it was outright insulting. And my lawyer did little to help. This wasn't his first time at the rodeo, as they say; no doubt he'd bore witness to this sort of thing countless times in the past. In response, he gave me the usual song and dance. "We'll schedule another hearing" was more or less his mantra.

As anticipated, I lost my benefits again. If I got a few bucks, I got a lot (on top of which was already being attached to pay back disability). All I knew is that I only wanted that to which I was rightfully entitled. What I didn't know was what to do to get it. In a world where everything was upside down, this was proving to be a stupendous feat. It just seemed so incredibly unfair.

I had known of an internal procedure (that is, within the comp board) for filing a discrimination complaint against an employer called a Section 120. I'd hoped that perhaps this would prove to be the way to put an end to NYCT's shenanigans, once and for all. The only problem was effectively presenting my case. As much as I knew the truth, and even with the amount of evidence I had behind me, I was in no position to go toe-to-toe with my former employer. And looking for another attorney was the last thing on earth I wanted to do. But I was desperate.

Trying to find an attorney to represent me on contingency was like a blind man trying to find his way cross country on a skateboard. Nobody seemed to be interested in taking on a case with a long, entangled history without first getting paid. It was not the kind of straightforward case that makes an attorney a quick, unfettered few bucks, but one that required a significant amount of time to put together and, due to its unusual nature, had an unpredictable chance of success. If I was able to come up with a bundle of cash, no doubt I would have had many takers. But that wasn't an option and, in the end, I was left to fend for myself.

When I appeared for what would prove to be the only hearing, I did the best I could to make my argument. I stood before the judge in a tiny hearing room with two men (presumably counsel) sitting to my right. Their close proximity to me was so unnerving that I had to ask the judge to remove them from the room while I said my piece. I had no idea whether that was even permissible, but I didn't care. Fortunately, the judge obliged me, but it didn't make a hint of difference. I realized in retrospect that if these hearings were 'for real', opposing counsel would never have stood for being directed to leave the room. As usual, they were a step ahead of me.

In the end, it was all for nothing. I nervously tried to convince the court there was a nexus between the withholding of comp benefits and my federal victory, but it didn't fly. They seemed stuck on the number of years that had passed since, and concluded it was too many for there to be a connection between the two events. Of course, such thinking defies common sense because there is no specific amount of time one can designate to say retaliation has positively not occurred, especially when one's employer is responsible for the delay. Fortunately, since then, The Supreme Court ruled that an employer can no longer necessarily use a lapse in time as an affirmative defense for retaliation; otherwise, all it would take to get away with such acts is stalling long enough to avoid litigation altogether. But it was too late for me.

The loss came as no surprise; I didn't expect much. Regardless, I had to do whatever I could to try to get my benefits. I didn't really have a choice. I began to see that this contest, too, would go on indefinitely until one of us gave up—and that one was not going to be me. There was far more to this than principle; it was a matter of survival. I didn't have many tools in my litigation toolbelt to make things happen any faster, and my lawyer did nothing to help. And now, after filing a Section 120, I sent out a very distinct message that I wasn't about to cower from anything my adversaries dished out, with or without him. Further retaliation was, henceforth, not far away.

In late 2002, amidst a second federal appellate decision, on the heels of a failed Section 120, and over five very long years after filing for benefits, the IME machine was fired up for its last strike in response to my ongoing efforts to secure the benefits that should never have been withheld from the start. Having learned by now from the past and realizing how important it was to become my own advocate, however, I had kept abreast of the comp world and was better prepared to defend my rights this time around. Being bullied was no longer acceptable.

IME guidelines had changed due to long overdue reform. Now, an insurance carrier could no longer spring one of these so-called medical exams on a claimant, particularly not one that caused any type of hardship such as having to travel far from home. This, of course, greatly limited the degree to which the IME could be used to inflict harm. But it didn't stop my disgruntled former employer from going full speed ahead with whatever ill-conceived plan they had in mind as a means by which to shut me down.

The day I received the IME notice, an all-out war ensued. The appointment was two days out with a doctor located far from home who, again, was not trained to evaluate my condition. I outright refused to comply. But the more I stood my ground, the more notices I received. I was bombarded with notices day after day after day. I was forced to timely respond or else risk losing my benefits so putting them aside for another time was not an option. I immediately called the TA and followed up each call with a letter. No sooner would it appear that they'd acquiesced than I'd get another notice, and another, and another, and another. Riddled with unbearable anxiety, I opened my mailbox each day like it was rigged to blow up. It got to where I was literally afraid to take in the mail.

Finally, at some point, they backed down—well, almost. While they managed to find a doctor closer to home, they were unable to find one trained in the field of psychology. It appeared that they didn't have a vast pool of candidates from which to choose that were willing to go along with the program.

On the day of the appointment, as I pulled into the parking lot, I got the distinct feeling this was not going to be good. I remember wanting to run like the wind. I just kept my sights set on reaching a conclusion to my case and told myself it would soon all be over, that this was the last IME I would ever be made to attend.

Once inside, I was again forced to relive the nightmare that had been my life for the previous ten years, the last thing in the world I wanted to do. So much as hearing the sound of my voice reverberating in my head was intolerable. *How many times am I going to have to relive this freaking ordeal?* I wondered. *It just gets worse and worse instead of ever getting any better.* There I sat, crying so uncontrollably before this stranger, you could've wrung me out like a wet rag. And what didn't come out of my tear ducts came out of my pores.

I was enormously relieved when, just as the doctors before him had done, this guy conceded a job-related illness and concluded, in his report, I was indefinitely unable to work. I wondered if my trusty tape recorder had anything to do with it. In addition to other impacting IME protocol reforms, a claimant now was able to tape his appointments, and there was no way I was going to pass up that opportunity. I had a cassette recorder that my father picked up at a yard sale for five dollars that I might never have used but for my desperation to keep the process honest. Boy, did that dusty old gadget come in handy! But, just as with the previous IMEs, I still was not out of the woods. Here, too, I had a follow-up appointment to contend with a few weeks later.

Although I'd rather have had needles stuck in my eyes than to go there again, I wasn't worried about the outcome; after all, I'd have the encounter on tape. Then I saw the report. I couldn't believe it even though I probably should've expected it: once again, I'd experienced a miracle recovery. It was déjà vu all over again. This time, however, I wasn't going to stand for it.

The only way I could challenge his findings outside of comp court, which I knew would prove fruitless and possibly protract the proceedings for yet another few years, was to file a fraud complaint against him to expose him for the crook that he was. I thought, *How dare he play with my life that way? How dare he even masquerade as a healer?* He needed to be stopped, not just for my sake but for the sake of all others who might ever have the misfortune of crossing his path.

I immediately got busy crafting a complaint that was sure to have him rethinking his affiliations. But before I even had the chance to mail it, I got the surprise of my life.

As I sat waiting my turn for yet another comp hearing—now nearly six years since having filed for benefits—my attorney approached me with the most astounding news. He said that the TA had conceded to establish my case on "total/permanent" basis. I thought I'd not heard him correctly, so I asked him to repeat what he'd said, because I knew I must be hallucinating. When he repeated the words I'd longed to hear, I stood in utter and absolute shock. I did everything possible to keep myself from collapsing onto the floor. A six-year battle that had ripped my guts out and kept me broke, finally reached its end. I must have said "Oh, my God" a hundred times—I was completely overwhelmed.

Despite the euphoria, I knew I had to get hold of myself. Was there more to this gesture than met the eye? Was it just that my argument was sound and irrefutable—and they simply had run out of ways to ward it off? Or, with another federal appeal looming, were they looking to clear the board of any extraneous issues that might muddy the waters? Or was it something I could not even conceive of? Whatever the reason, I was more concerned with sealing the deal and heading for the hills. So I pulled myself together promptly—as together as I could, anyway—and got ready to bid farewell to 30 Bay Street for good.

While I probably should have quickly signed the papers and ran, and as much as I wanted to dash out the door, there was something I needed to address with my adversaries that had been festering for years that would come to impact several matters yet unresolved—and this seemed the ideal time to put it to rest although I was aware that mere mention of it might possibly compromise the miracle that had just occurred. My gut told me to go for it. Besides, there'd be no other time like this where I had any bargaining power whatsoever. I approached Jon to ask that he present it to the TA's counsel. He agreed.

The position "offered" to me as part of my federal award carried with it a significantly higher salary, commensurate with what I'd have been earning at the time of the trial had I not been wrongfully demoted. A contract was signed to this effect and was officially in place (by this time) for seven years. Moreover, since that salary was calculated based upon what I'd have been earning at that time, it was my salary of record irrespective of the position I was "offered". But the TA, in usual form, refused to acknowledge the new salary; they continued to keep me on the payroll in my old position—at my old salary. In other words, they refused to accept that I beat them in court. For all the years since the time they terminated my employment, they held tightly to the view that I "failed to show up for work" as if to imply I never returned simply because I didn't feel like it, not because they had made me too sick to return. Over and over again, they would throw this false narrative around as though to convince the court that I was responsible for my own termination. Rather than ask the court to clarify the matter, they continued on in their signature style and refused to budge. Now, despite having been terminated, matters such as life insurance and other valuable benefits would be based on my salary of record and it was incumbent upon me to make sure I set that record straight.

Jon came back to me to say that the TA agreed to my stipulation, that they would concede to the higher salary—but that they also had a stipulation of their own.

They wanted me to agree that my condition was preexisting— that, in essence, I was somehow psychologically diminished prior to the claims I had made in conjunction with worker's comp. That just didn't make sense to me—they were agreeing to pay full benefits for the rest of my life for a work-induced illness, as long as I said the illness had nothing to do with work? I didn't like it one bit but agreed to it out of sheer and utter desperation.

I had lived scraping the bottom for so long that the idea of being able to pay bills without going into a frenzy was delightful. I was ready to move on and finally put this nightmare behind me. I saw the end of this six-year-long ordeal as the end of an era; I prayed I was finally getting my chance to move forward and could start the long-awaited process of healing I had been denied so many times before. It was the most positive I'd felt about the future in a long time.

CHAPTER 13

TAKING THE SUN
FROM MY EYES

BY NOW YOU ARE NO DOUBT aware that just because one is no longer physically in the workplace doesn't mean he and his employer have parted ways. As demonstrated by my experiences, there may be several loose ends to tie, especially in the wake of a legal battle as legal battles tend to breed the kind of bitterness that complicate otherwise purely straightforward business dealings. And I think it goes without saying that my case is no exception, not to mention a case of extremes.

After coming off the seemingly never-ending and equally emotionally exhausting worker's comp saga, unbeknownst to me, another one was about to begin. Not only was I facing the task of trying to collect $80,000 in differential pay in conjunction with workers comp, but I was also due another $11,000 for medical expenses that would already have been paid had it not been for the delay. Since I had no idea when or if I'd ever return to the workforce, I had to make certain that I accounted for and collected every dollar. To that end, foregoing some $90,000 was not an option, no matter that I was too sick to wrangle. Besides, I had already come so far in a war that all but consumed my life; this was yet another notch in the post of litigation of which I likely would not soon see the end. That didn't make it any easier to tolerate, just easier to accept. I was so deeply invested in this—it was now so tied to my survival—that I had to just hang in and tough it out.

Differential pay, for those of you unfamiliar with it, is the difference between one's weekly comp benefits and weekly gross salary—paid by one's employer *if* the employer offers it. At the time, the New York State Worker's Compensation Board's top comp benefit was $400 per week, making differential a potentially lucrative sum, especially when—at that time—there was no cap on the number of years an employee in my position could collect. However, it isn't until one establishes his comp case that he is entitled to differential pay. Hence, although six years has passed, my time had finally come to collect.

Rather than simply paying me, as they were obligated to do, the TA took the opportunity to turn this, as they did with all transactions prior, into a firestorm of litigation. They claimed I wasn't entitled to any differential whatsoever, because I'd failed to follow TA protocol, and even if I had followed protocol, I would be limited to two years' worth of benefits. Among the reasons cited for my alleged missteps were that I had not reported to medical (upon filing my workers comp application) and that the application itself was untimely. These—and all of the rest of their assertions—were outright lies.

In reality, the TA had nothing to support their claim. For instance, they never directed me to report to medical at any time. It wasn't until a year later, when they used the IME to cut off my benefits that I was directed to *any* medical of any kind, but an IME and a comp medical are two entirely different events. In addition, there was no way I could have filed an untimely application because there was no date upon which an injury occurred. This was an illness that came about over time for which I filed as soon as I'd realized I was too sick to return to work. These were ironclad, substantiated, irrefutable facts. But that didn't stop them.

Complicating matters further, was the $11,000 I'd paid toward medical care for which I was left holding the bag. Not only was I saddled with this added expense, but sometimes I had to forego medical care altogether. One instance, in particular, stands out in my mind when a lapse in insurance rendered me unable to pay for my prescriptions for a brief time thereby causing me to experience some pretty bad withdrawal. At my next hearing, I pleaded with the TA to allow me to fill my prescriptions under workers comp despite that I'd yet to establish my case. This was the first (and only) time I had broken down crying at a hearing—I just was unable to hold back. Expecting they'd find it in their hearts to do the right thing seeing the condition I was in, I was stunned when, without so much as pause for contemplation, they outright refused.

With this incident seared in my brain, now painfully aware that my adversaries were apparently unable to put our differences aside no matter what the reason, I was sure it would be a cold day in hell before they coughed up a penny more than they had already been forced to. It was clear to me that they did not see the things they failed to do as dishonored obligations so much as they saw them as victories. To do the right thing was to be defeated.

But I wasn't about to let their boundless defiance stand in my way. I decided to take my gripe directly to the TA. There, I had a liaison in the legal department, who I will call Rick, with whom I was specifically directed to correspond many years prior when it became evident to the powers that be that it was unwise to allow me to randomly deal with whomever happened to be available at the time, for those individuals proved themselves unworthy of how to effectively ward me off in order to negate their employer's obligations.

For some odd reason, Rick always seemed to take our dealings personally. No matter how many times I dealt with him, I was startled by his lack of ability to separate himself from the fact that it was his employer, not him, with whom I was at odds—that this was purely business. This made interacting with him (and thus, the TA) particularly difficult.

I had contacted Rick about my differential pay in 1998 as soon as my case had been partially established for that first brief time, but got the same resistance from him back then that I got five years later. He told me back then that I was not "yet" entitled to differential because the few weeks worth of comp benefits I received were levied to repay disability benefits (one is not entitled to "double dip" or collect from two separate entities at once). Because the money was levied to repay disability, he reasoned, the comp benefits were not actually mine to begin with. He concluded that if they weren't actually mine to begin with, I was not "yet" entitled to differential. This was a convoluted lie.

In 2003, five years later, the story completely changed. Instead of not "yet" being entitled, Rick said I was "not entitled"—never was and never would be. That is when he invented the story of my having failed to follow protocol; that it was my inaction that caused the forfeiture of differential pay. A back and forth ensued wherein I argued that it was not me but in fact the TA that had dropped the ball when they failed to ever send me to medical or inform me that I filed a late application. But none of that really mattered; it wasn't about protocol—only about keeping me at bay. I warned Rick that I would take further legal action if they did not cooperate even though I was sure they were going to push me to the edge. After all, they had no incentive to cooperate; the court had set the tone and it wasn't in my favor.

The very last thing in the world I wanted was to have to go to the mat again with my embittered employer, especially after what they had just put me through for the previous six years. While they were able to protract the process for an extraordinary amount of time, in the end, they had to pay and weren't happy about it. And although they beat me down, they knew I wasn't going away, not when there was so much at stake—attorney or no attorney.

Meanwhile, a comp judge ordered the TA to immediately audit the $11,000 in medical bills and to pay for all future symptomatic medical treatment. On top of that, I was given the go-ahead to continue to use private insurance for which they would have to reimburse costs. This was almost unheard of and in and of itself enough to fan the flames of our tumultuous relationship to epic proportions.

I waited and waited and waited and waited—long enough to know that I was never going to see a cent. Court orders apparently meant nothing to them despite that they had been given a "final opportunity" more than once to complete the audit and pay.

By this point in time, I'd given up on the prospect of *whether* I was going to stay the course, but instead accepted that every act of uncooperativeness on the part of my former employer was the prerequisite to another potential legal battle, and that this pattern could repeat itself for years to come. It was a game I'd become reluctantly accustomed to—me and my adversaries would circle the board as many times as it took until one of us had no moves left. The only problem is that in the end, I'm the only one who really had anything to lose.

By 2004, I had yet to a start a family, and it wasn't looking like that was going to happen any time soon. Stress, anxiety, depression, and prescription drugs make not a safe haven for a baby. Although I was told ad nauseum that the antidepressants were perfectly safe for an unborn child, I didn't buy it. Instead, I injected this thing I like to call common sense into my decision making, especially where having a baby was concerned. Moreover, I refused to bring a child into the middle of what felt to me like a war zone. Every so often, when I thought things were coming to a crescendo, I'd believed that time was still on my side, but these glimmers of hope were short-lived. Whenever I thought I had made meaningful progress, it seemed like I took two steps forward and one step back—or sometimes more steps back than I could recover from. And so I continued to keep my personal life on hold.

Around the same time, my therapist pushed me out of the nest after seven years. That was hard. She knew what she was doing, even though it didn't feel like it to me at the time. She said she felt strongly that as long as my employer continued to torment me, I would never be able to move forward to where I could achieve notable progress. She was right. All along, though, she gave me the tools to keep my head above water. She taught me so much, a lot more than I realized at the time. And when all was said and done with her, I continued to get by with the help of my beloved dog, Toto. It might sound crazy, but he truly kept me focused on life. Looking at him was usually all I needed to get that boost I so desperately needed. He was my go-to guy, and I will be forever grateful for his existence. But even with my faithful dog by my side as well as all of the wonderful friends and family with whom I was unquestionably blessed, my life was shrouded in darkness. I often wondered what eventually would become of me, whether I would ever get back to being the person I once knew, to the place that enabled me to work toward my American dream.

Whatever the future held, I knew the road there would be a rocky one; I had my work cut out for me and no time to sit around contemplating either. After the bomb I got handed last time around (missing the three-hundred-day filing deadline), I had no time to waste and quickly got to filing a (now third) EEOC charge.

No sooner had the ink dried than an unexpected financial opportunity presented itself, one that would allow me to put some funds aside to hire an attorney. I didn't really want to shop for another attorney nor could I really afford to spend any money on one regardless, but considering what was at stake, I thought it best not to take any chances even though I knew it wouldn't be easy to find someone I could both trust *and* that would want to take on a matter as entangled as mine. The amount of paper alone one would have to sift through just to see if he was interested—"interested" being positively correlated to the bottom line—was enough to whittle my prospects down to a challenge.

I composed an email with the subject line "Looking for the Right Attorney" and tapped every employment lawyer with an email address in the New York/New Jersey area. My goal was to find someone that was willing to work *for* me (as opposed to against me) who understood what it was I had been through and what it was I would continue to go through if I wasn't able to put an end to the madness once and for all. I was looking for one of that rare breed who actually gives a crap about more than the pot of gold at the end of the litigation rainbow. Truth is I had little to go on but my instincts. Short of your gut, there ain't much.

After communicating with countless attorneys—an incredibly arduous process unto itself when you have to repeat the same story over and over in such a way as to make it sound like a worthwhile (in lawyer terms, money-making) pursuit—I stumbled upon a young, enthusiastic guy named Pat. I immediately got a good feeling about him. Because he was young, I gathered he was not as seasoned as I would have liked, but I wasn't going to allow that to stand in the way. Pat was also not "familiar" with the Eastern District of the federal court where my case would be heard. I had no idea what that meant in terms of him being a good match for me, so I didn't ask. I never thought for a second that such a thing would make a lick of difference. But boy, was I about to get schooled.

Pat and I seemed a well-suited attorney/client team. We were on the same page, and I sincerely believed he had my best interests at heart. He realized the pitfalls of my legal claim, namely that the gist of my complaint—alleging a hostile work environment while absent from the workplace—was a novel theory upon which to proceed. Not that the law doesn't support acts of retaliation occurring outside the workplace, but to my knowledge, alleging a hostile work environment for someone who had been absent from the workplace for so long had never been done. Moreover, the concept of hostile work environment was (and still is) a somewhat murky legal one that has yet to be fully broken in. But as law is an art and not a science, its meaning was certainly open to interpretation.

During his first appearance before the court—before a magistrate under the judge who had been on my case from the start—Pat got pummeled. Not only was he pushing novel legal theory, but doing so on someone else's turf. He might as well have been facing a judge in a foreign country. That was two strikes against us before Pat even opened his mouth.

And things went downhill from there.

It became obvious right from jump street that the magistrate was unmoved by the fervent argument of the new kid on the block—one for a case with which she was all too familiar. To his credit, Pat put up a heck of a fight. The magistrate commended Pat's tenacity and commented that she was glad I had finally retained counsel. But that clearly wasn't enough. After a considerably lengthy exchange, she sent him packing.

When Pat called to tell me what had transpired, I burst into tears. He told me that he was ordered by the magistrate to amend my complaint such that anything and everything about it that made it a valid Title VII complaint in the first place was to be removed. I was stupefied and didn't understand how a judge—a magistrate, no less—could do such a thing. I kept asking Pat if we could appeal her order, an order she very vaguely put in writing, I assume, because she knew what she was asking him to do was wrong. All I knew was that the whole thing didn't pass the smell test for me, and I had strong suspicions as to her motivations. This was but the magistrate's way of telling me that I had become *persona non grata* in her courtroom, something, no doubt, the sitting judge was on board with if not behind.

From what I knew then and from what I still know now, it doesn't matter how many times an individual brings a complaint to the court; there is no law I know of against it short of the discretion a judge is allowed to impart on courtroom abuse such as when it is obvious that a plaintiff is wildly litigious, perhaps for the purpose of monetary gain or revenge. I am certain that the magistrate knew my claims were legitimate; after all, the very nature of retaliation itself increases the likelihood one might return. However, when the TA's counsel argued for the magistrate to threaten my attorney with Rule 11 sanctions—that being sanctions for frivolous or baseless complaints—she took them up on it, it appears, not because she truly believed they were, but rather that doing so comported with her apparent belief that once a litigant has had her (one) day in court, she has gotten all to which she is entitled. Ergo, Pat was being told, in so many words, that his client's return was unwelcome.

Pat was not as willing to push the envelope as far I wanted him to. While he was clearly disappointed—for he believed in my cause—he seemed equally concerned about not stepping on anyone's toes in an unfamiliar district, a place he would inevitably one day find himself back in. Still, I'd asked him a number of times about filing an appeal, something I would have done right off, even if it meant having the door slammed in my face once more. However, Pat insisted that we could not appeal, that there were no grounds for appeal. It just didn't make any sense whatsoever.

As per the magistrate's fuzzy order, Pat proceeded to amend the complaint, removing everything from it that otherwise made it viable under Title VII—namely, all of the background without which the complaint would unquestionably fall flat. Theoretically, if the judge did not know what led to the denial of differential, but rather only that it was denied based on the reasons set forth by the defendants, reasons they could not—and did not—support, retaliation could not possibly be proven. He did it begrudgingly, telling me it was all we had left to go on. He was almost as deflated as I was.

Left with a drastically pared down complaint that could easily be construed as nothing more than a garden-variety pay dispute, it was now up to the judge to decide whether I had brought a complaint worthy of going forward. Pat and I knew we were doomed.

In January 2009, summary judgment was granted to the TA. (Summary judgment, remember, is when it is decided that a complaint should be dismissed as a matter of law.) The only consolation was that I knew the outcome had nothing to do with the law, with justice, or with fairness, but rather with the acts of an ill-mannered governmental agency who had conveniently managed to hand the court precisely what it needed in order to impose its will under the guise of impartiality. Talk about judges abusing their discretion.

The whole thing was a big fat sham.

CHAPTER 14

ONE MORE ARROW

IT HAD NOW BEEN A mind-blowing fourteen years since this whole ugly mess began. Fourteen years—that's a long time by any standards. I would have thought that if nothing else, the TA would want to put the entire thing to rest by now; that no matter how far into the back pocket of the court they were, if they continued to roll the dice, even their luck could run out. Why take the chance? But this was not to be. The TA had an entire legal department and an endless supply of money while I clung on by my fingernails to the hope that if I was forced to keep on the path of litigation, I would catch a break.

Pat and I had parted ways, for unlike Tom, he had no vested interest in representing me on appeal. This time, I'd be flying solo. Handling my own appeal wasn't exactly something I relished; however, the odds weren't entirely against me. Because I lost "as a matter of law" (on summary judgment), I was guaranteed a de novo review—good news, especially for a pro se. De novo (as previously explained) simply means that the judicial panel is required to take a fresh look at the case—to consider it as though it had never been before the court. In so doing, I was optimistic they would see that the magistrate had erred, leaving them no choice but to reverse the lower court's decision. Hope springs eternal.

By now, it was August 2007, three years since I'd filed my complaint. It doesn't always take that long, but it did in this case, and I'm fairly certain it had something to do with having worn out my welcome. While no one would ever admit to such an inappropriate act, that is how things work in the real world. Perhaps my complaint had gotten "misplaced" long enough to further solidify the message that I should never have come back in the first place. This, though, was not about to stop me from at least trying to get the lower court's decision overturned.

With now fairly substantial experience in my personal legal arsenal after so many years of wrangling with my employer, I no longer felt like a fish out of water. I now had the confidence, if not the emotional wellness, to go it alone. I no longer viewed an appeal as the big, scary venture that lawyers make it out to be. Don't get me wrong—an appeal is by no means a piece of cake, but it isn't rocket science either. The tricky part of an appeal, as I came to learn, is often about almost everything but the merits of the case.

Before going forward, I had to file to proceed *in forma pauperis* (IFP) again. Fortunately, my IFP status in the lower court carried through to the appellate. But as is typical with all things government, I still had to file an application. And so I did. But the mean-spirited bureaucrats with whom I'd sparred over every minute transaction we'd engaged in sans the return of my pre-judgment interest check (albeit through an attorney) weren't going to miss any opportunity to retaliate. In fact they ratcheted up their campaign to yet new heights.

No sooner had I filed than I received an envelope in the mail that I was not looking forward to opening for I knew it could be only one thing. And it was. The TA had made a motion to permanently revoke my IFP status, a move the likes of which had become NYCT's signature modus operandi—to stop me before I even got out of the gate. So I expected it. What I didn't expect, though, was how they went about it. They simply knew no bounds.

The otherwise official-looking package contained all of the usual nonsense—until I got to the last page. I could not believe what I was looking at. There, staring me right in the eye, was a big, brightly colored, aerial photo of my home. I felt so violated, I nearly passed out. I had never been so filled with disgust in fourteen years as I was at that moment. This was truly the most devious, most disingenuous attempt to discredit me before the court that I had ever been subjected to, and one I could never have imagined—short of living it.

I didn't even need to read the motion to know what these scoundrels were up to. It was evident that they had scraped bottom. Using my house as a means by which to discredit me; to prevent me from getting something as inconsequential as a $450 fee? Could they stoop any lower? As far as I was concerned, they had truly crossed the line. They had invaded my private space. My home—my safe haven—had now officially become an environment as hostile as the workplace I'd left behind.

I was further sickened as I perused the remainder of the papers. Just as they had attempted in the past, the TA clumsily portrayed me as a well-off suburbanite, living in the lap of New Jersey luxury, pointing out my home's square footage and various amenities, including the "in-ground pool," "professional landscaping", and "patio area." These material items, they asserted, were grounds to revoke my status, for owning such things proved that I was much better off financially than I had claimed to be. In my opinion, this rather despicable collection of incorrect assumptions amounted to nothing more than one of the cheapest stunts they had ever pulled.

As always, I rebutted their vicious rhetoric with the facts. I prayed that common sense would prevail.

In the interim of their response, my adversaries (apparently) discovered that their prize aerial photo had been removed from the website where they found it. They quickly grabbed hold of this, asserting that I had removed it in an attempt to hide my assets. Again, I was floored. Not only was their entire argument baseless, but it defies all common sense and logic to suggest that an aerial photo is an accurate accounting of *anyone's* assets or that the absence (or removal) of it from a public website is anyone's attempt to hide them.

In the end, their big performance was for naught. The court wasn't impressed, and the TA's motion was denied accordingly. Certainly, I was relieved, despite the additional stress I did not need. And let's not forget all the time and money wasted over $450. No doubt it cost you, the taxpayer, a heck of a lot more than $450 in pay hours to put together such an elaborate package—but *that* is the true cost of revenge.

With the IFP ordeal finally put to rest, I was able to move forward—with the toughest part still ahead. Preparing an appellate brief is unto itself challenging, even with the bits and pieces of knowledge I had amassed. For a pro se, to whom the court gives very little leeway despite that the issue of self-representation has been before the Supreme Court who afforded them *some* accommodations, navigating around can be half the battle. The voluminous instruction packet provided to pro ses is somewhat helpful but otherwise useless for the inability to get a live person at the court to help you sift through it. You just do what you can and hope for the best. If you've screwed up bad enough, you'll know about it one way or the other.

Preparing an opening brief is all about research—and I did a lot of it. I had to pour over innumerable cases, some interesting and some so boring they nearly put me to sleep. Over the years, I developed an appreciation for the art of law, so I didn't so much mind doing the legwork, but that didn't stop my stomach from being in one big perpetual knot. One case would give me hope, another despair. Some cases were so ambiguous that it was impossible to ascertain whether mine fell within their scope or not. It can be a very emotionally taxing process when the case is yours—and you are not a lawyer.

I considered it a privilege to be able to bring my case to a higher court and was determined to give the opportunity everything I had despite the physical and emotional pain the process caused me, especially having to look back on the career-turned-nightmare I would much rather have left behind. But I believed in what I was doing and focused on the ultimate goal of winning even in the face of sadness that, at times forced me to pause, sometimes even for days at a clip, despite the looming deadline.

Once the brief was finally complete and all the many copies made, my husband trekked into the city to hand deliver the large, heavy box of paper to the Second Circuit Court of Appeals. After that, the long wait began.

I know beyond question from my myriad experiences with the various courts that there is no such thing as swift justice in civil court, especially for pro ses, who get treated like dirt, and worse yet, for one who has worn out her welcome. Four years passed from the time I filed my federal complaint to the time I appealed in July 2008. In all fairness, though, there were three separate filings along the way, including my pro se complaint, my first amended complaint with my new attorney, and the third, magistrate-ordered version. Before I knew it, another several precious years of my life were spent waiting, wondering when the day would come when this would all be behind me and I could begin to identify periods of my life by positive experiences rather than with the years that coincided with various legal actions.

In November 2008, I got the news that my appeal was defeated. I was hugely deflated but not entirely surprised. What did take me aback is that I had no idea why. The opinion was very brief and very vague. Excluding the two pages of standard legal citations, the opinion consisted of only one sentence, citing to the lower court's "thorough and well-thought-out opinion," a laughable statement unto itself when you consider that the defendants failed to proffer so much as a scintilla of evidence to support their argument. After so many months of toiling away through a boatload of emotional and physical pain, the appellate court shut me out with an opinion predicated on nothing more than its whims. Had the panel actually conducted a de novo review, as was their obligation, they would have had no choice but to overturn.

But this, I have come to learn, is the true nature of appeals. No matter how off-the-charts or how unfair you know the decision to be, you get what you get, and too bad if you don't like it. All of the bidding is done behind closed doors by individuals who have full immunity from prosecution. It is very frustrating, disappointing, and even frightening to think that although we have the right to appeal a lower court's decision, we have no right whatsoever to know how that decision was made.

After I had had a few days to percolate, I decided to call the court to see if there was any way I could find out more about the decision. They instructed me to make a motion for clarification but said there was no guarantee I'd get one. Of course, I might have overstepped my bounds by daring to make such a request in the first place, but I had nothing to lose.

My motion for clarification fell on deaf ears. My motion for rehearing and rehearing en banc, too, were denied. (That is where one asks the judicial panel of three and the entire sitting panel, respectively, to reconsider the original decision.) The only bright spot was that motions for rehearings are rarely granted, so I wasn't expecting much. Still, I wanted to exhaust all of my remedies and never think "what if."

Meanwhile, the TA was obviously busy conjuring up their next move. I had thought the whole mess was finally behind me, after all, I lost—what more could there be? Well, if there was ever an adversary who I could count on to find something, it was the TA. In all of their infinite mean-spiritedness, they slapped me with a whopping bill of costs for $2,000! These wasteful bureaucrats had the unbelievable audacity to ask the court to order me to pay the cost of producing their briefs. Until then, I had no idea that the successful party had the right to even ask for such a thing—and it's not the way I wanted to find out either! But still, the cost seemed exorbitant. I'd gone to the local UPS store and spent around fifty bucks (and I thought *that* was a lot).

Despite an all-out effort on my part to have the motion denied, the court ordered me to pay half of the excessive bill. I couldn't imagine what they were thinking. I was utterly perplexed by the notion that a person already deemed unable to pay a court fee of $450 could be saddled with a bill for more than double that. To me, it was like being punished for taking a stand, for exercising my right to seek justice.

In the end, I knew it was my duty to comply with the court's decision, whether I agreed with it or not. I tried to work out a payment plan with the TA, but that wasn't good enough. Rather, they wanted to set the terms of how much I would pay and when. Another back and forth ensued.

In my mailbox a few days later, I found a letter from a lawyer acting as a bill collector. As bad as things had gotten between us, this was somewhat of a shock coming even from them—to actually go to the extent of hiring a bill collector for $20 a month. (But there again, it's easy to do so with someone else's money.) Regardless of that I didn't agree with the court or the TA's handling of the matter, I originally decided to work with the guy—at least I then could avoid dealing directly with the TA. But on further contemplation, I realized I didn't have to deal with him *or* them.

The bill collector in tandem with the TA's counsel proceeded to harass me for weeks, even after I agreed to pay. I didn't know what else to do but contact the court. When I did, the woman with whom I spoke seemed thoroughly perplexed by what had transpired. She couldn't understand why it was the TA hired a bill collector for a matter borne out of workplace litigation in the first place. She told me to continue to pay them directly, and that if doing so didn't suffice, I could return to court to have the order clarified.

Still, I had bigger fish to fry. All of this extraneous nonsense did nothing but delay my next move—if I dared to make it. My last chance for justice lay before me. If I wanted to take advantage of what would prove to be my only hope to see justice finally served, that is, petitioning the Supreme Court, I had to decide soon. Petitioning the Supreme Court is a monumental endeavor that will almost definitely end in disappointment. With this in mind, I had to carefully consider whether I could withstand the pressure of such a process.

Meantime, there was, once again, unfinished business with the TA concerning medical reimbursements they had—in usual form—dragged their feet on paying. It was like I had broken away from them but for a thread on which they perpetually kept me dangling. I don't know about them, but the last thing I wanted was any more contact that wasn't productive if I had to have any contact at all. But as long as I was forced to deal with them on any level about anything, I had come to the realization that there remained a possibility things could heat back up again—that, or I walk away knowing they'd taken away my right to medical care (or whatever was at issue at the time)—something I was unwilling to accept.

The thought of actually having to go forward with *another* legal action was almost beyond comprehension. I didn't know what to do. One part of me felt ridiculous at this point, like I had myself become a litigious lunatic gunning for an employer with whom I'd had a tumultuous past. On the other hand, I knew that I was completely justified in asking for and receiving the benefits it was my employer's responsibility to pay. It's like they were pushing me and pushing me and then pointing at me as though I was the one who had committed the wrongdoing. I kept telling myself to not be concerned about what they or anyone else thought—that it would be far worse to allow anyone to succeed in making me retreat to the corner than it would to be looked at sideways for standing up for my rights.

And so, after exhausting all of the prospective remedies available through the workers comp system—namely, a string of hearings where the insurance carrier gets innumerable opportunities to comply with no punitive repercussions for failure to do so—there was only one option left, even though I knew my odds were painfully slim. But I tried to remain positive that if this vicious cycle of taking my employer back to court continued long enough, eventually the judge would see what was really going on and lose her cool with her fellow bureaucrats.

For eighteen months, I chased after my former employer, giving them what I believed to be more than ample time within which to cooperate. The audit they were ordered to conduct would have required an hour for them to complete, if that. I even went so far as to make things as easy as possible for them to process so they would have no reason to stonewall. But they did. They put forth a laughable defense, in which they claimed they were an "overburdened, understaffed" organization handling "an inordinate number of medical claims per year," and that "with a staff of six," they could not keep up.

If you did the fuzzy math, their numbers worked out to a preposterous two claims per each of 60,000 employees per year. That's pretty darn unlikely. Moreover, this was in direct contradiction to a previous deposition wherein a seasoned human resource veteran testified under oath that "even a lengthy submission could take up to three months"—up to three, not eighteen.

All things considered, I was confident that I could make a sound legal argument to put an end to my adversary's shenanigans once and for all. I had the case law behind me—but would I have the judge there too?

Federal law allows for a litigant to use previously tried or otherwise untimely acts as background to support a current claim, as long as one of the acts falls within the three-hundred-day statutory period of a current, timely filed EEOC charge. The law further allows for *any* act, no matter how trivial it might appear at first blush, to be characterized as retaliatory, when taken in proper context. On this, I had solid legal ground on which to proceed.

As a pro se counsel, this would be the first time I had to appear for deposition alone; I would face opposing counsel without the benefit of a safety net. Realizing what a bad idea this was, I requested and was granted permission to videotape the proceeding. Although I was tremendously relieved, the defendants were not. In true fashion, they objected, citing their concern that I might somehow alter the tape. This was simply ludicrous.

During the deposition, the TA's counsel tried their best to trip me up but were unable to do so, for as I always say, the truth is the truth and the truth doesn't change. In the end, there was no question—and video doesn't lie—as to the soundness of my argument, one based solely on Supreme Court case precedent. That alone should have been enough to advance me to the next level. But this time, no matter how solid I knew that my argument was, I had little hope.

In February 2010, I lost case number four. I wasn't at all surprised. To be perfectly honest, it was more like waiting for a loss than a decision. Again, unsupported, unsubstantiated lies won out over truth. The judge was determined to do whatever necessary to get me out of her courtroom—and out of the system for good—and it appeared she had finally accomplished her goal.

But the TA refused to let things be. They seemed to be unable to refrain from retaliation—especially as the courts had clearly given them permission to do so. Hence, I should have expected to open my mailbox to find yet another bill of costs, this time for the deposition transcript totaling $385. This from a bloated, wasteful governmental agency that virtually bleeds money for a deposition they *chose* to conduct. Heck, at least they could afford to conduct a deposition.

Once more, as they had done in the past, they went out of their way to attempt to portray me as a well-off suburbanite living in a spacious home with every amenity known to man, despite that I subsisted on a very modest sum that I don't doubt they knew to the cent. I'm not sure what they expected me to do—sell my house in order to pay them $385? In the end, this was little more than a weak attempt to infuriate the court, to dangle my possessions before it in order to try to convince the judge I was a fraud. As usual, I responded accordingly, praying the court would not turn a blind eye. And it didn't. Much to my utter shock and delight, the judge never responded—at all—even when the TA tried to resurrect the same matter a year later, upon the conclusion of the appeal. Maybe even the judge was turned off by this brand of sleaze. Finally, I caught a break.

CHAPTER 15

NOBODY WINS

IN THE SPRING OF 2010, I began the arduous process of petitioning the Supreme Court. At the same time, my second pro se appeal was looming. The timing couldn't have been worse, as that meant juggling two demanding legal matters simultaneously. While I had become accustomed to the mechanics of preparing legal documents, I can't say the same for dealing with the anxiety.

Initially, I came close to throwing in the towel, thinking it just wasn't worth it. *I'm gonna lose anyway*, I thought, *no matter how erroneous the lower court's decision was.* I was now incurably turned off by the entire court system; I had lost that idealistic hope that once kept me going. On top of that, I thought, *Ugh, they're gonna start with the whole IFP thing again. Do I really want to deal with that?* Nothing was ever easy with them. The TA, who no doubt had the benefit of dealing with many plaintiffs before me, knew all the legal tricks and never hesitated to use them. Further, they had the professional courtesies of the court extended to them as well as the benefit of knowing the court had already handed me my walking papers long ago. They had nothing to lose except your tax dollars. But I knew what my gut was telling me—and I just had to listen.

I had come to accept that any further legal action, especially something of this magnitude, inevitably would consume all of my time, cost more money that I didn't have to spare, wreak havoc on my back, and perhaps prove more anxiety-inducing than all of the previous actions combined. Oddly, however, by this time, anxiety had come to serve me in a way it hadn't in the past. Depression, the affliction that was once the biggest monkey on my back, had evolved into a form of mania. My inability to pick myself up to do anything had slowly evolved into an inability to sit still. While it did provide the fire that fueled the process, I knew it wasn't exactly a boon to my well-being. But if all the legal maneuvering was important enough to endure for all the years prior, it was certainly important enough now. I had come this far. There was no turning back. With that, I got down to business.

Petitioning the Supreme Court for what is called *certiorari* does not get one's case heard; it's not even getting one's foot in the door. It's like ringing a doorbell and waiting to see if someone answers. Without getting into the long, complicated process, petitioning is, in essence, merely a means by which to request to have one's case reviewed (to be heard)—and very few make it that far. And even then, if you are one of the lucky one or so percent that does, there's no guarantee you will be successful. The whole thing could take years.

The basic gist of a petition is to pose questions to the justices that are believed to be of national importance and/or that have resulted in conflicting decisions within the various appellate circuits. (Supposedly, the more conflict, the greater the chances of getting one's petition heard.) Although I posed a number of questions, the one that mattered most to me, and that I believed to be most pressing in general, is whether it is permissible for a magistrate judge to systematically (meaning indirectly) dismiss a federal complaint. Really, it isn't (they don't have the authority to outright dismiss complaints, so it goes without saying that doing so indirectly isn't permissible either), but the question was, would the court find this exceptional enough to entertain? It's difficult to know what they are going to choose to hear. No matter how misaligned the laws seem and no matter how far they might have deviated from the Constitution, the ideological values of the nine justices seem to more often than not take precedence over basic common sense and national good. What we have, then, is a game of politics with incredibly bad odds— and especially bad odds for a pro se petitioner like me.

In terms of the mechanics, preparing a petition is a full-time job. It is a demanding endeavor, requiring an extraordinary amount of work and infinite patience. If research isn't something you enjoy, this isn't a job for you. Your only alternative is then to hire an attorney, which requires a lot of money and/or a great sales pitch.

A pro se like me, on a tight budget, is relegated to being resourceful. Scouring the Internet for information, for example, is one way to get around subscribing to the pricey databases geared to legal professionals, even though this would have been the most efficient means of conducting research.

Painstaking hours upon days upon weeks and months were spent searching and digging and reading. My back ached from top to bottom as my brain spilled over with case law. But I was determined. As I toiled away, it became increasingly clearer that the issues upon which my petition relied were not only vastly important but also never had been entertained by the court. While they weren't likely to affect the general population (for example, the way national healthcare would), I believed their scope to be far-reaching, and thus my chances to be better than zero! Conversely, statistics on the number of petitions granted each year was staggeringly discouraging. As of the last I heard, each year, somewhere in the vicinity of eight to ten thousand petitions are filed, of which only around 100 are granted. Of the total filed, about 80 percent are filed in forma pauperis, and quite naturally, by pro se petitioners. Of those, the odds are even smaller of being heard.

Although the theories vary as to why pro se in forma pauperis petitions are so widely disregarded, my theory is simple: if there isn't a lawyer out there getting rich off of some unsuspecting slob's back, it probably isn't important enough to bother with. The theory I've heard espoused from the legal community and other pundits is that in forma pauperis pro se petitions are generally poorly written and often misdirected efforts. It's true that a pro se petition is not necessarily going to be the Hemingway of legal documents, but that doesn't mean that the issues contained therein are automatically not worth exploring.

Most pro se in forma pauperis petitions are generated by inmates—that alone may be enough to water down the attention pro se petitions are given. Having the financial resources of a Donald Trump, for instance, grants you unlimited access to the courts (and likely boosts your chances of a win). Conversely, if you are like me, the mere cost of filing is prohibitive. Average folks don't have $300 or $450 for appellate or federal filing fees, let alone money for legal counsel, and certainly not thousands for the professional printing required to produce a mandated-sized, impossible-to-duplicateat-home booklet. Without in forma pauperis status, I'd have been looking at a few thousand dollars, just for access to the court.

Like most pro se petitioners, I filed to proceed in forma pauperis because it was my only option. The only good thing about this was that my adversaries were not entitled to raise a stink over my claim, as they had in the past, because unlike with the lower courts, if the petitioner is granted IFP, so too is the respondent. On the downside, it wasn't until after I filed a completed petition that I would learn whether I had been granted IFP, as it is required that both applications be submitted simultaneously. Of course, this makes no sense, especially to a layperson, for if you knew ahead of time that you were going to be denied IFP, you wouldn't—because you couldn't—file a petition in the first place. I have no idea why it works this way, but it does.

Nevertheless, I was confident this would be a non-issue for me. After all, I had been granted IFP in both of the lower courts. I had little concern that all the hard work would be for naught and put life on hold for the better part of four months. The fact that it was summer didn't help matters any as I count on summer to recharge my mental battery—to get the sun that those of us who are prone to depression count on for a boost.

Nevertheless, as much of a sacrifice as it was and as overwhelming as it was to give as much of myself as I knew I had to in preparing my petition, I felt a sense of gratification every step of the way. I knew that what I was doing was a big deal, not just because it was something very few folks will ever have the opportunity to do, and not just because it was the highest court in the land, but because I knew I was wronged in ways that no employee should ever be (not to mention the complicity of the lower courts without whose hand in the matter I might have succeeded in putting a swift end to it all) *and* had this last—albeit infintessimal chance—to finally see justice served.

One day while trying to figure out how I was going to now pull together all of the information I had amassed in order so that it was on par with other "paid for" petitions, I got what I thought was a "sign" that I had indeed made the right choice to take on this monster of a project. As a pro se and a perfectionist, I wanted my petition to look as polished as humanly possible but wasn't quite sure how to go about getting it there. The fact that I couldn't afford the fancy, high-end booklets didn't mean I was going to settle. The pro se materials packet provided by the court just would not do. I thought, *This is the Supreme Court, not small claims court!* I searched the Internet exhaustively, but finding an acceptable prototype turned out to be far more challenging than I'd thought. After several hours, just as I reached the point of wanting to scream, the mail came. On my way to the dreaded mailbox, I wished aloud that when I returned to my desk, my luck would change, that I would find just what I didn't know I was looking for. With that, I pulled the mail out of the box and saw what appeared to be a printing company solicitation that I expected to open and toss in the trash. But when I popped it open, there it was, the best blueprint I could have ever hoped for— an authentic sample Supreme Court petition! I was flabbergasted. Bizarre coincidence—or a sign that my prayers would finally be answered?

This high, however, didn't last long.

When I got back to my desk, happy that this gift had been bestowed upon me, things quickly began to change. With a great deal of the work already completed and vulnerable to getting lost for I stupidly did not take steps to save it along the way, my laptop's hard drive crapped out. My irreplaceable work-in-progress was now effectively gone, unless I could find a way to recover it. Blood curdling panic immediately set in. The thought that I might have just forgone everything through no other fault but my own, was not something I could even bear to face.

The next day, I took my laptop to my local techies, who, after two days that felt like an eternity, miraculously recovered everything. By that time, however, I had already begun working at my old relic desktop and didn't see any reason to disrupt the flow—well, that and fear. Even though my laptop was supposed to be as good as new, I think the experience of almost having lost everything scared the heck out of me to the point that I viewed going back to it is as too risky. Then, the following day, just as I had settled back into my routine and thinking the worst was behind me, the desktops' hard drive went too! If it hadn't happened to me, I'd not have believed it. As if my nerves weren't already frazzled beyond belief, this was altogether too much. I think I would have died where I sat if not for having sent my work to e-mail "just in case," after the last crisis. And it's a good thing too. That data was gone for good, never to be seen again. The old relic was put to rest.

There was no time to waste. I quickly regrouped and got back to business on the laptop I should have stayed with in the first place! My nerves might have been shot, but my determination still was unwavering. After losing two hard drives within the space of a few days, I figured I had to be out of the woods. I thought, *What else could possibly go wrong?* Well, no sooner did I ask myself that question—and I should have known better than to ask—my printer died. I could not believe it.

The "miracle" sample petition was starting to look like the devil in disguise. But I wasn't about to let a failed hard drive or a silly printer slow me down. Nothing was going to slow me down now. And nothing did. I went on to finish my petition without further ado and felt an incredibly strong sense of pride not only for what I had accomplished but how I accomplished it. Ordinary, everyday citizen me, frazzled to the eyebrows and all, petitioned the United States Supreme Court.

But this was by no means the end. I had no time to exhale. I had already lost half of the 120 days allotted for my appeal brief and knew there was no way I could satisfactorily meet the deadline without an extension. And so, as I had done many times in the past, I made a motion for an extension—and forgot about it.

I didn't wait for a response. I kept right on researching, printing, and notating. The stress was so bad it felt like I was living under a giant boulder; just trying to breathe was a chore. Adding to all the mayhem was my cherished baby dog Toto's condition. We didn't quite know what was going on, but knew something wasn't right. My focus turned to him.

A few weeks later, I received a response from the court, denying my motion to extend. I was blown away. *What the heck is it to them to give me another month?* I wondered in amazement. I knew that there was often little rhyme or reason to the court's decision making, but was astonished nonetheless. Perhaps they, too, just wanted me gone.

Desperate, I called the court who told me to make a motion to reconsider. "Don't hold back; pour your heart out. People do it all the time," I was told by the clerk. Gee, there I was, trying to keep it professional, i.e., concise and unemotional, only to have it backfire on me. So I took the clerk's advice, and in so doing, ended up getting an extra three weeks which, as it turns out, was all I needed.

With my new September 28, 2010, deadline, I worked as if my life depended on it. Still, I couldn't help thinking how in the world it was possible that I could be sitting there after so many years devoting time to this seemingly fruitless war. It was almost beyond comprehension. But I wanted justice, and if giving so much of myself in the face of such repugnance was the road there, so be it.

Then, just when my day to exhale had finally come, on September 29, 2010, the day after filing what I prayed was the last legal paper of any kind I'd ever have to file in connection with my former employer for the rest of my days, my beloved Toto died. If there was ever a loss, ever a disappointment, ever a time when I felt like the world had come to an end, it paled in comparison to this. *Screw the TA, screw the courts, screw all of the folks who screwed me*, I thought. It was at that very moment after I watched him die before my eyes that everything came into focus. The impact that the rest of my upside down world had on me, the one I had gotten boxed into for the previous eighteen years, immediately melted away. All the years of legal wrangling that had effectively wiped my life clean of joy suddenly felt exponentially less tragic than it had only the day before.

I'm not saying that any aggrieved person shouldn't stand up for his or her rights, nor am I suggesting that I regretted standing up for mine, but in the scheme of things, nothing measures up to the worth of those we love, especially those who bring us such joy. For all the years I put my life on hold, battling with my mean-spirited employer, it took my dog a few tragic seconds to show me that in the end, I'd probably wasted a lot of precious time with small-minded folks who, with their penchant for vengeance and sheer desire to cavalierly wreak havoc on my life and perhaps the lives of others— all on the taxpayer's dime—weren't nearly worth all the effort I'd devoted to warding them off.

But everything happened as it did. I'd made my choices and decided to see them through to the end, regardless of the consequences. And it's a darn good thing I had by now come to some sort of acceptance, too, for my hopes would only continue to get dashed.

Not too long after having lost Toto, and still very much reeling from the shock, I received a skinny envelope from the Supreme Court long before I expected to hear from them. I knew it couldn't be good news. Any time I got a "skinny" envelope—one containing a single sheet of paper—it usually was bad news. And it was.

The Supreme Court denied my application to proceed in forma pauperis (and therefore my petition too). Just like that. I was dumbfounded. After all the work, all the anxiety, all the sacrifice, and all the obstacles I'd faced, the highest court in the land slammed the door in my face without ever so much as even knowing what it was I wanted to say. Whether or not it had anything to do with the fancy little booklets I couldn't afford, I'll never know. I pretty much chalked it up to a simple matter of the court's way of whittling down the unmanageable number of applications without having to actually take the time to look at them, no matter how important or how impacting the discarded petitions might have proved to be. In the scheme of things, I suppose I shouldn't have been at all surprised, considering what I had seen over the years in the courts below. It's just that I held the Supreme Court to a much higher standard.

I made a motion for reconsideration in a last-ditch attempt to convince the court to change its mind even though I was nearly certain it was an exercise in futility. And it was. It was all over. However, as disappointing as this defeat proved to be—and it was truly a blow to the gut knowing my petition was not even given a glance—I was oddly relieved. Yes, relieved. I didn't cry. I didn't fret. I didn't have to think of ways to overcome as I normally would under such disheartening circumstances. Instead, with "Toto's wisdom" firmly embedded in my soul, I turned myself toward the goal of writing this book, something I waited an incredibly long time to do–and had, in fact, tried to do some ten years prior.

It was in 2000 that I finally knew exactly what the book I had waited all my life to write was going to be about and made the not-so-prudent decision to start writing it back then. Some one hundred pages in, I stopped. I couldn't go on. The emotional fallout took me by surprise; I had no idea something like that would occur and was forced to put the project aside. I suppose all things have their time, and mine had not yet come. In the end, though, it all worked out for the best, as it wasn't until another ten years later that the whole ugly mess played itself out to a finish.

Sometime in early 2011, I lost my last appeal. I didn't bother to open the envelope because I knew what it was—and didn't care! I tucked it in my desk and smiled. That was it. Independence Day. I exhaled. I laughed out loud. My reaction took me aback. I was proud of it. I was finally liberated from the chains of New York City Transit. I instantly realized I finally had come to some semblance of peace with a very engrossing, almost alluring process that had stolen what should have been the best years of my life. And although life still has its ups and downs, and although the emotional scars of going through such an ordeal will forever remain, I rejoice. I am grateful for all the little things, more than ever.

Sadly, however, while I was set to move forward with life, my adversaries still were not satisfied to do the same. After losing my final appeal, as if it wasn't enough for them to once again emerge the victors, they made yet another motion to the court to have me pay for their printing. There it was—another bill of costs, this time for $150, as if to suggest that they were but a diligent pubic entity, carefully looking to be a good steward of the taxpayer dollar. If they sincerely did have any consideration for the public they serve, however, not only would they have exercised the same financial restraint after the last appeal—when they thought nothing of spending $2,000 they weren't guaranteed to recover—but they would never have treated anyone they way they treated me from the start. At best, they would have had the decency and dignity to accept their federal court defeat and walk away, focusing their resources on what really matters: the transit-riding public who count on them around the clock, 365 days a year, to safely get them where they need to be.

And so, in the end, I graciously agreed to pay the $150 and told them to tack it on my bill. No matter; something tells me that whatever quietude exists between my adversaries and me, and whatever I do to make things right, it will tragically never be forever.

PART II

HAVING WRAPPED UP THE LONG and sordid saga of nineteen years of litigation with an employer with whom I mistakenly believed I'd have a productive, meaningful, and positive career experience, I would be remiss not to take a trip behind the scenes to look at the players who made it all possible: doctors, lawyers, and bureaucrats. My story would not be complete otherwise.

Here, I take a closer look at what—and who—is behind the dismantling of the career of a hard-working, educated woman—one who did everything within her power to achieve the American dream in a nation that prides itself and was founded upon the concepts of liberty and the pursuit of happiness—and how theses forces come together to exacerbate an already sufficiently entangled workplace saga. Who are the people that drive the whole process, and what is the connection between them? And how is it that they care so little about the welfare of another human being that they would not only allow such a reprehensible ordeal to occur in the first place but to thrive?

While there is no definitive, one-size-fits-all explanation as to the trials and tribulations of workplace harassment, there exists a host of common-sense explanations as to how these situations arise and how they can readily take on lives of their own. When it comes right down to it, it's pretty scary to know how little control we actually have over our destinies when we enmesh ourselves in the lives of the people, that is doctors, lawyers, and bureaucrats, most of us have been raised to believe—and continue to believe—are obligated to serve and protect us.

Admittedly, there is nothing scientific about what I espouse herein; it is merely my own view of the individuals with whom I was forcibly surrounded when immersed in this grossly protracted legal battle. What I have learned—very much the hard way—is that it is a conglomeration of these three entities—doctors, lawyers, and bureaucrats—that, acting in concert, can make for the perfect storm of destruction for the aggrieved who seek retribution from workplace harassment.

I'd like to think my experiences could prove helpful to those who work in the public sector, in particular, although I believe they can very well serve to help those in the private sector too. It's just that working in the public sector—or being a bureaucrat—brings with it some painfully unique circumstances that require a certain kind of disposition of the folks who seek to have their bread buttered therein.

My naiveté and hopelessly idealistic views brought me happily skipping to the public sector for what I expected to be a fulfilling and prosperous career. Never did I imagine that government employment would be so starkly different compared to that which I had become accustomed. I also could never have predicted it would be so incredibly cruel. In retrospect, I realize I probably didn't belong there, no matter how much I wanted to be. And when I was told that I'd probably not fit in because I'd get "frustrated" by the red tape government bureaucracies are infamous for, I refused to believe it. It took being there and having the emotional crap kicked out of me to see the light.

I'm writing this book as our country teeters on the brink of financial ruin, and as talk about how government and its ubiquitous bureaucrats are the primary force behind it all fills the airways day in and day out. Not a day goes by that I don't hear about corrupt politicians, belligerent unions, or rogue judges that do nothing but further destabilize a country that has slowly but surely fallen from its place at the top of the heap of society. As a result, the enormous anti-government sentiment out there will not soon go away—not until things change—if they ever do.

If you trust what you hear in the media, you might believe that employment litigation is a get-rich-quick scheme for anybody who dares to jump in the game. I'm here to tell you, you have been seriously misled. I have nothing to gain from painting a more colorful picture, nor would I want to. I'd like to think my saga contains enough "natural color" without needing to be peppered with gratuitous embellishment. Nevertheless, whether or not you've actually taken away anything from my story that will help you navigate through your own life, or whether or not you have, ever had or ever will have such career troubles, your eyes will likely have been opened, if only a bit more than before.

So many things attract scores of applicants to government employment such as job security, great benefits, the hope of early retirement, and a whole host of other perks. It remains an ideal opportunity for some folks, not the least of who are women and minorities, groups at one time faced with insurmountable obstacles getting any kind of employment, never mind meaningful employment. But whether you are a minority looking for better prospects; an idealist, like me, who believed public service is noble; or just someone in search of the ultimate in job security, still, government employment will never be without its drawbacks.

For me, it was not only the pitfalls of the public sector that proved to wreak havoc on my life, but the entities they acted in concert with—those that share top billing in Part II that were purposefully pulled into the mix—that made it the unbelievably and unnecessarily painful experience it proved to be.

CHAPTER 16

LIONS AND TIGERS AND BEARS, OH MY!

I LOVE *THE WIZARD OF OZ*—what a great film. So many things about it make it great, but one in particular—its message—stands out for me: many of us have the heart, the brains, and the courage we need to get by in life, but usually don't realize it until faced with extreme adversity.

My life-altering workplace fiasco made me see just that: I am infinitely wiser, braver, and more passionate than I ever realized. After being forced to tap into my very core for survival, it became apparent I possessed enormous intestinal fortitude. Courage kept me from fearing the enemy, from being intimidated by those with infinitely more abundant resources, even when I thought my well had run dry. Brains enabled me to reach far outside my sphere of intellect, to never refrain from learning and using that knowledge for good. And more than anything else, heart kept me from quitting, from throwing in the towel, even when I would've rather died.

I liken what I went through to navigating a forest strewn with lions and tigers and bears. For Dorothy, the adventure was as cute as it was scary. For me, there was nothing cute about it—except

Toto. For Dorothy, the lions and tigers and bears became her closest confidants. For me, they were the force far greater than I could singlehandedly conquer, even though, when all was said and done, I conjured up the wherewithal to hold my own in my plight for justice.

What I learned over time is that my experience was not something many folks could wrap their minds around. I first realized this early on when many of my male colleagues attempted to offer comfort and reassurance by reminding me about the plethora of "secretarial jobs out there," as if that was going to somehow to counter what I was going through. This was the very last thing I wanted to hear at the time even though I know they meant well.

My boyfriend at that time was almost no better. He couldn't relate at all. And where family and friends were concerned, while they were always supportive, it was clear that they couldn't really grasp how I could win a lawsuit and end up where I did. It was far too complicated (and painful) to explain over and over again, so I didn't. In the end, I thanked God for those who truly cared for my well-being and called it a day. Outside of that, I was really on my own.

Among the countless doctors, lawyers, and bureaucrats— lions and tigers and bears—with whom I was forced to deal, there was a general lack of humanity that's hard to believe exists. These three entities, which I've dubbed the "triangle of doom," were the necessary evil force of public sector workplace litigation, that, when working in concert, wreaked a brand of havoc all their own. From the outside, each of these entities has a certain societal gravitas that perhaps would make us want to know more about their seemingly untouchable and equally curious worlds. But get ensnared in the vortex of these three presumed forces for good, and you're likely to find that this is one trifecta that does not pay off!

The number of doctors, lawyers, and bureaucrats with whom I dealt throughout the nineteen years still makes my head spin. In fact, I'm not sure I even remember all of their names. I probably spent more collective time with these relative strangers than I did with my mate. They were the people of my surreal alternate universe, the people who would have more control and influence over my future than any human beings should ever have over each other. But I didn't really have much of a choice. Mired in illness and desperate for answers, I quickly acclimated to this strange, new world into which I was thrust.

Throughout my life prior, I avoided doctors like The Plague, steered clear of the courts, and worked only in the private sector. To suddenly have all of these entities raining down on me at once in the face of desperation was overwhelming. Dealing with each one of them requires a certain kind of savvy, a task even more challenging for someone as naive and idealistic as I was. To say this was one hellish learning curve is an understatement. But after nearly twenty years "in the system," I can say with complete certainty that I have changed. Everything has changed. What I have come to know, I feel compelled, if not downright obligated, to share, in hopes of shedding at least a flicker of light on these three groups of folks who otherwise have long been considered upstanding pillars of society.

Throughout this long, painful journey, I sought to find my way back to normalcy, to be made whole, get healthy, and to resume a productive livelihood. Instead, I ended up sicker, poorer, and much less capable of living a happy, meaningful life, in spite of a successful lawsuit promising to set my world back on its axis. The justice system I once trusted, the medical profession I once respected, and the workplace I looked to as a springboard to a fabulous career in what I perceived as a noble profession all let me down. In effect, these three entities, whether or not any of them intended to do so, raped me of the American dream. And no one in this great land of ours should ever be given the latitude to do that.

CHAPTER 17

DOCTORS:
THE *REAL* COWARDLY LIONS?

WHEN WE THINK OF LIONS, most of us think of majestic, brave, and revered creatures, much the way we think of doctors. As a society, we put doctors high up on a pedestal; we see them as being a cut above the rest, relying on them to work miracles, when the truth is, they're really no different from the rest of us.

Sure, they might have a leg up on the masses. How many other professions can claim to be on the front lines of endeavoring to preserve and better human life? And let's not discount what is required to get to be called an "MD": enduring the long and arduous process that includes countless years of schooling followed by the medical version of boot camp, and a demanding job that perhaps all but consumes one's life. But even all this doesn't elevate them to sainthood.

I'm not implying that the role of doctors in our lives isn't necessary. It is. Very. I'm just saying that being a doctor in our society is perceived as *the* most important job, one that only the very best and brightest could possibly think to hold, where the importance of all other jobs pales in comparison. This elevates doctors to a level beyond reproach.

I look at the work, for example, of an air traffic controller or firefighter or border patrol agent. They're all supremely important jobs too. Sure, they are first and foremost in the business of pubic safety, but they, too, have a hand in the preservation of human life. Yet there seems to be a mystique surrounding doctors and their alleged wizardry that mesmerizes us, simply because most of us are mystified by how they do what they do. It's the not knowing how exactly they do what they do—and believing we never could do it if we tried—that makes many of us step back and bow blindly to the magic they presume to be working. In turn, we have empowered doctors to such a degree that we often fail to question them or hold them to the high standard anyone we trust with our lives should be held to. We have given them carte blanche to operate above and apart from the rest of society, even when their skills are subpar. When it comes right down to it, we have foolishly placed doctors at the top of the societal heap due to our collective ignorance, not because they necessarily belong there.

I've never been a big fan of doctors. As a tot, I had a crippling fear of them. My doctor, Dr. Taylor, the standard general practitioner of that time, was a very kind and gentle man. He was, nevertheless, the man with the needle. I recall how worked up I would get, knowing an injection was inevitable (the apparent cornerstone of his healing philosophy) and that every time I was there, I'd hope he'd spare me the grief of poking me with that shiny, giant pin. That never happened. Now, as an adult, I realize I probably gave that nice man far more grief than he gave me, with all my crying and carrying on, in one visit than he could possibly have given me in all the years he treated me.

Regardless of whether or not I liked it, my mother had blind trust in the man who provided her and her children with medical care. That's a very scary prospect—especially today.

Of course, back in the '60s, health care was vastly different on many levels. The practice of medicine was, at that time and in my humble opinion, still a mostly noble profession, because it wasn't yet more about money than it was about healing. The process of seeing one's physician was a fairly straightforward one. For a run-of-the-mill visit, you got examined, you paid a reasonable, affordable fee, and that was the end of it.

But in the 1960s things also began to drastically change. Health insurance reared its unsuspectingly ugly head, and things have never been the same since.

Even though some form of health insurance has actually been around since way back in the mid 1800s, it wasn't until more recent times that it has become *the* way most of us pay for medical care. While that sounds great in theory, someone else footing the bill for the bulk of our medical bills is not without serious drawbacks, not the least of which is what happens to its overall cost and quality.

Under the Clinton administration, things took a turn for the worse. Early in his presidency, when Bill Clinton mandated businesses employing over forty-nine persons to provide health insurance as part of the comprehensive employment compensation package, called the Comprehensive Occupational Safety and Health Reform Act, or COSHRA, the cost of health care went up and the quality down, exponentially. This didn't happen overnight, of course, but it was the beginning of the end of health insurance as we knew it.

Although I know that there are folks among us who refuse to believe it (or just don't know it), the truth of the matter is that when doctors begin to see a decrease in what they recover on insurance claims due to the increase in the number of people an insurance company must cover (thereby prompting insurance companies to negotiate fees down), two things necessarily occur. First, fees go up such that the portion of a claim the insurance company refuses to pay, the doctor will seek to recover by increasing his fees as well as increasing his patient load. Second, as a result of the increase in patient load, the quality of his care necessarily goes down such that he will have less time to devote to each patient. It's a simple matter of attempting to preserve and shore up the bottom line. Over time, as a result of the insurance companies continuing to renegotiate their fees down (which they will presumably do), doctors will jack their rates up even higher to make up the difference to where, without insurance, very few folks will be able to afford to pay those over-inflated rates. Of course, this does not take into account the cost of navigating the red tape that goes hand in hand with an insurance-driven system that can force doctors to drop out of participating in insurance altogether. I can't tell you how many times over the recent past I've not been able to see the doctor of my choice because he doesn't take any insurance whatsoever (or sometimes not mine) and charges (what I consider to be) astronomical rates. Sadly, these are often the more reputable doctors who can afford to charge more for their services. Eventually, what we are bound to face is a system where only the very well off will be fortunate enough to have quality healthcare—just the opposite of the intended effect of, for instance, The Affordable Care Act.

We cannot, however, place the blame solely on health insurance. The skyrocketing cost of malpractice insurance to cover the rapidly growing number of class action and other individual lawsuits is sure to drive prices up, if nothing else does. It is just plain sad that we have become so incredibly litigious as a society that we feel compelled to sue for every little miniscule thing we perceive to have gone wrong, rather than reserving lawsuits for the more egregious acts genuinely warranting such harsh action. This, no doubt, is a reflection of the overall deterioration of our society in general and not necessarily attributable to doctors or the practice of medicine. As we descend downward, ignoring common decency and all that goes with it, we contribute to the collapse of a system already run amok. When all is said and done, no matter the reasons—and there are likely enough to fill another book—I can say without a doubt that good old Marcus Welby, MD, is gone, and we will never see the likes of him again.

Fortunately for me, up until 1992, I'd enjoyed good health for most of my life and was therefore able to avoid doctors for the most part. I attribute this to good nutrition and plenty of meaningful exercise. Even when I wasn't particularly active (such as all the years before working out when I sat at a desk most of the day), I tried to avoid many of the standard workplace hazards such as greasy, high calorie fast food, donuts and whatever other "goodies" found their way into the office —not easy but well worth the effort.

After 1992, however, things changed. Stress gave way to a host of psychological and physical ailments I had never known. Concerned, I began seeing doctors. The fear I once had of this otherwise everyday occurrence, suddenly took the backseat to getting to the bottom of what was going on with my body. That, coupled with being forced to see doctors for no other reason than to justify my legal claims—if I could even dare refer to them as doctor's visits—suddenly brought the medical profession front and center in my life. All told, I went through more doctors from that period to the present than I had in my thirty or so years prior—by far.

As I mentioned earlier in the book, for the year prior to the onset of the whole ugly work debacle, I wasn't feeling quite right and went for a full blood work-up. Normally, I would never engage in such an undertaking due to my crippling fear of needles; I'd just tough it out. But as I was about to embark on a rigorous physical fitness regimen, I thought it wise to make the effort no matter how freaked out I was. When I found out that I was the picture of health, I was thrilled. Who wouldn't be? So when the harassment escalated and the various physical ailments began to plague me, I was perplexed. Eventually, when it came to where I was juggling more ailments at one time than I had collectively experienced in my entire life, I decided it was time to see my general practitioner for a check-up. This was the doctor who, when summoned to testify for me at trial, told Tom that she didn't believe anything about that matter that I had said. Her lack of integrity floored me to the core.

I had apprised her of the workplace harassment, having given her a rather detailed account of what had been transpiring at the office. She seemed rather sympathetic at the time, although perhaps a bit skeptical too. I didn't expect that reaction, because she was a doctor; I expected her to listen and to at least *attempt* to treat me for the ailments about which I complained. And if she couldn't, she should have referred me to someone who could.

Among the list of things about which I complained, the constipation and the severe rectal bleeding it caused were particularly troubling at that time. She recommended fiber wafers and lots of water to help with the constipation, the severity of which I never thought possible. But what about the stress? It certainly wasn't going to go away by itself, not to mention that it was more than likely the culprit behind every bothersome physical thing I was experiencing. But that didn't seem to matter to her. When I asked her for something to take the edge off, she refused to accommodate me and told me to see a psychiatrist. But my insurance didn't allow for "behavioral health" at the time, so I was more or less at her mercy—and she knew it.

In the end, nothing she did or said helped me in any way. In retrospect, she was either ill-equipped to treat me (an inexperienced or seriously undertrained doctor), *or* it was simply that she smelled litigation and decided to stay as far out of the mix as she possibly could without coming out and telling me to get treatment elsewhere (which in a way she did). I suspect the latter—that she wanted to cut me off before I pulled her in. Whatever the case, that is when I took to self-medicating—drinking myself to sleep at night, when at 2 a.m. or later, I still lay awake, staring at the ceiling, panicking over what was in store for me the following day.

Now, I am fully aware that what I experienced was pretty extreme, perhaps difficult for the average person to swallow, but it was hard to believe that this woman made her way through medical school, a residency, her career and life up to that time *as a woman* without ever seeing or experiencing *some* kind of discrimination. And even so, I'd have to have been a sociopath and a magician to make up the kind of stuff I presented with. Tangible ailments don't come from fairytales. Hence, it's fair to say that it is clear who the real liar was here. What that did to me, both on an emotional and humanistic level—I can't even describe the impact. I was deceived by a medical professional I trusted implicitly, during a time of utter despair, who never once questioned my legitimacy at the time I saw her. And worse yet, this was only the first of many such mind-numbing experiences I had with doctors during that time.

Doctors in the field of psychology were without a doubt the ones that most took me by surprise. Certainly, psychology isn't without its vulnerabilities due to its very nature to begin with, but when someone presents with suicidal ideation or any other potentially life-threatening condition, most of us would expect to be treated with a kind of delicacy that perhaps other conditions do not warrant. Well, don't hold your breath. Add litigation into the mix, and you're *really* on your own.

I was so naïve that I believed, without question, that I would get treated for the issues I faced, and never rejected for the reasons I faced them. When an individual becomes involved in workplace litigation, suddenly whatever he says and does with his caregivers is not about him and his health, but about his caregivers' quest to avoid having to go beyond the call of duty. In fact, a physician may refuse to treat a patient at all upon learning he is enmeshed in litigation that might possibly ever involve him in some way—unless, of course, in the case of a high-profile patient willing to pay handsomely for his caregiver's testimony and/or one apt to generate free publicity (in which case, the end result is the same: they both generate income). As for us regular folks who happen to fall ill as a result of an employer's wrongful actions, "First Do No Harm" goes right out the window.

Of course, doctors are supposed to treat prospective patients, regardless of whether they happen to be involved in a lawsuit. It is grossly unethical to turn them away on such a premise. But doctors do not want to be called, under any circumstances, for depositions, nor do they want to end up testifying. This is for a number of reasons, not the least of which is being put under the microscope. And although there are privacy laws to protect the patient, it's risky business when a doctor is called upon to testify on a patient's behalf. Some therapists, for instance, take few if any notes for that very reason—if subpoenaed, they are better able to protect a patient's privacy. This is a sad commentary, for sure. But the reality is that if put on the stand, a health-care professional generally will be fiercely challenged by opposing counsel, who will fish for testimony about a client's business, with reckless disregard for his privacy. I was the victim of this sort of thing when one day when I'd gone to my chiropractor who informed me—very much to my consternation— that two men posing as some sort of NYCT investigators had been there at her office asking questions about the care I was receiving. She knew better than to disclose anything except to say that I was in fact a patient. Turns out, the two men were coworkers from SID sent there by George to find out whether I was indeed receiving care for the spinal condition about which I had taken sick leave. I was beyond disgusted—I was outraged. I thanked her for her professional handling of the matter, and asked that she never speak to anyone ever again without first consulting me. Hence, I strongly advise anyone who finds himself in need of medical care, whether or not the result of a workplace illness or injury, to be candid with his doctor about the prospect of litigation to which he might become a party or for which he may be asked to provide medical documentation. It is not wise to ambush a physician who is reluctant to testify, or worse, to subpoena him against his will for he will not serve your cause well, nor it is beneficial to try to establish a last-minute doctor/patient relationship from which testimony might be relied on to support one's case.

From my personal experience, I have seen that the world of medicine, in large part, has become little more than a business, replete with folks more concerned about making a profit than with healing. Not all doctors. I don't want to condemn an entire profession, as I trust that there are doctors among us doing what they love, and doing it well, whether or not the money follows. But from what I have seen and heard over the course of my existence, including what I have been made privy to by family, friends, acquaintances, (and even through the media outlets I consider to be reputable), doctoring has lost its nobility. It has devolved from a profession focused on people to a business obsessed with the bottom line.

While it is true that the insurance industry has had what I believe to be the most damning impact on the quality of healthcare, there are numerous other, perhaps less obvious, factors that contribute to the decline of doctoring, some to which the doctors themselves knowingly and willingly contribute, and others to which they fall prey in their quest for professional survival.

Let's take pharmaceuticals, for example, and how they impact doctoring. How often do you leave your doctor's office *without* a prescription? Not often, I'd bet. Aside from meds prescribed for the occasional illness, millions of us are on maintenance meds, too, for everything from high blood pressure to depression to cholesterol. And then there's a generation of kids who are being medicated for … well, for being kids. While I have my theories as to why (that I won't get into here), the point is that medication is doled out to children like Halloween candy. In years past, putting a child on medication for becoming easily distracted, for instance, was virtually unheard of. Now, it is commonplace. The point is that the rate at which we—and our children—pop pills in this country is astounding—and we don't need statistics to prove it. Just look around! We've gotten so far away from nature that we have come to rely on synthetic substances as a substitute for common sense and the preservation of good health. And we implicitly trust the men and women who tell us to do so.

But why is it that doctors prescribe medication as readily as they do? The reasons are plentiful—some borne out of good intent, and others not so much.

Let's start with the obvious reasons. Sometimes drugs are necessary. If the drug works, it works. Then there's plain old bad doctoring. Some doctors are just not good at what they do, just as folks in any other profession or job, and maybe never will be. Who knows how many meds are unnecessarily prescribed simply because one's doctor is incapable of making a sound diagnosis. The third most obvious reason is when a good doctor makes a bad call. Even the good ones are bound to goof up every now and again. We just have to pray it isn't fatal. And finally, what I believe to be the most prevalent reason of all: philosophy. American doctors seem to put a great deal of stock in western medicine where the synthetic substance trumps the natural one. And as medicine is a practice and not a science, it is conceivable that drugs are but a tool in the process of elimination that is diagnosis. If one doesn't work, there's always another to try.

Alas, there are a host of less obvious reasons why meds have become so commonplace, namely those instigated by the pharmaceutical industry itself. After all, who has a greater stake in pushing meds than the people who manufacture them? The way I see it, there are two key factors in how the pharmaceutical industry plays a role in getting those drugs into our bodies: salesmanship and advertising. First, let's take good old fashioned salesmanship. An individual with the ability to hawk his wares might close the deal on a drug a doctor would otherwise not have considered using, whether or not it's as great as the salesperson claims. And the free samples probably don't hurt either. Second, there's the alluring world of advertising. Drug ads abound. They are everywhere, filling up the airways, magazines and newspapers with promises of stabilized mood, shrinking prostates, lowered cholesterol, and whole host of other good stuff. But are all of these drugs as good as they are purported to be? It's difficult to know for sure except to say that doctors often prescribe them just the same. For the patient, it's very easy to get caught up in wanting to jump on the bandwagon, too. Years ago, before these ads existed, patients had nothing else to go on but the word of their doctors. But today, everyone decides which drug is right for him—and then asks his doctor to prescribe it.

Finally, this discussion of the decline of medicine and how it has become a business would not be complete without touching on medical testing. Did you ever wonder why we are summoned to so many tests in some circumstances and none in others? And why there are so many more tests administered when we're hospitalized? Do you think all those tests and procedures (and operations) are actually necessary, or that sometimes we don't get tests when we should, and vice versa? After all, we trust that if our doctors say we need or don't need a test, they know what they're talking about. But the truth is that tests generate big bucks. That's not to say that every doctor administers tests in pursuit of money, but if a doctor gets paid "x" amount for every test and "y" for every procedure, then he's probably going to order more tests and perform more procedures—even if you don't need them!

Again, health insurance plays a role. In the end, it dictates the testing you can and can't have done by virtue of how much is or isn't covered by your insurance plan. Doctors are compelled to yield to this lunacy because they can't order tests they know aren't covered even when they believe you need them. Case in point: I was told to go for physical therapy for serious spinal issues before any testing had been administered because the mind-set of the doctor who prescribed it (and most other doctors I've seen as well as those friends, family and acquaintances have seen) is that insurance companies 'don't approve MRIs'. So they tend to avoid them.

My spinal issues are congenital. It took ten years for me to get a proper diagnosis. Early on, I'd sought the care of a chiropractor, that helped to some extent to manage pain and improve function. But as time went on, and I knew my condition was progressing—not to mention a fall down the stairs a number of years ago that did nothing to help matters—I had to take steps to find out exactly what was wrong, so I could receive proper treatment. I'd seen one specialist after the next, sometimes waiting years in between, purely out of disgust.

The first specialist from a prominent hospital in New York City, who, to his credit, ordered an MRI, told me there was nothing wrong. Well, he sort of told me. He rather directed his speech to my husband, as I sat there like an idiot, listening. Regardless of his blatant male chauvinism, I left there, frustrated to bits. I knew something was wrong and was determined to find out.

A couple of years later, I went to another specialist. He took an X-ray and saw a bunch of stuff on my lower spine but refused to order an MRI. I told him I had just fallen down the stairs, thereby exacerbating the problem. He pressed on the spot where I had fallen and said nothing was wrong, even though his touch was enough to incite some pretty excruciating pain. I later learned that this guy was a foot specialist, and that because the back and spine guy didn't accept my insurance, I was assigned to someone else in their practice who did. Too bad they failed to tell me this.

I saw the next specialist a couple of years after that. I was already feeling hopeless but nonetheless undeterred. This particular doctor, the one that ordered physical therapy in lieu of an MRI, was an older man who had been in practice for a very long time. I didn't choose him for his presumed experience, however; it was insurance constraints that led me to his door. The most he was willing to do was take a very blurry X-ray and write a scrip for six weeks of physical therapy. This perplexed me. He didn't even know what was wrong, but he told me to do exercises that (I feared) might make things worse. But like the guy before him, he proclaimed it would be nearly impossible to get approval for an MRI and didn't want to spend time trying. I suppose the opportunity cost of wrangling with an insurance company was money lost attending to another patient.

A couple of years ago, a total of ten years and three specialists after the first attempt to get a proper diagnosis, I gave it another shot. Again, the doctor was an older man with many years of experience under his belt. After all I had already been through, I was prepared to put my foot down and insist upon a prescription for an MRI. And it's a good thing too. After relying on the blurry X-ray from the doctor prior, he told me that if the previous doctor and the other doctors before him said there was nothing wrong, then there was nothing wrong. I was utterly flabbergasted. He didn't even try to come up with a diagnosis but rather deferred blindly to others he did not know. I finally demanded an MRI, explaining to him I had called my insurance company who said I was entitled to one without pre-approval. A couple of weeks later, a sheepish man on the other end of phone began the conversation with "As you suspected …" As I suspected. Yes, I did. For a very long time indeed.

Another great example of the testing dilemma is what my best friend went through trying to get a diagnosis of her leg and foot, where her skin hurt so bad she couldn't let a sheet touch it. She had sleepless nights and was truly frightened about what could be wrong. It was perplexing. She went to nine different doctors, from her general practitioner to a rheumatologist, an allergist, a cardiologist, a hematologist, a neurologist, an internist, an orthopedist, an ENT, and back to another allergist, each of whom ordered a battery of blood workups and tests, including one for stool (which left the both of us scratching our heads). My head was spinning just getting the updates. While she was busy being poked, prodded, and scanned,

I was fiercely perusing the Internet, trying to figure out what was wrong with her. Some of the stuff she was told along the way was both ridiculous and outrageous, and I feared by the time they came up with an answer, it would be too late. For instance, there was the neurologist who was completely at a loss to make a proper diagnosis and said, "Now, if this was Star Trek, I'd be able to tell you what was wrong." If this was Star Trek? If that doesn't take the cake of excuses for a lack of concern, I do not know what does. But this is reality. I've seen it with her, experienced it myself, and heard innumerable stories from others just as stunning. The one common denominator, though, is that, competence aside, each doctor tended to order tests that were "insurance friendly" rather than those that were truly necessary. Not only that, each round of testing perpetuated the doctor/patient process such that there was a follow-up visit. And the cycle continued. Sadly, after all my friend was put through, she never got to the bottom of things.

Insurance is, without a doubt, to blame for a lot of the unnecessary testing—but not entirely. One simply cannot blame insurance for a doctor's general lack of professionalism or the ability to administer a proper diagnosis—or at least try. Treating me as though I was just another woman with an imaginary condition, or using a blurry X-ray, or telling me to get physical therapy for a condition not yet diagnosed, or worst yet, relying on the word of another doctor to tell me nothing's wrong are all disgraceful examples of medicine gone wrong.

With all I've witnessed both personally and from afar, I've come to realize the importance of becoming my own health advocate. There is a time and place for doctors, but I firmly believe that if

I do see one, I must show up for appointments armed to the eye teeth with whatever info I can reasonably manage to collect. It really is imperative today to do the kind of research necessary to ask intelligent questions. Challenging the findings of a doctor rather than deferring to him, as if he has all the answers merely because he is a doctor, makes a world of difference. I have found, time and time again, that once they see that I am on top of what's going on, they take notice. I gave this advice to my best friend and although she never got to the bottom of things, she saw an immediate difference in the way she was treated, mostly that suddenly she wasn't being tested and retested for the same things over and over again.

For me, it wasn't until I had been subjected to the world of medicine for the purpose of justifying my work-related illness that my eyes were truly opened. It certainly forced me to become a more informed consumer.

Unfortunately, I had little choice in being subjected to a plethora of doctors during the seemingly countless years of litigation. As time went on and the litigation thickened, I found myself enmeshed in a medical quandary that forced me to keep the ball rolling, whether I liked it or not; whether I needed to really be there or not.

Of all of the disheartening and downright frightening experiences—the one that solidified my disgust with the medical profession to the nth degree—was with Dr. E., the brilliant psychiatrist who had no idea, after two whole years, why he was treating me. It's difficult to ascertain his true motives, what with his five-minute assembly line appointments and an obsession with his watch. And let's not forget how he humiliated me in his waiting room for being a few minutes late for a five minute appointment it took me nearly an hour to get to—and all for what?

I actually never liked Dr. E. from the start. My spider senses told me something wasn't quite right about him. And I was dead on. Not only did he compromise my comp benefits with his gross indifference, but when I sought an explanation, he avoided me entirely. He knew he had screwed up and wasn't man enough to admit it.

Dr. E. might have been the worst of the bunch, but the other psychiatrists with whom I dealt also proved to test my wits. After switching from one to another and to another yet again, I found they were pretty much all the same. I always found myself getting increasingly worked up as my appointments drew closer. It's as though most of them did more harm than good.

One doctor, in particular, was so blatantly awful, I didn't make it past the first visit. After taking my history and whatnot, she blurted out, in her rather intimidating, thick, Eastern Bloc accent, "I don't testify. I don't do depositions. I don't provide documentation." Point blank. Just like that. Not that I had asked for or even intimated that I would ask for anything, mind you. Certainly not a good start to a doctor/patient relationship, especially considering some of the sensitive stuff I shared with her.

I assured her I didn't want anything from her but treatment; that I wasn't there to ensnare her into the net of litigation, and we left it at that. A few days later, I received a call from her saying that she could no longer see me. She said that the TA informed her she shouldn't be treating me because my comp case had not yet been established (yes, they never missed an opportunity!). Although I was immensely upset at the time for what they had done, in retrospect, I know I was all the better for it. Who wants to see a doctor who doesn't want you there in the first place?

Another horrible psychiatrist that epitomizes my less-than-fruitful experiences was one I chose out of default from a list of those doctors willing to take worker's comp insurance at a time when I had no other options. I didn't like this guy right from the start—he was robotic and cold, and the fact that he hadn't quite mastered English didn't help matters any. After a few cursory minutes together during our first meeting, he prescribed meds and sent me on my merry way. Just knowing I had to go back there—over an hour drive away—was anxiety-inducing enough. But to have to then sit waiting in a jam-packed reception area for another hour was too much to endure.

One day I sat watching as a slew of other patients, who came in after me, got called in before me. This ostensible healer looked me right in the face each time he came out for his next patient, without even acknowledging my presence. I tried to remain calm, but it's hard to remain calm when you're already riddled with anxiety. Although I certainly can't prove why I was left sitting there, it might have had something to do with my ethnic background not being the same as that of the doctor and the bulk of his patients. Nevertheless, whatever the reason, I got up and left and never looked back.

On a bright note, I did have one positive experience with a psychiatrist. The last psychiatrist with whom I dealt, was not only different from the rest, but also partially responsible for encouraging me to start writing this book when I did. During an appointment in late 2010, when I told her about the book I intended to begin writing, she was immensely receptive; she thought it was a wonderful idea. She saw it as an important step in moving on, as well as a way to enlighten others. Not only that, she actually spent more than five minutes with me, listened intently to what I had to say, and remembered what I said too! I wish more doctors could be like her, but I don't delude myself anymore, especially where psychiatrists are concerned. Seeing a psychiatrist is nothing like the way it is portrayed in the movies. Nix the couch, the pad, the note taking, and niceties. Forget the "tell me about your childhood" too. It is strictly reserved for the purpose of administering medication. If you want to talk to someone about your woes, call a friend. Or go to a therapist—although even that, too, is a crap shoot, at best.

Fortunately for me, I struck gold the first time around. I couldn't have found a better therapist if I'd tried. I don't know what I would've done or how much worse things would've become without Marion. After we parted ways, I saw a handful of folks over the years who paled in comparison. One was so bad, in fact, that she would repeatedly counter my statements with problematic situations of her own. Before long, I realized she was, in effect, using her patients as *her* therapists! Obviously, our relationship was short-lived.

I can't entirely lob all the blame on the backs of doctors and therapists and the like, however, as some unwittingly become pawns in the game. It's often their partners in crime, lawyers, who, in seeking to carve another notch in the bedpost of litigation, push the envelope to the detriment of the medical profession. Just look at how the TA tried to manipulate the outcome of my workers comp case for six years by using doctors to achieve their goal. While this doesn't give the doctors who willingly participate a free pass, it shows that sometimes a doctor's services are inadvertently used in unseemly ways over which he might not always have control.

I don't need charts, graphs, statistics, or so-called experts to know that the practice of medicine has sadly become a business so overrun with fear of litigation, regulations, and insurance constraints that the new Hippocratic Oath should be "First Break No Law." Rather than a profession underscored by physical and emotional wellness, it is one preoccupied by extraneous circumstances that have little or nothing to do with healing. As such, it is imperative for us, the patients, to get more involved in our care. Most importantly, we need to be proactive; the more we take the wellness onus off ourselves and place it on strangers who may not be sufficiently capable of addressing what ails us, the more we come to rely on this once noble group of individuals who have been, whether by choice or not, relegated to placing cash over care.

To that I say, "caveat emptor."

CHAPTER 18

LAWYERS: YOU WON'T CATCH THESE CATS BY THEIR TALES!

AH, LAWYERS. THEY ARE THE fierce and handsome bunch that we look to for the administration of justice. Like the tiger, they have great aesthetic appeal. Decked in fancy duds and driving high-end cars, we look at them and up to them. And just as with the lion, the tiger's allure makes us want to get close enough to know more about a creature most of us have only seen from afar. But watch out! Looks can be very deceiving. This otherwise upstanding officer of the court and disseminator of justice isn't necessarily all that.

It's astonishing how much tigers and lawyers have in common. Tigers are the largest cat of the big cat family, and if by large we mean most dangerous, then there you have it. Even though we hold doctors in higher esteem than lawyers in America, they aren't nearly as dangerous, despite that they often hold the fate of our lives in their hands. Powerful, yes. Revered, absolutely. If you say you're a doctor, chances are you're bound to get a slice more respect than a lawyer. But in terms of wreaking havoc on society, lawyers (tigers) still pose a far greater threat to humankind as they go around devouring our liberties, bit by juicy bit.

Tigers, like lions, are referred to as apex predators—that is, those who have no predators of their own. This couldn't be truer of lawyers. They are virtually bulletproof. Tigers are also known as keystone predators. This means that they have a disproportionately large effect on the environment, relative to their abundance, and it is suggested that society would collapse without them. Quite frankly, the way lawyers conduct themselves today, I'm not so sure society would be hurting if lawyers ceased to exist. We *could* simplify our legal code and fend for ourselves, but sadly, that will never happen.

But why have lawyers become so loathed? Why is there no joke more gratifying than a lawyer joke? I can tell you it certainly isn't coincidence; they have, in my opinion, earned their sullied reputations. Truth is most lawyers simply do not act in a manner befitting those who embody and uphold the law. *They* might think they do. And I suppose that they'd have to hold tight to a mantra to that effect in order to carry on without the risk of crumbling under an albatross of guilt.

I grew up believing lawyers were a force for good. And I still believe they once were—at least to some extent. My father's sage philosophy was that lawyers were useless, that anyone could learn the law (or how to build a second story on a house) and represent (or build it) himself. I might have looked sideways at him back then, but not anymore. He always successfully represented himself whenever the rare occasion arose, *and* he built a second story on his house applying the same principle. He taught me by example that sometimes what looks like an insurmountable task, reserved only for the select few, is nothing more than an illusion created by those who want others to believe that. Trouble is, I didn't quite realize the magnitude of his wisdom until well into my legal odyssey, but at least I realized it.

Unlike with my father's experiences, what I was entrenched in was far too complex to instantly parlay into successful self-representation. And besides, I was far too lost in the beginning to even think along those lines. But over the years, being forced to sink or swim, I got to know where my father was coming from. Being thrust into the legal arena opened my eyes to exactly how our so-called justice system *really* operates and that the practice of law isn't rocket science but rather an entanglement of politics and personal bias with a dash of common sense and a pinch of good luck. And that brings me to ponder why in the world we put so much stock in lawyers and why they have become such prominent, powerful figures in American society, when what they do and how they do it barely warrants such respect.

What we're really faced with is a vicious societal cycle in which lawyers have become a key component. As our country's collective values have diminished, we look more and more to laws to keep the masses in line, and the more we do that, the more we look to lawyers to help us control a society running amok. We have become a society of helpless, vindictive, and morally bankrupt people who look to the courts for answers, rather than trying to find them ourselves. We don't consider the consequences of our actions until it's too late, and we see dollar signs every time we don't like how things go. We behave badly and then sue each other! How civilized is our society when lawyers are cradling us, falsely lulling us into believing the responsibility of acting civilized lies in their hands, and that there is a monetary reward for everything, right down to hurt feelings?

Part of me knows there is undoubtedly a need for lawyers, as much as I'd rather not admit it. If not for lawyers, to whom would we turn to disseminate our vast laws and navigate our complex legal system when we believe we've been wronged? On the other hand, if we'd just treat each other with more respect and consideration, we wouldn't need so many lawyers. Okay, I know that's unrealistic. Truth is, though, we've surrendered our individual responsibility to litigation as a surrogate conscience and continue to empower lawyers who are well aware of the force that they've become. How sad is that? For us. Not for them.

The way I see it, lawyering requires a certain kind of mentality that isn't necessarily one with which the well intentioned college graduate starts off. If he's smart, he quickly learns that being a successful lawyer means keeping with the culture of the profession. The reality is that if the idealistic, aspiring young lawyer thinks he's going to change the world without ever compromising his principles, he likely will be sadly disappointed. In time, he will be required to settle into a different universe, where reality is but the culture of lawyering, and everything he knew before then ceases to exist. He who starts out all bright eyed and bushy-tailed will be forced to fall in line with his legal community brethren or he won't stand a chance. It's a simple matter of survival.

My first lawyer, Tom, and last lawyer, Pat, are a good illustration of the evolution that takes place from being fresh out of the box to a worn-in veteran. Pat was a young, ambitious guy, brimming with idealism. While he was a go-getter, someone who really fought hard for me, he played by the books—and fell flat on his face. Conversely, Tom was a wily veteran who knew how to maneuver around the courts and sometimes broke the rules to make sure he won—and for him, winning was getting paid. Tom knew where to tread and how in order to stay comfortably in the black, even though he sometimes tread where he shouldn't, for instance, when he filed suit against me after walking away with a sizeable purse. That aside, he was well aware of how to balance his resources to maximize his bottom line, in other words, he knew just how much time to put into a case without putting in too much. Pat, on the other hand, was still finding himself. His sights seemed set more on following the rules and not pissing off the judge than how much he could bill for his services, even at the expense of winning.

I recall how stunned Pat was after his initial encounter with the TA's counsel. He was completely taken aback by the way they spoke to him; they really did go all out to treat him despicably, barking nastily at him and hanging up on phone conversations. Granted, and in all fairness, this was extreme, even for the bureaucrats that they were. Tom, on the other hand, took his not-so-pleasant encounters with our adversaries more in stride, even though they did manage to get under his skin every now and again, like when they mocked him in open court right under the judge's nose. Nevertheless, it was pretty obvious that a few years made a big difference in how each lawyer operated, especially in terms of how thick their skin had become as well as how they viewed justice in light of the bottom line.

In Tom's defense, at least to the extent that it is a challenge all sole practitioners face (not that it necessarily excuses any of their decision making), opportunity cost does, in fact, become, in large part, their professional compass. Pat, employed by a law firm, wasn't forced to sink or swim, unlike Tom, a small-business owner, who had learned through his years of experience that justice had to take the back seat to the almighty dollar in order to survive. Those in Tom's position cannot devote too much time to a client from whom there will be little return and must quickly move on to the next case in order to maximize profits irrespective of the justice to which each client may be entitled. This doesn't mean a lawyer does not truly believe in your cause, but unless is it profitable—or more profitable than other of his cases, yours will likely get less attention than it might rightfully deserve. Moreover, the sole practitioner will not gamble on a case he cannot readily "sell" to a jury by taking it on contingency for there is no guarantee he will get paid at all. Rather, it is the plaintiff that will have to come up with the money if he wants to even try to get justice, a very difficult thing for someone whose employment has been terminated—or is dangling on a thread—to do. In the end, it's a numbers game, and the surest bet gets the most play.

Of course, it's perfectly acceptable for lawyers to seek to make money, even large sums. But when justice is totally forgone for the sake of money, that's another story. And unfortunately, it usually is. Anyone who thinks for one fleeting moment that money isn't the impetus for the pursuit of so-called justice—on both ends— probably has never been thrust into the legal arena. Not only are the lawyers in pursuit of a big payday, but I learned early on that even plaintiff's must think along those lines as monetary awards are the predominant means by which the aggrieved are made restitution.

I will never forget how deflated I'd gotten when told Tom me that George, Fred, and Carmine would never be held personally accountable for what they had done to me—at least not through the courts. I would much rather have seen them stew in a jail cell for a while than waste time shaking down my employer for taxpayer dollars better spent elsewise. I'd perceived what happened to me as criminal, rather than "civil". But there is no such thing as incarceration in civil matters. Instead, the three men would not be held accountable except to the extent the TA saw fit. And so, I was forced to shift gears.

I suddenly found myself thinking along monetary lines as much as I didn't want to. Not that I'd know what a fair jail term would be, but I had no idea how to determine a dollar amount sufficient to say that justice had been served, or in the case of Title VII, to make one "whole". I still don't. But my attorney certainly knew how to steer me there. In due time, I no longer thought about seeing the perpetrators behind bars but rather how much money it would take to fill a void that could never really be filled regardless. Lawyers tell you how much your pain is worth, not because they know how much it's worth (or even care) but because it often gets more money into their pockets. And sometimes they even walk away much better off than those they were hired to represent.

What this means for you, the prospective client, is never believe you are the apple of your lawyer's eye, no matter how badly you've been treated by your employer or how sympathetic your lawyer appears to be, unless, of course, you're the guy whose case will yield the greatest return. There is, after all, a direct, positive correlation between a case's chance of success and how much time is devoted to it.

I've had my share of horrific experiences with lawyers. I know others who have as well. But it's not until you've been there more than once that you understand how the game is really played. That is why you will rarely hear someone who's been around the block, as have I, praise lawyers. Once you've had sufficient dealings with them, you'll likely get to where you will try to avoid them almost at all cost. Conversely, in their lifetime, most folks never experience more than the garden-variety legal matter or two, such as with real estate and wills and the like, which, for the most part, are simple and straightforward transactions, requiring little more than a signature. Get entrenched in something infinitely more complex, and you could find yourself ready to pull your hair out of your head. Ignorance—as in never having to go down the path of litigation—truly is bliss.

That said, I am far from blissful. I admit I don't have all the answers, but I have inarguably amassed a fair amount of knowledge along the way that I think is worth sharing. Namely, there are a few basic principles one needs to keep in mind when dealing with his attorney that might sound much like common sense but that can go right out the window when one is emotionally distraught, which is often the case when one in immersed in a legal dispute.

First and foremost: *your lawyer is **not** your friend*, no matter how sympathetic or empathetic he appears to be and no matter how much you want him to be. While it's a natural instinct for us to develop an emotional bond with those we perceive as our protectors, lawyers are not wired that way. They aren't in business to make new friends; they have a bottom line to protect, and they're already going to pick your pocket in many creative ways, so don't help them! I personally know someone who once told her attorney "money is no object" (another thing I suggest you *never* do!) and then proceeded to chat up the firm's staff as if they were her lifelong buddies. I don't want to tell you how badly that whole thing turned out.

Second, lawyers learn early on how to handle their clients and go by the cues they get from them to keep them in line. The more seasoned the lawyer, the craftier he is at manipulating you in ways you don't even realize. If your lawyer is adept at calming you into a false sense of trust, chances are, you, the distraught soul, will leave the lawyering to the lawyer, keeping far out of his hair, refraining from asking questions that might upset his apple cart. If you happen to be the inquisitive type, as I was, you will likely frustrate your lawyer, and may be the recipient of a lot of b.s. intended to get you to retreat into the corner, so he can proceed without interference.

Third, preying on your emotions, as Tom handily did with me, is a famous tactic that also works like a charm. Lawyers are very adept at smelling desperation, and I, for one, stunk to high heaven. I emptied my meager pension fund, the only money I had to my name, without putting up a fuss, because I was desperate *and* made the fatal mistake of revealing my finances, foolishly thinking Tom would be sympathetic to my financial woes. Turns out he couldn't have cared less if I ended up living in a cardboard box on the corner. After forking over that initial thousand, I was unknowingly on my way to hell. But my empty pension fund would prove to be the least of my problems.

While Tom might have been successful at keeping the TA at bay, I realize in retrospect that any lawyer with half a brain and a lick of experience could have won that case. It was textbook Title VII. For Tom, it was all about how much he would make rather than how he was going to make me "whole." In the end, he rather made a "hole" in me. A permanent one. He screwed me worse than those he was hired to implicate. Not the conclusion I expected.

I now know, after a long history of having tried, there is no formula for finding the right attorney. There are no guarantees as to their integrity or abilities, no matter how successful they might have been for someone else. From where I stand, it's not just "a win" that matters but that you are appropriately compensated to the extent that your adversaries pay for their wrongdoing, whether it's cash, a job, or whatever it is that a victim believes to be fair and equitable compensation. It is, after all, your case. You are the victim, not your attorney. Though with what some of them charge and the amount they walk off with, you'd never know it.

So how does one go about making the most informed decision possible when looking for a reputable, qualified lawyer? The best he can do is poke around the Net, ask a lot of questions, and pray, because the process of educating himself to the point of being able to take matters into his own hands takes far too long to master within the short window of time he has when faced with a legal crisis. That, coupled with the prospect of a diminished emotional state, is a recipe for potential disaster.

Lawyers have it all figured out, so that no matter how you fare, they somehow come out on top. The whole system works to their benefit, whether or not they've done the job you hired them to do. While one can sue his lawyer for malpractice, it is not something you often hear about, nor is it something I personally recommend, because it isn't easy. I know; I started down that road only to waste more money on another attorney who I couldn't afford to continue to pay to finish the job. Lawyers, like union workers, have a tight-knit brethren that, even if they despise one another, will go out on a limb to make certain they preserve the sanctity of the profession. Short of trying to sue, imagine asking a lawyer with whom you are not happy for a refund? Good luck with that too.

With this kind of built-in safeguard, it behooves lawyers to jump in wherever they see an opening to make a buck because they don't have to worry about any negative repercussions. They are almost guaranteed to be compensated for whatever it is they profess to want to try to do for you, even if, in the end, they don't. The fact is that when anyone can go about earning a living without being held to a certain quality standard, he will sure try. And since lawyering is about a paycheck, just like any other job, there are a lot of lawyers out there who just assume check their morals at the door. Sure, they all sound good, like they sincerely care about your rights and the rights of citizens in general. But if it really was about justice, you'd hear about more attorneys extending themselves, whether pro bono or even on a discounted basis, to represent financially challenged folks with worthy causes.

While there are attorneys that do pro bono work, even the motives behind these seemingly selfless acts can be questionable. Pro bono is no more a champion of justice but rather about firms investing in building or fostering their reputations. While advertising is an effective way to drum up business too, putting oneself out there for a "good cause" goes much farther for a lot less, toward accomplishing this goal.

That brings me to the court-appointed "pro bono" lawyers often assigned to the indigent (as in those granted an IFP status), a status for which there is no standard. For the truly abject poor, there's little doubt as to their inability to pay for an attorney. But what about the folks who work, make a decent living, pay their bills, and still cannot afford to hire legal counsel: the working poor? The term "indigent" or even "*pauperis*" connotes poverty, when in reality, it's just as much the plight of the middle class as it is the poor to scrape together funds to pay for legal representation. Hence, as is often the case, the middle-class are considered too well-off to be considered poor thereby presenting them with the most insurmountable obstacles of all litigants in search of justice.

Is it that the courts simply don't understand the plight of the middle class? That's not very likely. The appointment of counsel appears to have less to do with one's finances or with fairness and more to do with control. The way I see it, it is a mechanism to regulate caseload, to rid the courts of cases in which they have no interest. The middle class just happen to be the ideal targets. The courts might as well just come right out and say, "Middle class need not apply: justice for the rich and poor only—oh, and we must like your cause too." Something is seriously wrong with that.

One might then wonder how it is that lawyers can charge such crazy amounts of money for employment-related cases (defending people who often times no longer have jobs) when the court fees alone can be prohibitive. Let's face it—even a relatively small, nominal court fee—never mind modest retainers—can be enough to knock a lot of folks right out of the box, as it did to me. As I touched on earlier, Title VII suits provide for the victor to collect attorney's fees from his opponent, making it very easy to ring up a steep tab. Of course, one must generally have a case his prospective attorney believes he can win too.

Although Tom kept mum as to his strategy, he took my case almost entirely on contingency because he knew it was a virtual slam dunk. There was little risk for him to take on a fresh, winnable case with no baggage. He could easily employ all of the tactics he had learned along the way to maximize his award, including extracting a sizeable sum from his struggling client just for good measure. After our successful run, however, and after I was hung out to dry, retaining counsel on contingency was no longer an easy feat. Just because I had a win under my belt and had presented a sound, defensible argument for retaliation thereabout, there was no longer a pot of gold waiting for an attorney at the end of the rainbow.

With a long, complicated history that got longer and more complicated as the years unfolded, my case became a hard sell. The amount of work it would require just to go through the boxes of paperwork was enough to send any lawyer packing, even if he truly believed in the cause. A lawyer is not about to devote weeks going through stacks of paper when he could be looking at the next clean, unencumbered case he is bound to win and guaranteed to get paid for. Since my case didn't fit the mold, I was ultimately reduced to a vulnerable pro se bound to fail. It was either that or walk away.

Walking away, for me, was not an option, so when the legal community turned its back on me, I had no choice but to take matters into my own hands. Operating in a pro se capacity is no walk in the park for someone in a sound emotional state, never mind someone who is clinging on to sanity for dear life. On top of that, there are as many risks inherent in operating as a pro se as there are opening the phone book up and choosing an attorney you know nothing about.

For one thing, courts frown upon pro ses, despite our long-held right to self-representation in the United States under Section 35 of the Judiciary Act of 1789, dating back to the days of George Washington. This means (theoretically, anyway) that one does not need to be wealthy to seek (and get) justice. It sounds so American, being given the right to stand up for oneself without prejudice. But in reality, it's more or less a bunch of malarkey that, outside of small claims court, I don't necessarily recommend. While it should be both permissible and honorable to represent oneself—and *was* back in 1789—it is clearly frowned upon today.

Judges make it clear, as did mine, that they do not want to deal with pro ses. Pro ses are generally viewed as nuisance litigants with baseless cases, not fit to waste the time of our already seriously backlogged courts. The unspoken reasoning of the court is that if you don't have an attorney, it's because your case lacks merit. Moreover, who wants a pro se clumsily navigating his way through a process with which he is unfamiliar, thereby taking valuable resources away from "serious" litigants? Sure, the courts are staffed to assist pro ses with the technical aspects of one's case. But don't expect much. My experiences have been hit-or-miss, and as the years went on, much more miss than hit. But one cannot expect much from bureaucratic clerks bombarded by repetitive questions with which they'd presumably rather not be bothered. And in my particular case, after seeing my name so many times, they, too, likely put me on the back burner.

Pro ses are also frowned upon because they are not supporting the cause. Judges, now relegated to dealing directly with the layperson, were once lawyers themselves. There's something to be said about loyalty to one's own, to keeping the cause impenetrably thriving. The fewer pro ses there are, the better it is all around. I mean who wants outsiders learning the tricks of the trade? It's much harder to operate when everyone knows what you're really up to. And so, in the end, the only thing having a lawyer will guarantee you is the nod of respect you'll get for supporting the cause. Being a represented litigant is a show of good sportsmanship, if it's anything at all.

As much as it is difficult to be disregarded by the courts in the face of desperation, and as much as it hurts to know that justice could have been served but for the corruption that has all but consumed our justice system, there is one last but equally important aspect of employment law just as egregious that warrants discussion.

What I went through is deemed an act of civil (versus criminal) proportions within the scope of our penal code when there is nothing about it I know that was particularly civil. In fact, the more I contemplate the thinking behind what constitutes a civil act versus a criminal one in this country, the more it makes me wonder how far from common sense we have migrated.

In my case, not only did the perpetrators not get punished— at least not by the courts—but had I been a criminal, or a crime victim, rather than the victim of some rather heinous workplace violations, money would never have been an issue. Criminals—or should I say the "innocent until proven guilty"—are guaranteed free legal representation, no questions asked, while crime victims have prosecutors to look out for their interests. While the latter is perfectly understandable, the former is not necessarily, at least not when someone knowingly sets out to commit a crime. I seethe knowing that a child molester, rapist, or serial killer is afforded an attorney on our tax dollars, while I was forced to spend countless sleepless nights and angst-ridden days, trying to figure out the next creative way to move forward and, when all else failed, was left to my own devices in a diminished capacity. That makes my blood boil. It should make yours boil too.

I have nothing against the concept of reserving judgment until which time an individual has gotten his day in court. Any one of us would want that, for anyone of us could be wrongfully accused tomorrow of a crime we didn't commit. I even understand the concept of "the right to representation" on the taxpayer's dime, for again, if it was you or me, the last thing we'd want is to be incarcerated for being necessitous. But that's where I draw the line.

The problem lies not so much in the criminal justice system, although it is one aptly named for vehemently protecting the criminal at all costs, and in that regard, we have gone way off the deep end. What really whips me into a frenzy of utter disgust is that criminals have far more rights than dedicated, hard-working folks who are violated by their employers. This is just plain wrong. I profess that we need a serious revamping of our legal code, one that allows for holding employers who knowingly commit workplace atrocities criminally liable. I firmly believe that incidents of workplace harassment would plummet downward, to where we'd see a fraction of the lawsuits, if this type of offense were to suddenly be on par with, for instance, assault. Although it might not always prove to be a simple task to ascertain where the line is drawn between civil and criminal, I can say with relative certainty that had George, Fred, and

Carmine been facing even the remote prospect of serving jail time or even so little as the shame of a criminal record, I'm fairly certain none of what I went through would have ever occurred, because most of the folks who commit these types of infractions aren't hardened criminals with the propensity to act heinously in the face of harsh punishment; rather, they usually are nothing more than bullies who recoil at the thought of so much as posing for a mug shot, never mind spending the night—or longer—in jail. The humiliation alone would serve to keep most workplace bullies in line.

I fear, however, that the so-called justice system will never change, and in fact, it will continue to deteriorate into more of a cesspool than it already has become. And as long that is the case, we will unfortunately need lawyers to help us navigate through the lunacy they helped to create. However, as my experiences have shown me, having a lawyer by no means guarantees one more liberty than one would otherwise have, and can often serve to exacerbate an already bad situation—especially when the judge is unimpressed by the person you've hired to advocate your cause. Judges, by all means—and make no mistake, jury trial or not—can and do have the greatest impact on the outcome of your case.

I used to believe, like most of us do, that if a litigant was adequately able to present a sound argument (sufficiently supported by case law), he would have to prevail. I found out the hard way, however, that it doesn't work that way in the real world. Legal precedents, most notably those set by the Supreme Court, can be as flimsy as the paper they were printed on. I would get very excited when I'd discovered a Supreme Court case clearly aligned with any of my many arguments. I thought, *Okay, there's no way I can lose; how could a judge possibly rule against me with the Supreme Court on my side?* Little did I know, lady justice is not blind; instead she is the puppet of judges who impose their personal bias in ways only a judge can. If a judge has his or her mind made up about the way things will go, his or her whims can carry a great deal more weight than the highest court in the land, a group also known for handing down some truly bewildering, uneven-handed decisions.

It is no secret that the justices of our Supreme Court are known to demonstrate some pretty blatant courtroom bias. Decisions handed down by the nine justices are often reflective of their political ideology, rather than common sense and logic. One can almost predict the outcome of a case, based on the number of those to the "left" and "right" of the political spectrum seated at a given time. Hence, much against the dynamic set forth by our founding fathers, it is political ideology, not necessarily the tenets of the United States Constitution, that ultimately shape the laws of our land, making even our most powerful judges of all far from beyond reproach

The lower courts are no better. From the inside, that is, from the vantage point of a litigant, you will find out, if not sooner, later, that there are no guarantees of success no matter how tight you believe your argument to be. Picture it: You know the law is on your side. You know you've presented a sound argument chock full of legal precedent. You move forward expecting there to be no other possible outcome. And then—*pow!* You don't know what hit you. You go over and over it, trying to figure out where your argument went wrong but can't. That's because it's not your argument that went wrong—it was the judge. The fact is that anything imaginable could have swayed him, from his political ideology to his personal philosophies to his cronies to his mood that day. It's hard to say which trumps the other except to say that impartiality is not always part of the equation. One never knows what he's going to get despite the merits of his case, and he will be hard pressed to prove anything fishy occurred short of a taped confession.

The judge who presided over my case started out as someone I regarded as a fair and impartial arbiter of the law, even when she ruled against me on this issue or that. But somewhere along the way, she seemed to have had a change of heart. As the years rolled on, and it became glaringly obvious that both the judge and her magistrate were displeased with my repeat filings, things continued downhill. They seem to have perceived what I characterize as the courageous efforts of a pro se litigant in her valiant struggle for justice as an overstepping of bounds and overall waste of the court's time. That's unfortunate.

The fact is that there is no limit to the number of times an individual may file complaints within the same jurisdiction, and unless he is blatantly committing some kind of abuse, he will be allowed to proceed. In my particular situation, when the TA implored the judge to order what are called Rule 11 sanctions for what they deemed "a frivolous suit", it was nothing but another paltry courtroom tactic. The defendants knew it, the magistrate knew it, and I'm sure as heck the judge knew it too. Nevertheless, although the sanctions were never ordered, the threat alone worked to stop me in my tracks, proving that a judge can and will find ways to dissuade unwanted litigants, represented or not.

Quite frankly, I'm not sure where else I was supposed to turn (or where anyone else would have turned), heck, there was no place else to turn. Suffice it to say, being shown the proverbial door when I needed the court to protect me was a hurtful experience that both surprised and disgusted me—but it's not quite as souring as knowing how many genuinely frivolous suits are filed (and entertained) every day. In fact, not a week goes by that I don't hear about another workplace incident or other type of civil suit about something that— at least on face value—screams absurdity.

Take, for instance, the fairly recent case of the woman who had a head scarf yanked off her head at work, after which time she alleged her life had been devastated. Don't get me wrong: I'm not insensitive to such things. I completely understand that acts of this nature are hurtful and wrong and perhaps even grounds for serious repercussions for the perpetrators, including termination. But that something of that nature could warrant a firestorm of litigation and a small fortune in monetary compensation is entirely over the top (perhaps an assault charge would have done the trick?). By cherry-picking cases that align with courts' political ideologies, even when they do not truly comport with Title VII statutes but are rather stretched to appear that they do, and tossing to the curb those that are sound legal arguments but for having lost their political sparkle, we reduce our justice system to a bona fide carnival of opportunists that seriously diminish its standing.

If not for the veritable blizzard of cash to be made off of these cases, they would never make into the courts in the first place. What's worse is that it's the lawyers themselves that are often the ones to incite litigants to file these outrageously exorbitant suits over slights that might otherwise have been resolved with an apology and a handshake. There again, handshakes don't buy Mercedes.

Genuinely frivolous lawsuits hurt everyone. They contribute to the moral deterioration of our culture while driving up the price of goods and services and, in some cases, bankrupt businesses. The mom-and-pop operations upon which this country was built have become sitting ducks in a society gone litigation-wild. In fact, small businesses are at great risk of ceasing to exist as the result of just one frivolous lawsuit. That is a very scary prospect and discourages people from going into business at all. Imagine spending your entire life building and running a business that's been in your family for generations, only to one day get a knock on the door that later proves to be the beginning of the end. You are rendered powerless by a lawyer who will force you to settle, just to make him go away. And over what? A customer frightened by a store's display claiming it has traumatized him for life or another who acts recklessly and then turns around and blames the business owner for his own irresponsibility. I hear about ridiculous suits like this all the time. The question is: why do they even make it into our courts?

If these little pieces of Americana were no longer around, we'd be forced to rely on giant corporations for everything. That would be disastrous. They would continue to buy each other out until we were left with no choice but to shop at the one place that dictates what we buy and how much we pay for it. Nobody else would be able to compete! We've already seen this happening to a degree over the past couple of decades. Walmart comes immediately to mind. I love Walmart. Target, too. But I also love the quaint little shops where I can find unique items and those made still made here in the good old USA. We need to preserve that. But if we keep on the path we're going down, if we continue to legally nitpick small businesses into obscurity, we're toast. So, the next time you trip or bump your head or get frightened by a display, don't take it out on the guy toiling away, day in and day out, trying to keep his precious business afloat because some lawyer whispered in your ear about how you've been wronged and how much money you stand to make. Tell him to move on; accept an apology from good old "Pop," and call it a day, as tempting as the prospect of rolling around in a vat of money might sound. (I know, easier said than done.)

Telling the average Joe to walk away from the prospect of a windfall of cash is not an easy feat. After all, it takes a person of genuine integrity to steer clear of potentially lucrative litigation, when we, as a society, are sending out the message that it's okay to sue the crud out of each other like it's for sport. Lawyers, on the whole, have conditioned us, worn us down; they have succeeded in controlling almost everything we do without us even knowing it. Every time you use a product, walk into a store, buy anything (and the list goes on and on), you are subject to restrictions put in place as the result of another lawsuit. Did you ever read the packaging for a product and wonder why it contains a laundry list of warnings? Chances are they ended up there as the result of litigation. It's gotten to where some folks steer clear of certain products out of fear of being harmed when in fact it was probably only one person who claimed to have been injured. But just that one claim is enough to force the manufacturer to add another warning to the list to avoid further litigation.

Inasmuch as you might never have considered suing a business or anyone over anything, you are more likely now than ever to get the fever, as our society sinks further into the depths of litigious hell. Take, for instance, the TV ads with which we are bombarded. Today, lawyers are so intent on tapping into every potential well, they've resorted to reaching into our living rooms all day long to let us know they're there to bail us out of a jam anytime we need them. Countless ads purporting to be looking out for our welfare abound. Everything from the ill effects of antidepressants to mesh implants and everything in between could entitle even you to "a cash settlement ." These ads might sound innocent enough, but they're not. There's a lot more going on there than most folks could even imagine. And it has nothing to do with protecting you, the consumer.

Trial lawyers are actually "gaming" the system by casting large nets to ensnare as many potential litigants as possible, in order to get around state caps on damages. By trying to "recruit" plaintiffs in several states (through TV ads), they attempt to steer class action litigation into more favorable court jurisdictions (away from state and into federal), where they can avoid damage award caps (to make more money for themselves). How seedy is it to lure potential litigants, some likely not even legitimately injured, by telling them they're entitled to "a cash settlement" for their injuries, when the true motivation is hitting the class action jackpot?

Before the 1970s, lawyers didn't advertise. The legal profession itself banned the practice of advertising until 1977, when the Supreme Court made it entirely permissible (as per the First Amendment), when they decided that two lawyers in Arizona who were banned from practicing law by the bar were well within their rights to have done so. I could easily criticize this decision as yet another of the highest court's worst for what has come from it, but it isn't the nature of the decision that's the problem. It's those who take wrongful advantage. And with the toothpaste already out of the tube, this practice will most likely live on.

I have nothing against lawyers advertising or even seeking out the aggrieved who might not otherwise be savvy enough to recognize what they have experienced as an honest-to-goodness compensable injury. But when they hunt you down for their own personal gain and nothing else, they should be disbarred or at the very least sanctioned. Realistically, however, the best we can hope for are jurors who are cunning enough to see past the smoke and mirrors, who weed out these ambulance-chasers and the innocents they use for personal monetary gain.

Occasionally, we are fortunate to have some of these cases make it all the way to the Supreme Court—fortunate because it (presumably) will put an end to a flurry of similar baseless cases. Case in point: a landmark decision handed down in June 2011 involving my friends at Walmart. Thankfully, the court put the brakes on that runaway train, where some 1.5 million female employees were lumped into a multi-billion dollar suit alleging gender bias. In my humble opinion, the Supreme Court was correct in determining that there was no common triable legal thread connecting all 1.5 million litigants, thereby putting the matter to rest; it shut down the greedy bastards whose only objective was to abscond with billions made off the backs of vulnerable women. While I don't ever want to see any woman (or any individual) needlessly wronged, I also don't want to see countless ill-intentioned lawyers making a living out of taking advantage of folks who, for all their trouble, would have walked away with a few bucks each at best. This is, however, the slippery slope we are headed down—and we are moving at record speed.

Surely, it is not easy to navigate our judicial system. It's not easy to know who to trust or how to make prudent legal decisions or how to plan for life after litigation. With this is mind, I hope to be able to lighten your load a bit by leaving you with the following tidbits of wisdom with which I have come away over the course of my nineteen year journey. I pray you never need them, but I implore you to consider these general time-tested insights in the event you ever find yourself in a legal bind.

1. Shop carefully for your lawyer. For matters of life-altering proportions, shop like it's the last purchase you'll ever make. In the end, it is about you and your future. Put your emotions aside as best as you can. This is the greatest pitfall, the one that causes us to jump at the first thing that looks good. Lawyers are truly a dime a dozen. And always keep in mind that this person will be working for you, not the other way around. If he doesn't like your high standards, chances are he lacks the kind of integrity you would expect of an individual who holds another's fate in his hands. I didn't know any better and allowed the first person I dealt with to place me under his spell. Although I asked tons of questions, I didn't push when not provided with acceptable answers. That proved to be the worst mistake ever. Be your own advocate.

2. Do not allow any attorney, no matter how confident and knowledgeable he seems, to take your case solely into his hands. Get online (or go to the library) and do your

homework. If something sounds fishy, it probably is. Ask as many questions as you need to and demand answers. Consult with other attorneys to obtain a consensus of opinions, if need be. There are lots of attorneys out there who will answer basic questions without having an attorney/client relationship. I found this to be hit or miss, but the hits were usually very helpful. The misses were typically the paranoid types who immediately recoiled in fear that any little thing they said could be turned on them if things didn't go my way. Nevertheless, educate yourself the best you can and be realistic about what to expect in terms of results.

3. Discuss the fact that you are about to embark on a lawsuit with your family. Lawsuits can be very time consuming and emotionally draining. While it's nonproductive to be negative, it's imperative to be honest with yourself about what such an endeavor can do to your life. A lawsuit can last far more years than you could imagine. Lawyers have a nasty tendency of minimizing the time frame of a case and then explaining away all of the interruptions and holdups as everyone's fault but theirs. But in all fairness, be aware that our courts are very slow-moving. Civil matters are not given the same respect and attention as criminal matters, and the incidents of employment suits ebb and flow with the political climate. There is no right to a speedy trial in civil matters, so be prepared for a potentially protracted ordeal that seems to never end.

4. Get all you're entitled to. Don't be fooled by thinking, as did I, that you have much less say in your case than your lawyer.

Demand what you believe is fair in order to achieve the wholeness the system is (purportedly) designed to deliver. Seriously distraught and hopelessly idealistic, I allowed my attorney to dictate the demands because I trusted that he was looking out for me. But he wasn't. He got what he wanted with complete disregard for my suffering. His reasoning sounded good at the time but never felt quite right. Intentionally minimizing my complaint so the jury wouldn't think I was too litigious is absurd. I was told to keep quiet about the sexual harassment and focus on the discrimination aspect of my case. I listened to him because I thought he was representing my best interests. Turns out that sexual harassment is just tougher to prove; it would have gotten in the way of his fast track to a big payday. But sex discrimination and sexual harassment often overlap and can be equally devastating. So, listen to your inner voice, and don't let anyone tell you what is truly important to you in terms of how you might have been harmed. Demand everything you believe you're entitled to without being greedy. It's not a get-rich-quick scheme but rather (hopefully) a path to justice and healing.

5. Make the contract between you and attorney as much about you as it is about him. Retainer agreements and contracts are put in place to benefit the lawyers, not the litigants, no matter much you are told otherwise. It ultimately protects them to ensure they get paid as well as limits liability for screwing up. But it doesn't have to be an entirely one-sided contract. A truly upstanding attorney won't have a problem

making sure your interests are equally protected. Everything is negotiable.

It pains me to say, but would be disingenuous not to, that lawyers have become the termites in the wood of the foundation of our great nation. Money is the goal and justice merely a by-product. As such, it has now become our duty, our obligation, to question the trustworthiness and reliability of those we used to take for granted as among the most revered pillars of our society. Every man for himself has never been truer, at a time when it should be the farthest thing from our minds. Truly selfless fellow human beings, you will find, are few and far between, especially among lawyers.

CHAPTER 19

BUREAUCRATS: PLEASE DON'T FEED THE BEARS

THE BUREAUCRAT IS SURELY IN A class by himself. He might not have the aesthetic advantage of the attorney, nor might he have the majestic allure of the doctor, but he certainly has misleading characteristics of his own. The bureaucrat is the bear of the "lions, tigers, and bears." He's not a fancy sort, like the tiger or lion. He is rather a more understated creature who is always on the take for as much as he can sock away for his long slumber. And if you feed him—that is, give him what he needs to survive (or worse yet thrive)—he will surely never go away.

There are many different types of bureaucrats, however, not just the garden-variety federal government pencil-pushers that generally come to mind when we hear that term. A bureaucrat, or civil or public servant, as they are often called, is anyone who works in a government setting, whether at the federal, state, or local level, from bus operators to prosecutors to judges.

Government employment, or better yet, government as an employer, has grown, of late, out of control. There are, as such, a lot more of these workers among us today than ever before. Taking a closer look at them, that is, trying to learn what they are all about, is all the more imperative, for the more we know, the easier it will be to spare ourselves the grief of being overrun by an entity so ambiguous as to wreak unnecessary havoc on our lives.

Working for the government is very different from working in the private-sector in many ways, not the least of which is the concept of civil service. One who is a civil servant, albeit a term sometimes used to describe any governmental worker apart from the military, is one who has achieved a status that makes him virtually bulletproof. This so-called competitive method of weeding out prospective employees on the basis of professional merit, established in the United States in 1871, practically guarantees one's employment for life, and that is something that cannot be said about any other group of workers. Although the preponderance of civil servants are employed by the federal branch, some state and local government entities have competitive civil service systems modeled after the federal. Among these Teflon Toms are bus drivers, police officers, sanitation workers, teachers, mail carriers, and a whole host of others who provide necessary community services.

While this competitive method of hiring may have begun with the intent to benefit the employer (i.e., if one passes the exam, he is capable of performing the duties required of him more competently than others who may not have passed the exam), it now actually serves to benefit the worker, who, once achieving his civil service standing, is nearly impossible to fire, even if he is the laziest, most incompetent individual that ever was. Getting out the "dead wood" becomes a mammoth task for an employer that is often so cumbersome, it's not worth the entanglement of red tape he is bound to get caught up in.

The concept of passing a test for employment meant something way back when Imperial China first instituted the concept some 2,000 years ago. I imagine it was an honor to be one of the fortunate souls who achieved this status and that loyalty, not an expectation of excess, instilled one with the kind of pride that motivated him to do a good job. Today, no such altruism exists that inspires an employee to respect the process once meant to elevate and protect him. There is no longer a need for individuals on the path to civil service to strive for excellence, as we've lowered the bar to getting and staying there as low as it can go.

As we have continued over the years to lower (test) standards, it's become increasingly more difficult to separate the wheat from the chaff. Every Tom, Dick, and Sally that comes along, complaining about unfair (discriminatory) practices, (usually attributable to nothing more than their intellectual or physical inability to pass the exam), contributes to the watering down of those standards when he files suit, for example, regarding the weight-lifting requirement of a firefighter. I've always been an advocate of women competing for and doing whatever job their male counterparts do for the same pay, unless they need to lower legitimate minimum requirements to get there. I'm not saying that there haven't been legitimate gripes over the years about exam questions intentionally or unintentionally favoring particular groups to the exclusion of others, but I also say if you can't perform the most difficult tasks required of a specific job, don't ruin it for everyone else with your whining. Next, civil service exams do not ensure that the guy with the highest score will be any more valuable than the guy at the bottom of the list.

A productive employee does not a high test score make. Also, test taking doesn't do much to ensure against corruption. For instance, it isn't uncommon for higher-scoring candidates to be passed up by their lower-scoring colleagues for promotions. I've seen it happen, and let's just say it doesn't make for a peaceful workplace, whether the impetus is cronyism, racism, or anything else. Finally, enter the civil servant who is also part of a union, and you have an employee about as darn near impenetrable as they come. He who cannot be fired, especially absent productivity incentives generally not found in the public sector, will more than likely have little reason to achieve, let alone excel.

Civil service (or unionism for that matter), however, isn't at the center of the problem in the public sector—the absence of a profit motive is. Government's gross inefficiency can mostly be blamed on the fact that it operates on somebody else's money, other wise known as our tax dollars. Not having to turn a profit to stay "in business" is the root from which all other problems stem. Throw in civil servants who are also under the protective cloak of a union, and you have the greatest productivity killer of all.

For the very same reason—the absence of a profit motive—government also has no rationale to limit the number of employees it hires. For a whole host of reasons, including political ideology espousing that the public sector is better able to perform services than its private sector counterparts, government employment continues to thrive, even in the face of national financial uncertainty. Unions vie to increase membership for it strengthens their power base, namely for the huge vats of cash that enable them to manipulate Washington. But we cannot lay all the blame at the feet of the unions either. In government, management's hands are dirty too. For them, increasing the size of the workforce not only justifies their existence (and employs their buddies) but also spreads out the work. I can't tell you how many times I witnessed a group of colleagues perform tasks that could easily have been performed by one person. This is what makes the "use-it-or-lose-it" principle so vitally important.

"Use-it-or-lose-it" is the concept that perpetuates the practice of quickly filling jobs with unqualified individuals for no other reason than to give the appearance that a particular position is vital to the operation of a department—which, sometimes it is. But rather than diligently searching for the right person, a process that generally takes time, sometimes any old body (such as was the case with both Fred and Carmine) is thrust into a position he has no business being in for no other reason than to "place mark" the spot until a suitable replacement can be found (or not). Of course, sometimes there is no need for a particular job to be filled at all. Case in point: I have a friend who works at a place where there are three supervisors and a director who are all paid well over six figures a year. They try to give the impression that they are an integral part of the operation, when the truth is, they do almost nothing to contribute anything meaningful to the day to day operation. In so doing, they breed a great deal of resentment among the staff members who are expected to follow an entirely different set of organizational rules. Nothing has changed in many years despite that this conundrum has been brought to the attention of upper management a number of times. Instead of simply cutting the dead wood out and perhaps increasing the salaries of the highest achievers whose functions are critical to the organization's success, management perplexingly sits on its thumbs while the infighting ensues. What their reasoning is, I can't claim to know, but, in the end, the bottom line—and those that they are in business to serve—suffer.

Only recently, as we find ourselves staring down the barrel of the economic ruin of our great nation, are many of us finally waking up to the fact that government is more of a purveyor of waste than an ideal employer. As a result, the public has engaged in some of the most lively and controversial political debate that this country has ever witnessed. Taxpayers are putting their collective foot down against the abuses of government, including the exorbitant salaries, outrageously decadent benefits (including trips to Vegas, hot tubs, and champagne), and other privileges bestowed upon many who in the private sector wouldn't be nearly as endowed. How is it that government employees are entitled to higher pay and better benefits for the same work? Or less work? Or since when is it that "We, The People" have permitted government to ignore the basic tenets of decency? Of our Constitution? Feverishly answering the call of duty, scores of fed-up citizens have begun to rise from complacency to take an unprecedented stand against big government. As such, the once safely cloaked bureaucrat is now facing enormous backlash that has him uneasy about whether the gravy train will soon come to a screeching halt.

Unions, in particular, have recently found themselves in the center of the hotbed of "wasteful spending" controversy. The public has seemingly lost its tolerance for the over-the-top compensation packages and iron-clad job security bestowed upon those who, in many instances, have resorted to hostile hostage-taking negotiations to secure and maintain excesses the likes of which most other hard working Americans will never know.

Just the other day, I heard a union member on TV going on and on about how they (union workers) make less than their non-union counterparts. I laughed out loud. *Could she possibly believe this?* These folks are the quintessential spoiled children. Give them everything they want and protect them from ever having to work too hard, and they will believe that what they're getting isn't enough, no matter how much it is. Try to step in to take it away, and they throw a fit. It's easy to see why the other "kids" who are made to work hard doing chores aren't too happy.

In particular, teachers are a shining example of unions gone rogue. While teachers don't all necessarily earn excessive salaries, they are ensured an enviable benefits package, including a two-month-long vacation, and iron-clad job security. The job security alone is priceless. Make no mistake; I'm in no way against teachers. Heck, I spent my childhood wanting to be one (until the women's movement bored a temporary hole in my brain and had me believing that being a teacher was beneath me). I respect teachers and firmly believe they deserve to be handsomely compensated (the good ones, anyway). But taking on a bad one and not being able to get rid of him, or having a dismissal process so circuitous it might as well not exist, tends to attract subpar people who might have more interest in the perks than sufficiently teaching our children. It is this misdirected path that we have paved for ourselves, one that has led to the deterioration of the public school system, which has placed teachers, in particular, under immense scrutiny. For better or worse, teachers have become the new poster children for everything that is wrong with unions.

In response to all the union mayhem, teachers have, as of late, found themselves facing some serious challenges. Once untouchable benefits such as early retirement (along with enviable pensions) have been targeted as wasteful and are now in serious jeopardy. For some, retirement hopes have been dashed as many states seek to slash spending in an attempt to balance budgets. For instance, some teachers planning for retirement only a year or two out are suddenly finding they've got five more years to go. I doubt that anyone ever saw that coming. It is an earth-shattering wake-up call to unions from a public clearly determined to put the brakes on a system overwrought with corruption and abuse. And if it can happen to our beloved teachers, it can happen to anyone.

When I first worked for NYCT, I knew nothing of a union-driven work environment. Not to say I didn't know any union workers, it's just that I had never before worked among them. It was extraordinarily eye-opening to go from white-collar Wall Street to hard-core, blue-collar Main Street. Public-sector workers are already a whole different breed from their private-sector counterparts. Throw in the union presence, especially one as strong as the Transport Workers Union (TWU), and you've got quite an arrogant and indestructible group of Teflon Toms.

Like many things initially fueled by good intent, such as welfare, unions, too, have devolved from a form of protectionism to a practice of exploitation. The TA's TWU is just one example of a powerful union that, in my opinion, takes full advantage of the latter. And to say these guys are a force to reckon with is an understatement. Let's face it; they'd have to be pretty solid to get away with keeping a guy with a toothache out of work and on the payroll for three years!

During my years with the TA, I witnessed stuff I simply couldn't believe. Many times, I stood in utter amazement at behavior I never knew existed in the workplace. The guy with the eternal toothache was but one mere example. Of course, there was also the aforementioned guy with the back injury who looked like he was preparing for a bodybuilding contest. While he was supposedly incapacitated to where he couldn't so much as drive a bus, a fairly physically non-demanding job, he'd come to collect his paycheck in a muscle shirt as though he was there for a beer with the guys— because it didn't matter, and he knew it.

One of the most outrageous incidents I can recall, however, is the guy who decided to sell the merchandise he stole from work out of his house! This bus mechanic, on the cusp of retirement, got caught in a sting operation, with somewhere in the vicinity of a million dollars' worth of goods (or at least that's what they found in his possession at that time). Although terminated (and possibly even prosecuted), he kept his pension. I don't know if he ever got jail time, but does it really matter? He got to keep the pension for which he had hung in twenty years, and that he would have begun collecting anyway in a year, had he not gotten caught.

Had any one of these situations occurred in a private-sector setting, or what I refer to as "the real world", Muscleman, Stickyfingers and the Tooth Fairy would have been sent packing. But not in government—and not at the TA. The reps watched over their members like a momma bear protecting her cubs. Whatever management might have viewed as wrongdoing, management was dead wrong, even when they were dead right. But that is what unionism has unfortunately come to: a shield from behavior that would otherwise never be tolerated—behavior that sets a poor example for every worker, stifles productivity, and drives costs through the roof.

I once got a taste of what it is like to be on the receiving end of a disgruntled union worker. I found out first-hand that these guys (and gals too) can be awfully mean when they want to be. While I managed to play nice with my union colleagues for the most part, including the union reps with whom I often worked closely and got along famously, there were a few times when I guess some of the less evolved chaps saw the need to "school" me for something I had no idea I had done wrong—and they weren't in the business of necessarily talking things out.

It was a Friday, and, as always, I could not wait for quitting time. This particular Friday, however, I was jazzed about going away for the weekend. But when I headed out to my car, parked in its usual spot on the street, I was met with quite a surprise. One of the guys had taken the liberty of throwing a wrench through my back window, shattering it into oblivion. I was stunned and devastated.

At first, I had no idea what to think, as it wasn't the greatest of neighborhoods. But when I opened the car door and found a greasy wrench sitting on my back seat, my heart sank knowing it was one of my co-workers who had carried out this dirty deed. After I scooped up the wrench, making certain not to put any finger prints on it, all I could think about was how I was going to get my window fixed in a jiffy so as not to forfeit my trip. But that wasn't to be. After reporting the incident to management and filling out all the pertinent paperwork, I proceeded home, where I patched my window until I could get it replaced. Talk about a stress balloon.

I never found out for certain who the culprit was, but I had a fairly good idea. Could it have been the guy whose advances I spurned? Or the guy who didn't agree with something I said the day before? I just never knew if what I said or did was something potentially explosive. These guys were nasty as heck when they wanted to be and made certain to leave a calling card you'd soon not forget if you crossed them—it was just tough to know when and if you did. While the wrench ordeal was totally uncalled for, I had slowly but surely come to learn that this was the culture of unionism.

Unfortunately, the impervious world of government unionism imparts far more widespread damage than that to the windshield of my car. Their misguided efforts are epidemic—a downright detriment to society. If these workers were truly at risk of being exploited to the degree they needed to be so obsessively coddled, I'd say go for it. No worker should be exploited or treated badly—this, I know. But unions have turned the table on us; they use their power-in-numbers advantage and political muscle to take more than their rightful piece of the pie. They are fiercely single-minded entities that have no consideration for anything whatsoever except protecting what they believe to be theirs. What that does to others is of little to no consequence.

Recently, I saw a John Stossel TV special that summed up my sentiments perfectly. The show was entitled *Freeloaders,* and in it, Mr. Stossel explored an array of government programs failing to achieve their intended goals. One such program involved the promotion of public safety by handing out free bicycle helmets to the less fortunate. Problem is they weren't getting to the people that truly needed them. I recall the long line of folks waiting for helmets, most of whom were very well off and, upon being interviewed, had no shame in telling Mr. Stossel how they were entitled to government hand-outs, despite their obviously enviable socioeconomic lots. Disturbing. But not nearly as much as what followed.

When Mr. Stossel interviewed a snarky, arrogant union rep from the TWU Local 100, my ears perked right up, and I was glued to the TV. Stossel's barrage of no-nonsense questioning irritated his guest to no end, as he made a number of excellent points to which there were no viable answers. As the interview progressed, the union rep became increasingly agitated. In particular, when asked about the ridiculously high average number of sick absences per year per employee in the TWU, he had the utter audacity to assert (after dancing around the issue for as long as he could get away with it) that the only reason they had an average of some fifty plus absences per year per employee was because of the extraordinarily high number of pregnant woman in the workforce. I suppose I should have expected some sort of ludicrous response—but that one almost knocked me out of my chair. Blaming pregnant women for the blatant abuses inherent to the culture of their union? Talk about going out to the tip of a limb.

I last worked in the TA some fifteen years ago, when there was only a handful of female bus operators, and absenteeism was just as much a problem back then (with no pregnancies that I ever knew about). I've already cited a number of examples of workers who took extended "vacations" under the guise of illness—need I say more?

Those under the titanium umbrella of the TWU couldn't lose their jobs if they killed someone. Oh yeah—I saw that happen too.

What I learned from my stint in the TA is that the public sector's lack of profit motive goes a long way toward gross incompetence and unimaginable waste, to which unions contribute in large part. Couple that with civil service and you have a tough road to hoe if you ever want to engender efficiency. Moreover, it has opened my eyes to government in general. It is by far not the TA or any other federal, state, or local government agency, organization, or program alone that wastes taxpayer dollars with reckless abandon; all of them do.

There are hundreds, if not thousands, of government-sponsored programs that create as much waste as unions. Shrimp on treadmills comes instantly to mind. One of our nation's science foundations, funded entirely by taxpayer dollars, spent half a million-plus dollars testing the metabolism of sick shrimp. I'm all for exploring different avenues of curing deadly disease and ways to improve our overall standard of living, but this study and innumerable others conducted by the same agency are nothing more than some nimrod bureaucrats' pet projects that have little, if any, bearing at all on society. It's not just the shrimp that chap my scampi. This kind of thing goes on all the time; we just aren't privileged to know about it—we are only expected to pay for it.

When you are someone, like myself, who has had the experience of spending many years working in a government setting, little comes as a surprise. As I've said, I witnessed the out-of-control spending firsthand. These folks spent other people's money like they'd won the lottery, then, on the other hand, refused to spend when and where it was really necessary (recall the cheap lock for the ladies room that I had fought tooth and nail for and never got). The gross misappropriation of funds incensed me, and I naively thought everyone else should be as concerned as I. But they weren't. "It's your tax dollars too!" I'd say. So what? To care required effort. And besides, nothing was going to happen to them for spending too much on office supplies or working unnecessary overtime. Even on a systemic level, there were many failed multi-million dollar projects that got scrapped like yesterday's paper.

Perhaps I just didn't belong in the public sector. The perfect match I once believed I'd found unraveled into the bureaucratic disaster of a lifetime. When I decided to flee Wall Street to take the plunge, I recall my exasperated broker colleagues asking why in the world I would leave a place where I could make "a killing," to go to "a place like that." But at that time, I viewed brokers and the whole Wall Street scene as the bastion of meaningless money mongering and saw my future with NYCT as a potentially substantive stint of sunshine and lollipops. I knew little about what I was getting into but didn't care. I was warned of the pitfalls of the public sector by others but didn't really take heed. They couldn't have penetrated my wall of enthusiasm if they'd tried. I had my rose-colored glasses firmly in place and was headed for what I believed to be the beginning of something great.

In the beginning, when things were looking up, I think the worst I could say about working in the public sector was how robotic I found bureaucrats to be. I witnessed my colleagues' glee as they thrived on sailing through a relatively unproductive, uneventful twenty- or thirty-year career. For the vast majority, it was a matter of going with the flow of the daily grind: punching a clock (at the precise right time), refraining from questioning authority (that would be disloyal), accepting that they wouldn't get ahead in the absence of cronyism (even though it was frowned upon), not being inclined toward individualism (God forbid!), and not giving a hoot about efficiency (which most of them had no clue about). There's not a lot of room for creativity in the government setting where hard work and enthusiasm are often viewed as threatening. It is a mundane, one-dimensional world, where most of my counterparts seemed quite content—but where bubbly old me just didn't fit in.

Even working as a budget analyst had its robotic attributes. Although my job wasn't altogether flat, it wasn't exactly the bastion of excitement either. The more repetitious tasks made for some pretty dull days I had to drag myself through. Still, it was a start.

When I first began my stint at the TA, I thought the work of a budget analyst was important. After all, you can't run a successful business without sound financial planning, right? Well, just imagine my surprise when I began to see that what I did every day was really nothing more than an exercise in futility. Government budgets are a joke, I quickly learned. What gets spent, gets spent, despite the big hoopla budget process and the production of lengthy budget reports month after month that we were led to believe were the pinnacle of our existence as analysts. The real bottom line is that there was never a genuine consequence for going over budget—and nobody ever seemed to notice.

To prove my point, I had a counterpart in another borough who once decided to test the waters by injecting random gibberish into his monthly budget reports. He went on about Mickey Mouse and a bunch of other stuff to see if anyone would notice. He was sure that no one really read those reports, and this would prove his theory correct. His suspicions were confirmed. Nobody ever noticed. I suppose all we really were doing, as we suspected, was justifying our existences.

But this is government. Budgets are but a front for the wildly irresponsible squandering of our tax dollars. We wouldn't be in such deep doo-doo today if this wasn't true. In fact, just as with filling open positions with dimwits in order to not lose them, the same principle applied to the budgets themselves. Spend it whether you need to or not—or lose it. Rather than be lauded for one's efficiency, one is forced to spend every last dime, and then some, in order to ensure his budget remains intact. Alas, there is no incentive to be efficient, to be productive, to hire the best and brightest, or be the best and brightest.

Call me crazy but I always believed that NYCT could have been run like a business if anyone higher up cared—or dared—to try to do so. This goes for any governmental agency, including the townships in my home state of New Jersey, where we pay the highest property taxes in the nation. Local government officials tell you it's impossible, that they can barely make ends meet, and that in the face of hard times they've managed to refrain from imposing increases— all of which might be so. But if you look closely at the way a private business is run, in comparison to just about any government agency, I'd be willing to bet there's a lot of room for improvement—union presence or not. People like myself who are trained to identify problem areas, can offer sound suggestions on how to achieve efficiency. But the nature of government isn't conducive to efficiency; they'd rather run folks like me out of town before surrendering to a more sensible way of doing business because it behooves them to do so.

NYCT would definitely cease to exist but for the subsidies it receives from the federal, state, and local governments. Although it takes in around half of its operating budget from revenue, it would sink like the Titanic if not for the endless flow of taxpayer dollars, because it prevents itself from surviving elsewise. When it comes right down to it, this public-sector giant is, as has been said about the many (failing) private-sector giants, "too big to fail," and so, despite its ability to generate more revenue (by the very nature of the service it provides) than a lot of governmental entities do, it will nonetheless forever continue to thrive, no matter how poorly it performs. It is public transportation—something New York City simply cannot live without at any cost.

Often, I got to thinking about ways in which my employer could motivate its employees to do a better job; to care more about the consequences of failure. As someone with aspirations of someday becoming a public sector exec, this was the prism through which I looked at the workplace. It's easy to complain about what's wrong with it; it's harder to come to the table with solutions. And I always came to the table with solutions.

Organizations like the TA are virtually devoid of incentives. No one really has a reason outside of himself to do any better than he is doing because there's nothing more to offer him than what he's already getting. Sure, now and again, one of us gets rewarded for a job well done, as did I when I got the unexpected promotion to manager of Budget and Personnel. I was blown away when I found out, as I had already gotten used to the cronyism that would have immediately claimed that position for someone's friend or relative, no matter how deserving I—or someone else—might have been. So I can't say it never happens. It does, albeit rarely.

I am a huge proponent of a merit-based system of reward, despite its drawbacks. Merit can be used for good, as I saw in the private sector, but it also can be used for bad, as I saw at the TA. What I had seen in the private sector, at least to a greater degree, was that if you worked hard—that is, you produced for the company by increasing productivity in some meaningful way—you got rewarded. Using merit to bolster productivity doesn't seem to work as well in government, however.

The TA used merit increases to manipulate rather than motivate. First, they were only given to management. And second, if you were persona non grata, you'd know it when review time came around, no matter how impressively you'd performed throughout the year. The whole thing was pointless; it only served to grease the palms of some and weaken the platform of others. I recall how the guys used to wait impatiently to see their performance evaluations for no other reason than to find out if they were going to see a bigger paycheck. Once the process had run its course, they knew exactly where they stood. Then the resentment kicked in as the guys compared raises that were not usually commensurate with one's level of achievement, but rather a testament of his relationship with the boss. There was no impartiality, and without it, instituting a reward-based system cannot possibly work to motivate anyone.

Outside of merit or some other tangible incentive, there is only one thing left that can motivate us: pride. Call me old fashioned, but I still believe in pride. Pride is free. Pride used to matter. I have a theory that if someone takes pride in what he does, he will never surrender his integrity to anyone. Maybe that sounds corny, but there is something to be said for doing one's job—and doing it well just for the sake of his own gratification. At least he can look himself in the mirror each day and lay his head down on his pillow at night, knowing he did his best, whether or not others took notice. This philosophy was solidified for me when I continued to put forth my best effort even when I was being mercilessly harassed. I had a job to do, regardless, and if my name was on it, the end result had to be a quality product, because I don't allow others to dictate my standards. I got the distinct impression that I was being laughed at for my efforts, but I didn't care. Sadly, I didn't see much pride among bureaucrats. It's almost as though the only pride was in knowing they got a big check for doing little. It was mediocrity at its best.

What I experienced as a government worker was pretty disheartening; it really opened my eyes to the true meaning of the word bureaucrat. I can't say that I ever came to accept the concept for what it is, even though it didn't make me like my coworkers any less. But after a while, and it took a lot for me to get to that point, I realized that nothing I did or would ever do was going to change things much—mediocrity was the norm. However, I wasn't quite as tolerant of the ubiquitous bureaucrat when I came to discover that our court system was, too, overrun by the same laissez-faire attitude toward achievement that sunk the TA to these sorrowful depths.

Although I touched on judges earlier in the legal setting, they have a place here—amongst the bureaucrats—too. I never thought of judges as bureaucrats; to me, they were always in a class by themselves—a cut above the rest. After all, judges are the very people we look to to disseminate legal issues that shape society as we know it. However, these perceived pillars of our communities, that I believe most of us tend to hold in the highest esteem and trust to engender fairness and civility, are bureaucrats too. Judges might be looked upon as being cut from a different cloth, but the fact is that they are no different than bus operators, teachers, and whole host of other folks doing the daily government grind. When it comes right down to it, judges are susceptible to the same pitfalls as any of their bureaucratic counterparts.

The men and women we look to as the ultimate arbiters of justice are as vulnerable to bureaucratic stagnation, cronyism, and bias as any of their public-sector brethren, despite that their duties are by and large more involved and infinitely more complex than those of the average bureaucrat. And I don't doubt that being a judge can be an incredibly demanding job at times to which some 'of the robe' sincerely devote themselves. But they are indeed bountifully compensated for the duration of their careers and beyond to fulfill, with the utmost of integrity, the duties bestowed upon them even though that is not always the case.

Most of these once-upon-a-time lawyers endeavored as prosecutors and public defenders. More bureaucrats. Unfortunately, there is no such thing as a private sector judge. While some judges are elected, some—namely federal judges—are appointed. Beyond knowing this about them, which isn't much, judges are a pretty elusive group despite being some of the most influential people in the country.

True, it's nearly impossible to know what really goes on behind the scenes, unless you work in the courts or had the misfortune of having been enmeshed in a legal battle. And even then, depending upon all the variables of one's case, he can still be left in the dark. Most of us probably rely on TV to paint the portrait of judges, but I can tell you that those TV shows aren't at all realistic. "Reality TV" is hogwash, depicting judges as consistently fair beings who always operate in accordance with the law. So if you think watching Judge Judy or any one of those other shows is enough to get the inside track on the judicial process, think again.

While I'd venture to say that not all judges are cookie cutter bureaucrats, I am convinced that there exists a vast pool of them who would be better put out to pasture, especially some of the more extreme ideologues we've been privy to as of late who have no shame in handing down decisions that are but a reflection of their (sometimes extreme) personally held beliefs. This is an incredibly dangerous reality considering most judges are seated for life and almost entirely immune from prosecution. This equates to a legal free-for-all for them and no guarantee of justice for us.

I've had more than my fair share of dealings with judges over the past twenty or so years. In addition to my own legal woes, I was simultaneously involved in my husband's twelve-year-long custody battle. Between the two court battles, a total of twenty-nine years worth of court time, I have concluded that it doesn't matter what's at stake: a child's welfare or one's livelihood—each can get treated with the same reckless disregard. Most striking was finding out that the judges we trust to protect our children are no more devoted to the cause than the ones I've faced in small-claims court. In fact, I've experienced a higher caliber of judges in small claims.

My husband's dealings with the court (along with those of many other folks I personally know whom have been engaged in custody battles) showed me just how upside down our "justice" system really is. Each court appearance (and they were countless) was a gut-wrenching, emotionally draining ordeal. We would walk out of the courtroom absolutely stunned and amazed, eyes glazed over, as though we had just seen a UFO. And each and every appearance was just as mind-blowing, if not more so, than the one before, as we never knew what to expect. The lawyers unnecessarily protracted the whole process, more than likely for the benefit of their wallets, while the judges acted as though the law was theirs to mold into whatever suited their fancy on that particular day. Then, as if that wasn't enough to rip our hearts square out of our chests, the judges never stuck around long enough to get to know my husband, his child, or the circumstances. On the couple of occasions he got a judge that was passable, one or two hearings at best and—poof—he was gone. The majority of them clearly bought into the "fathers are nothing but cash machines with feet" theory that seems to pervade the entire custody enterprise. All I can say is that the expression "in the best interest of the children," the standard by which all decisions regarding child custody are *supposed to be* made, is the biggest bunch of bullshit you will ever hear in your life. The only "interest" that is "best" is that of the lawyers and judges. But this is what you can expect when bureaucrats make life-altering decisions for you and your family.

As I approach wrapping up my peak into the world of bureaucrats, there is one last group of them without discussion of whom this topic wouldn't be complete. While not nearly as glamorous as judges and not quite as familiar as teachers and bus operators, they are every bit—and then some—as guilty of mediocrity. The group to whom I refer is my friends at the Equal Employment Opportunity Commission.

No bureaucrats have been as utterly inadequate, as much of a waste of taxpayer dollars—in my opinion—as those to whom I turned for help in my darkest hour. While New York City Transit was, in my opinion, filled to the brim with depraved indifference, the EEOC was filled with … well … much of nothing. This bastion of incompetence disguised as the aggrieved workers' superhero is *the* saddest excuse for an oversight agency I've ever had the grave misfortune of dealing with in my entire existence.

The EEOC is, for the most part, a shameful, colossal waste of resources. Unless my senses have taken compete leave of me, I believe they spent more time stringing me along than looking into any one of my charges. If not for the Right to Sue letter being necessary for one to move forward with a federal complaint, it's best to stay far away from this place. They almost make family court look good. The EEOC is a purely governmental agency with no incentive whatsoever to succeed. This agency has no profit motive or any other kind of motive, except to fill an imaginary role that folks are falsely lulled into believing they can competently fill. After having gone several rounds with them, I can attest that these public servants are undoubtedly *the* quintessential bureaucrats.

I discovered very much by virtue of being taken for a long, bumpy ride to nowhere that the EEOC is really more of a *symbol* of workplace equality than any kind of purveyor of justice. It exists for political and ideological reasons, not practical ones. Like me, most aggrieved employees look to this agency for guidance in desperate times of need, sometimes as their last hope in the face of losing their livelihoods (or sanity) and short of filing suit. But there is no reason to believe that the EEOC will do anything more for the aggrieved employee than eyeglasses would do for a bat.

I feel for anyone who has to deal with the EEOC. Not only will this over-staffed, under-managed bureaucracy definitely not find in your favor (that being the equivalent of finding for your employer, which, if they also happen to be part of the public sector brethren, likely puts you in an even more disadvantaged position), but they will likely send you on a wild goose chase at a time when that's the last thing you need. Then, after you've finally pinned them down, if you do, you'll probably wait eons for a response that, at best, will leave you worse off than when you began. Although they can be sued, it will be a cold day in hell before you will be able to hold them accountable for their gross incompetence. They are almost as immune to prosecution as judges.

Once again: caveat emptor.

Here, I leave you with the advice to tread lightly where bureaucrats are concerned. While it might just seem like business as usual when your path crosses one of a bureaucrat, business can be quite unusual. Bureaucrats might come in all shapes and sizes but are really one big conglomerate of workers disincentivized by a perennial flow of tax dollars—even as well meaning as many of them surely are. As this equates to you in your daily lives, don't expect much.

MY FINAL THOUGHTS

WRITING THIS BOOK HAS BEEN an incredible process for me, more cathartic than any therapy, pill, or self-help book was or could ever be. I knew one day I'd set out to write a book, but I never imagined it would be about a gaping nineteen-year black hole that snuffed out my livelihood and what should have been some of the best years of my life. How life takes such unexpected turns.

While doing research about getting published, I immediately came across a website that really hit the nail on the head. The author's sage advice resonated with me. In short, he advised to never write for money but rather as a labor of love. In so doing, whatever you strive to get across, you will. Conversely, if your writing comes from the desire to prosper, you might well miss the mark. So true. I find that with a lot of things in life. Activities I enjoy doing are so pleasurable until suddenly I must do them, rather than simply want to, and then no longer enjoy them as much. Add doing them out of desperation, and it's a real buzz kill—like writing legal papers to save one's job.

I took this guy's advice to heart and as a result, writing has never been so rewarding, even though it has dredged up a ton of negative emotions. I promised myself on the day I began that I would take it slowly and not allow the experience to add to my already over-the-top anxiety. The last thing I wanted to do was to turn the process into a stressful venture. I've had more than my share of that. Rather,

I wanted to bring this painful ordeal full circle, to get much needed closure. Moreover, I wanted to share my insights with others. If I only had a manual of sorts to guide me through this bizarre journey, I sincerely believe I would have been able to get by with far fewer battle scars.

What I thought I knew about our so-called justice system turned out to be fantasy. What I learned about the public sector was gravely disappointing. What was perpetrated on me by doctors was shocking. Maybe my experiences—all my trials and tribulations— can spare others the gut-wrenching agony of meeting a similar fate.

I have tried to paint an accurate picture of what really goes on behind the scenes. Admittedly, I still have some ill feelings for the various groups and individuals with whom I dealt along the way, but I consider myself a fair and impartial arbiter of information, even though I often wear my heart on my sleeve. While I believe it is an author's responsibility to step back and be as unemotional in disseminating the facts as possible, it is exponentially more difficult to do so in a tragic personal memoir. In spite of this, however, I believe I accomplished that goal. I want you, the reader, to walk away with untainted, useful information—information you can apply not only to workplace litigation but to a host of other day-to-day situations where you need a little boost or a bit of sound advice. I hope I've done this by sharing my story.

The most important goal when writing about a horrific experience is demonstrating that there is a silver lining, no matter how hopeless things seem. I still believe in silver linings—despite that I spent a heck of a lot of time asking God why this had to happen to me, I spent just as much counting the ways in which it made me a better, stronger, more resilient person. While it is true that it took a long time before I saw a light at the end of the tunnel, I scratched and clawed to hang on to hope that justice would prevail and that I would come out the other side in one piece. And I almost did.

As you are aware, my dog, Toto, was enormously instrumental in getting me through the toughest times. He wasn't in my life until 1999, but when he arrived, he helped save my sanity. I can't express enough the healing power of animals. When things got so bad I wanted to die, I'd look at Toto (and my kitties too, of course) and know I could go on, no matter how much I was suffering. When I lost him in September 2010, it was the day after I filed my last appeal. To me, it was God's way of telling me it was time to move on, time to take the bold step of writing the book I had always dreamed of writing. Thank you, God, and thank you, Toto. With both of you at my sides, it's no wonder I was able to succeed.

Today, when I stop to think about the whole thing, I still get nauseated by the realization that although I survived and although I have become a better woman in some respects, almost all I invested in achieving my dream was for naught. Not having a career (or children) is quite hard to accept. I'd always envisioned having a super successful career and nice, traditional, American family to complete the picture. But all is not lost. I don't discount the greatness of having achieved a higher education and amassing a body of knowledge to tap into to carry me through whatever I do in life. I wouldn't trade that for anything. I vow not to forsake its value for the likes of any evil persons and to continue to use it for good as long as I live.

When I look back to the beginning of my life, I sit in awe of the enterprising little urchin I was—the drive and tenacity I had even at the ripe old age of five. If there was a kid you'd have bet was going make something of herself, your money would have been safe on me. I tried everything, never with the fear of failing. It makes me sad to know that I had all the makings of a successful life but for the savvy to navigate evil. I got the rude awakening of a lifetime as I learned firsthand that not only does evil lurk in the most unexpected places but that our society so often allows evil-doers off the hook with little to no repercussions. That's a hard pill to swallow for me. I didn't ask for anything—no handouts, no special treatment, no favors. I did what I thought needed to be done and got where I wanted to be with good old-fashioned hard work and dedication. I'd like to believe, though, that in the end, it is how we handle life's tribulations that ultimately makes us who we are and how we parlay those experiences into daily living that measures our success, rather than the titles we hold or the size of our paychecks.

Believe it or not, the thing I walk away most frustrated about after all these years goes beyond what my colleagues perpetrated on me. It is rather the warped way in which we characterize civil versus criminal behavior in our society that gets to me even more. I can barely wrap my brain around that one. If our justice system characterizes what happened to me as "civil," we've got a long way to go before we can even begin to say our justice system is just. Those of us who have suffered at the hands of our employers surely don't think there is anything civil about the treatment we receive, and no one has any more right to rape you of your career than they do your virtue. Each is criminal in its own right.

In the end, I am fortunate to be able to close this long chapter of my life sharing my story with others—a dose of redemption I can hardly put into words. And while there are times I still look to God for answers to why my life took the unexpected turn it did, as the fallout will forever be woven into the fabric of my being, I'd like to believe that He only gives to us in life what He knows we can handle—if I'd dare to think I'm even worthy of such praise.

I think Friedrich Nietzsche said it best when he said 'He who has a why to live can bear almost any how'.

www.ingramcontent.com/pod-product-compliance
Lightning Source LLC
Chambersburg PA
CBHW070535120726
47909CB00007B/2145